Little White Lies

by

Sara Ackerman

The Westby Sisters, Book One

This is a work of fiction. Names, characters, places, and incidents are either the product of the author's imagination or are used fictitiously, and any resemblance to actual persons living or dead, business establishments, events, or locales, is entirely coincidental.

Little White Lies

COPYRIGHT © 2016 by Sara Ackerman

Cover Art by *Debbie Taylor*

The Wild Rose Press, Inc.
PO Box 708
Adams Basin, NY 14410-0708
Visit us at www.thewildrosepress.com

Publishing History
First Tea Rose Edition, 2016
Print ISBN 978-1-5092-0651-3
Digital ISBN 978-1-5092-0652-0

The Westby Sisters, Book One
Published in the United States of America

She swayed toward him, ensnared by his provocative words and enticing nearness.

He seemed to hesitate a moment, perhaps tempted by what he saw written on her face. Shaking his head, he turned to leave, but stopped and faced her again. "Then run away with me, Amelia."

"Wh-what?" she stuttered, backing away from Tavis. She didn't know which of them was more shocked. "We hardly know each other!"

"Many marriages begin on less," Tavis persuaded, crossing his arms over his chest.

"I don't even know who you are. You could be anybody!"

She turned her head to the side and closed her eyes, more tempted by his offer than she was willing to admit to herself. He was giving her a chance to leave behind the solitude and misery her curse had imposed on her from the age of eight. She could leave and start a new life away from London and the gossips of the *ton*. She could finally have a normal life. A husband. A home. A family of her own. She would no longer be the awkward spinster sister of the lovely Beatrice or the bane of her mother's existence. She could be free…

What he is saying is crazy! Respectable gentlemen don't go around offering marriage to near strangers.

Proper young women did not accept offers of marriage from near strangers, either. But, oh, how she was tempted nonetheless to accept and live a life where nobody knew about her curse.

"I could be anybody, 'tis true, lass." Tavis grabbed her chin between his fingers, forcing her to look at him. "But I also could be somebody, Amelia. Somebody you could care for. Somebody you could marry."

Praise for Sara Ackerman

"Ackerman whisks readers to a magical time and place where lust, betrayal, and a gypsy's curse enchant each page. Readers will want to travel back in time and make Tavis their own."

~*Ava Black, Crimespree Magazine*

~*~

SILENCE IS GOLDEN
and
SILVER-TONGUED TEMPTRESS
follow *LITTLE WHITE LIES*
in The Westby Sisters Series
available from The Wild Rose Press, Inc.

Dedication

To R.
Sorry I almost stabbed you with a fork
on our first date.

Chapter 1

London, 1810

"It is a lovely evening tonight, my lord."

Amelia Westby smiled and fluttered her lashes, a coy attempt at sincerity, but she received no response. Holding back a frustrated sigh, she took a deep breath and counted to ten before checking her progress once more. Nothing happened.

Drat! I'll have to try again.

"I do like to dance." Amelia waited and grew anxious when she didn't sense a twinge or a tic or even a gurgle. Never had it taken more than these two simple phrases to achieve her desired results.

The ticking clock in the room competed with the worried voice in her head, both reminding her of the limited time she had before being caught. Soon her mother or her sister would barge in and end her attempt to sabotage the evening.

For this to work, she needed a convincing lie, not one which could be confused with the normal pleasantries exchanged between acquaintances of the *ton.*

Think, Amelia! What do you hate more than anything?

In a flash, it came to her, and Amelia braced herself for what was to come. With a toss of her copper curls and a saucy smile, she said, "Yes, my lord, I love attending balls, especially when you are here."

There it was. A large pang rippled across her stomach causing Amelia to wince in pain. She looked into her vanity mirror. Despite the agony she was in, her sparkling green eyes reflected only happiness at her success. But she wasn't done yet. It wasn't over until she cast her accounts on her vanity or she passed out on her bedroom floor. Either would work for her purposes this evening.

Pushing past the bile rising in her throat, Amelia bared her teeth at her reflection, knowing what she needed to say to end this madness. "Of course, my lord, I'd love to—"

"Yoo-hoo, Amelia! I've come to rescue you!"

Huffing out an impatient breath, Amelia tried to ignore the cheery intrusion of her longtime friend, Lady Clarisse Thornston, and to concentrate on the agony her lie generated. But it was gone, leaving not even a dull ache. The familiar nausea receded, and her stomach was fine. Lady Amelia Westby was well and truly stuck.

"Clarisse, you do have the worst timing!" Amelia turned away from the mirror to gift her friend with a baleful glare. "I almost had it this time."

With a swish of pink skirts, Clarisse was by her side, giving her a rather unsympathetic pat on the shoulder. "As your mother thought, so she sent me up."

Amelia wanted to scold her friend for colluding with the enemy, but the kind brown eyes staring into her own stopped Amelia short. Clarisse did not deserve her anger, no matter if she did agree to help her mother drag her to the ball. She contented herself by mumbling, "Traitor," like a petulant child instead.

"You may call me any name you please, Miss Amelia, but I'm not sorry I did it. I happen to agree with your mother on this."

Hopping up from her chair, Amelia stood over Clarisse and plunked her balled fists on her hips. "You're supposed to have my best interests at heart, Clarisse, not hers!" Amelia gestured to the door where her mother most likely lurked listening to everything the two women said. "You know how I dread going to dances!" Amelia turned away and wrapped her arms around herself, all her anger and resentment from years of being barely tolerated by society returning to tear apart her self-confidence.

Since her come-out three years ago, Amelia could count on one hand the number of times a gentleman had asked her to dance. In her first season she had alienated most of the eligible bachelors with her blunt honesty. It wasn't her fault her partners insisted on asking inane questions. Nor was it her fault she was required to give a completely honest answer—or suffer the consequences. Soon it was rumored Lady Amelia was odd, rude even, and the number of gentlemen who asked her to dance dwindled until she no longer had any partners at all.

Nowadays, her father had to bribe men to dance with her. Except for one. Jeremy Michelson continued to seek her company in spite of her oddities. It didn't help that he lived in her home, either. When Jeremy's father was lost at sea, Lord Westby had invited his old friend's son to live at Westby house, where he was forever underfoot and in her business. Had he a pleasant disposition, she might have grown to admire him. She did not. Jeremy was a foul-mouthed, ill-tempered bully who enjoyed tormenting her and her sisters. She despised him almost as much as she despised going to balls.

Thanks to Clarisse's untimely interference, she was going to her sister Evie's debut ball, which meant there was no way to avoid dancing with Jeremy. Amelia shivered, remembering the last time they had danced and his pursuit of her down a distant, empty hallway. If Beatrice hadn't happened along... Amelia jerked her mind away from those dark remembrances and willed her pounding heart to calm.

Tears welled in her eyes, and Amelia wiped at them hoping Clarisse didn't see. Amelia did not want to talk about what had happened all those weeks ago, and she certainly did not want Clarisse to convince her to leave her room.

This really has been a most disappointing evening. She sniffled quietly and wanted to stamp her foot in frustration when she felt Clarisse move to her side.

She had not been quiet enough.

Pulling Amelia down onto the vanity chair, Clarisse placed a comforting arm around her shoulder. "Now what has you scowling so?"

Amelia knew she couldn't lie, nor could she avoid answering honestly. It was an annoying problem to have, especially when well-intentioned friends asked questions she didn't want to answer.

At this point, Amelia didn't even contemplate lying to make herself sick. Knowing Clarisse, she'd slap some powder on her face and lug Amelia below stairs regardless of her state of consciousness. Better to save her the trouble and answer with the truth.

"Jeremy Michelson."

"Yuck!" Clarisse wrinkled her nose in disgust. "I thought he had taken his own residence after returning from the Continent. I haven't seen him skulking about in ages."

"No. He's here all the time, Clarisse." Amelia had her own theory about why her father had given Jeremy an invitation to live with them, and after the events following her last dance with him, Amelia suspected she was right. "I think Father wants us to make a match, Clarisse, and I'm worried he will force my hand if I refuse."

Clarisse wrapped her arms about Amelia's shoulder, comforting Amelia with her embrace. "I won't allow it," Clarisse said with her usual pragmatic calm.

With a watery laugh, Amelia straightened and saw the light of determination in her friend's eyes. "What? You can't be serious."

"Sure I am. We'll run away together, you and I, and…and travel to the Americas."

"The Americas? Isn't it a little rustic over there? Perhaps we might go to Italy or France. Of course, there's a war, so France might not be the best option, but surely Italy is a far better choice than the Americas."

"No, no. Forget refinement and luxury. We want to get as far away as possible. It has to be America." Clarisse's brown eyes had a mischievous gleam in them as she warmed up to her idea of life in the New World. "Think of it, Mimi, the adventures we'll have. We'll learn to survive off the land by picking nuts and berries. And…and in the winter we'll hunt wild chickens!"

Amelia giggled, imagining the two of them in their

finery—Clarisse in her pink dress and voluminous skirts and Amelia in her blue—traipsing through the forests of America hunting chickens. "We don't know the first thing about hunting, Clarisse, and I'm not entirely sure chickens are wild."

"Details, details. Now, the first thing to do is…"

Embracing her friend in a tight hug, Amelia silenced Clarisse's wild imaginings with her gratitude. "Thank you, Clarisse," she whispered into her ear.

"So we're staying tonight?" Clarisse asked, holding Amelia at arm's length, her dear face ever encouraging and hopeful.

Amelia nodded. "I think it's best if we do."

"And we're going down to the ball?" Clarisse emphasized, giving Amelia a significant look.

"Yes, Clarisse. I will go to the ball."

Clarisse squealed and clapped her hands. "We're going to have such fun!"

Amelia gulped and turned to face her vanity before plopping her chin on her fists. "I'm doomed."

"No, Mimi," Clarisse said as she grabbed Amelia's hairbrush and started brushing through the tangled mass of thick, red curls. "Not doomed. Only cursed."

Chapter 2

After another half hour in her room, during which time Clarisse repaired Amelia's hair and helped her to finish dressing, Amelia was ready to endure another one of her mother's soirées. She had just stepped off the last stair when a small whirlwind with pale blonde hair and snapping blue eyes stopped her in her tracks.

It was Evie, Amelia's younger sister. "Where have you been?" she hissed. "Papa is going to announce my betrothal any minute. He's been waiting until you arrived."

Unruffled by Evie's outburst, Amelia did her best to appear indifferent to her lateness, knowing how it irritated Evie. "As you see, I am here."

"It's about time," Evie huffed, her impatience at Amelia's tardiness evident in every taut line of her small body. She was aquiver with nervous excitement, and Amelia bit back a retort at her sister's insensitivity. Evie was young, and it was a special night for her. It was not her fault Amelia hated balls.

Evie grabbed onto Amelia's hands and squeezed, smiling into her sister's eyes. "I'm glad you're here, Amelia." Amelia softened and returned her sister's smile, reminding herself of Evie's good qualities. She was a loyal sister, and Amelia cared for her. Most of the time.

"I want this evening to be perfect, and now you're

7

here."

Some of Amelia's anxiety melted at the sincerity of her sister's words, shaming Amelia for her selfish actions earlier this evening. She had opened her mouth to apologize for her lateness when Evie said, "It's perfect timing, really. Now I can remind you to be on your best behavior." Waving a stern finger at Amelia, she said, "No more missteps tonight, Amelia. This is my night, so try not to offend anyone." Having delivered her final warning, Evie sashayed away, her head held high and her white gown shimmering with every step she took.

"I...what..." Amelia spluttered. "What happened, Clarisse?"

"My poor dear," Clarisse giggled, mirth illuminating her eyes and lightening her face. "How Evie can insult a person to his face while making him feel grateful for the experience is beyond me! Even if I were as beautiful as Evie, I don't think I could get away with it. She has a flair for getting under a person's skin."

Amelia's confusion past, the full sting of Evie's insult penetrated her usual cloud of nervousness. She lunged after Evie, wanting nothing more than to make her younger sister feel the bite her words had caused.

Clarisse stopped her with a firm hand to her shoulder and shook her head. "Count to ten, Mimi, and let her go."

Gritting her teeth, Amelia took the advice. After all, it wouldn't do for the debutante to arrive at her betrothal announcement with a torn gown and chunks of hair missing, so she started counting. As she got to twenty, some of the anger had receded. By the time she reached fifty, she had cooled off, and all thoughts of revenge on the petite hellion who called herself sister were gone. "Remind me again why I came?"

"Even though she didn't say it in as many words, your presence tonight is important to your sister."

Amelia rolled her eyes. *Clarisse, ever the diplomat.* She'd spent most of her acquaintance with Amelia soothing the ruffled feathers of the Westby sisters. Amelia often thought Clarisse should join Parliament. She'd have those men in agreement within a matter of days, and they'd think it was their idea in the process. Though Clarisse almost always spoke sense, Amelia wasn't ready to roll over and let Clarisse sweet talk her out of her bad mood yet.

Leave it to Evie to take a perfectly rotten evening and make it even worse. "Evie's a spoiled brat." Amelia crossed her arms and sulked.

"She's your sister."

"Which does not negate the fact she is spoiled rotten."

"It's not her fault she was cursed, poor lamb. She was so young when it all happened."

"Are you forgetting something, Clarisse? I was right there getting cursed by the old gypsy hag, too! Where's my 'poor lamb?' "

"And mine?" a distant voice called.

Both women turned and watched as Lady Beatrice Westby, Amelia's elder sister, sauntered the length of the hallway. "I want a 'poor lamb,' too, Clarisse. Mine is the worst of all!" Bea clutched Amelia's shoulder and pressed the back of her hand to her forehead in true dramatic fashion.

"Oh, you two!" Clarisse scolded. "You know very

well Evie took the worst of it. Why, to be mute must be horrid!"

"Mostly mute," Amelia clarified. "You forget Evie can speak to family, if not acquaintances or strangers."

"Why are we speaking of our curse anyway? It's old news." Bea pretended to look bored while she smoothed invisible wrinkles from her dress. It was a gorgeous creation of silky gold, falling in a graceful stream from her cinched bosom to the tops of her matching satin slippers. A single ivory ribbon adorned her swan-like neck, its tail fluttering onto the smooth expanse of her open back. In her golden locks, her maid had woven strands of pearls through the intricate loops of her hair. The overall effect was stunning.

As her sister, it would be easy to hate Bea. Gorgeous, intelligent, and witty—women had been despised for less, but Amelia never could. She alone knew the guilt Beatrice carried with her every day. After all, it was Bea who had convinced them to lie and thus gotten them cursed in the first place. Both she and Evie had forgiven Bea long ago, but Beatrice never forgot.

So in spite of Clarisse's protestation it was Evie who bore the harshest curse of the three sisters, Amelia knew it was Beatrice. For not only did she carry the weight of the gypsy's spell, but she had to live with the knowledge that their one lie had cost an innocent man his life. Amelia would rather be forced to tell the truth than forever bear the hardship of that guilt.

Amelia rubbed her arms against the sudden chill accompanying her musings and noted the conversation had moved on without her. Clarisse, as usual, was defending her. "We are speaking of the curse because your sister is having a difficult time with it this evening."

"It's only going to get worse, I'm afraid," Bea said with uncharacteristic sympathy. "Mother wants you to meet someone."

Oh, no. Not again! As she was unable to secure a proposal within her first season, her mother, Lady Anne Westby, had made it her personal mission to see Amelia married. It didn't matter to whom, and as long as he was male and had a title, Amelia was forced to meet him. The last gentleman she met had been over seventy and deaf as a post. When Amelia resisted due to his advanced years, her mother had said he'd be dead soon, leaving her a wealthy widow. As tempting as the promise of independence was, Amelia refused to marry a man over three times her age.

"Who has mother picked out for me this time?" Amelia asked Bea and Clarisse, with a feeling of impending doom. "It must be someone important, because she sent both of you to get me."

"I don't know his name," Bea hedged, "but Mother says he hasn't been in London since your debut. I know almost everyone who is in Town for the Season, and I don't recall seeing any new faces."

"Maybe he's recently arrived?" Amelia wondered, trying to recall if she'd heard any gossip about new arrivals in the last several weeks. If the Season weren't still so young, there would already be rumors circulating regarding a new face in the crowd. Too bad the gossip mill was not functioning at full capacity yet.

"Oh! I know who it might be!" Clarisse said, interrupting Amelia and Bea's conversation. "It could be Lord Stanton."

"Lord Stanton? I've never heard of him. Have you, Bea?"

"No, I haven't." Amelia didn't quite believe her, and that was the problem with Beatrice's curse. It was always difficult to tell whether she was lying or telling the truth, and right now Amelia was almost certain her sister was lying to her.

Amelia noted Beatrice avoided her eyes and looked to Clarisse for answers instead. "What do you know about him, Clarisse?"

"He's recently inherited the title, and I heard Mother telling Father he's come to Town to look for a wife."

Lord Stanton? Amelia scanned her list of acquaintances, a woefully short list for a young unmarried woman, and realized his name was unknown. "Where is he from, do you know?"

"I think Scotland," Clarisse responded, but she was no longer paying attention to Amelia and Beatrice. She moved to the open door of the ballroom and peered inside. Whispering over her shoulder, she beckoned the two of them. "Your father is announcing Evie's betrothal to Lord Newgate."

Beatrice and Amelia hurried over and stood behind Clarisse, craning to see over the crowd of people who had gathered for her father's announcement. With a few words from Lord Westby, a ready blush from Evie, and a chaste kiss from her betrothed, Amelia's baby sister was engaged.

Backing away from the door, Amelia felt a strange hollowness having nothing to do with her curse and everything to do with her status as spinster. Amelia didn't want to be alone the rest of her life. She wanted happiness like Evie had. Maybe she had been too hasty in dismissing all those suitors her mother had arranged for her to meet. Maybe it was past time for her to find her own special someone.

"Mimi?" Beatrice asked, following Amelia into the shadows of the hallway. "Are you well?"

"When am I to meet this man, this Lord Stanton?"

"Are you sure? No one will force you to meet him. I'll talk to Mother and—"

"No, Beatrice. I…I want to do it, so please tell me when."

"Midnight."

Amelia nodded, determined to grab whatever happiness she could find. If Lord Stanton was new to Town, as Clarisse said, then perhaps she had a chance at establishing a relationship with the one man in London who didn't know of her affliction.

"I'm sure," she repeated, as much for Bea's sake as for her own.

"Then I wish you luck, darling."

The opening chords of Evie and Lord Newgate's first waltz started as the clock chimed the half hour.

"Oh, la! Is it that time already?" Beatrice drawled. "I'm off to a card game, and you"—here she adjusted Amelia's bodice so it showed more of her ample bosom—"have a date with a Scotsman."

Amelia watched Beatrice disappear down the hall before turning to Clarisse. But her friend wasn't standing by the door, nor was she in the hallway. Looking into the ballroom, Amelia was scanning the sides of the dance floor when a familiar pink dress floated past. Clarisse was dancing with a gentleman she had long admired.

With no one left to distract her from her thoughts, Amelia paced the hallway, obsessing about her decision to meet Lord Stanton. The mere idea of meeting another strange man had her flushing as perspiration dotted her brow.

Why am I doing this? Men find me too direct. This one won't be any different, and I'll be back where I started, unwanted and alone.

Tears pricked her eyes at those ugly unbidden thoughts, but Amelia recognized them as truth. Men didn't like her, and meeting Lord Stanton would only show her again she was unworthy of finding love. A clawing panic worked its way up from her stomach to lodge in her throat. Amelia wasn't up to the task of meeting the mysterious Scotsman. She might never be. On an impulse born of desperation, she fled the house.

The moment Amelia stepped outside she was calmed, always finding comfort and peace in the outdoors. She looked up at the clear evening sky and found her favorite stars twinkling above. On a deep breath, Amelia detected the faint scent of the honeysuckle and roses that bordered the walkway to the stables. She sniffed again, alerted to a more potent odor. *And cigar smoke?* No one was supposed to be smoking near the stables. All the groomsmen knew it, too. Her father would dismiss any one of them on the spot if they so much as puffed a cigar near his beloved thoroughbreds.

Picking up her skirts, she raced down the pathway to the stables. As she rounded the far side of the building, she ran into something solid and warm and definitely male.

"Oof!" she screeched. Strong arms reached out to

steady her, and Amelia, caught unawares and frightened, kicked her leg into what she hoped was a gentleman's "sweet spot."

She heard a grunt of pain, and a rough voice close to her ear hissed, "You little minx!" before Amelia's world turned upside down.

Chapter 3

Tavis McGuire was having a bad night. His informant had arrived with nothing of import to tell him. In fact, he wasn't telling Tavis anything he didn't already know. Tavis stared at the younger man, the moonlight on this side of the stable illuminating his beady eyes and sullen face.

"How is it in your six weeks of surveillance with the family you have yet to find any concrete evidence implicating our target?"

The man shifted on his feet and whined, "He's very secretive, my lord, and keeps his affairs close to himself."

"You can't even tell me if there have been frequent visitors to the house for his lordship, or if he leaves home for long periods of time?" At the uneasy look on the other man's face, Tavis sighed and ran his fingers through his hair. "Meeks, you must have something you can tell me!" he exploded in exasperation.

"The ladies do receive frequent visitors, and one visitor in particular is at the house on a daily basis."

"Yes, yes, Meeks. You've already mentioned Lady Clarisse Thornston, and I believe I've already told you we have cleared her and her family of any suspicion."

"I am sorry, my lord. There's not much more I can tell you."

"Your search of his study yielded nothing useful?

No hidden compartments or secret doors you can investigate later?"

With only continued silence from Meeks, Tavis gave up. "Go away, Meeks. Unless you have something useful for me by tomorrow morning, you will be reassigned and no longer connected to this mission."

"Yes, sir," Meeks replied and skulked away into the night, leaving Tavis to ponder what he had learned. Or not learned, as was the case. Six weeks of surveillance gone, and he was no closer than he was when he started. Without the documentation he needed Meeks to find... Tavis groaned. *I'll have to proceed to Plan B.* His hand grasped his neck, already contemplating the hangman's noose tightening if he didn't ferret out the traitor's secrets.

Pulling out his pocket watch, Tavis checked the time. "One more hour." He felt the noose pull tighter.

"Hell," he snorted, patting his horse on the rump. "This whole year has been some sort of Shakespearean tragedy." Tavis lit a cigar and walked out into the warm evening air to lean against the smooth wooden stable walls. He assessed the expansive Mayfair mansion alight with glittering candles. Even from where he stood, puffing on his cigar, he heard the faint strains of music spilling from the house into the May night. He sighed. This was not how he wanted to spend the evening. But ever since his brother's solicitor had tracked him down on the Continent almost three months ago to inform him of his brother's death, Tavis's life had not been his own. Now the heir to the earldom of Stanton, Tavis had all the responsibilities which accompanied the title.

And none of the fun.

He remembered the day the solicitor found him on a battlefield in France and told him he must come home.

"Home?" Tavis demanded. "Stanton hasn't been my home for years, not since John assumed the title of earl, and Ballywith has never been my home. I will not return."

The solicitor, a Mr. Alfred T. Coombes, had been nervous and a little afraid of him. Tavis supposed he had looked less than civilized in his torn and bloodied uniform, having recently survived a hellish battle against the French. Mr. Coombes had taken one look at his blood-streaked dirty face, saw the musket Tavis had grabbed upon his arrival, and paled, but he did not back down.

"Mr. McGuire, sir, while you may not have made Stanton and the Ballywith estate your home for several years, it is now yours. You must return and assume your responsibilities. It is imperative."

Tavis had never liked being told what to do. In fact, most of Tavis's life had been in the pursuit of doing exactly what he wanted to do. Being the second son, he always knew he was not destined for the earldom or the entailed responsibilities which accompanied the title. From the day he was born and sent to live with his aunt, he lived a carefree life, never bothering to learn about estate management, finances, and the like because he knew the earldom was in the capable hands of his elder brother, John.

So when this nervous solicitor tracked him down and told him he had to return to take over the responsibilities of the title, Tavis objected.

"What do you mean I must assume my

responsibilities?" He advanced on Mr. Alfred T. Coombes, his voice calm but menacing. "Who gave you the authority to uproot my life and to tell me what I should be doing?" Tavis had cornered the solicitor in his tent. The man had by now a kind of wild-eyed look to him, and Tavis grabbed him by the jacket.

But Mr. Alfred T. Coombes was not a complete idiot. Realizing his words had angered the new Earl of Stanton, he backtracked. Adam's apple bobbing, he said, "Ah, well, you see, it's…ahem, aside from your inheriting the title, it was also the express wish of your brother that you be found and brought home."

Tavis's grip on the solicitor's jacket tightened. "What do you mean it was the express wish of my brother?" Tavis and John had never been close; a twelve-year gap had separated the two brothers. By the time Tavis was old enough to be of interest to his brother, John had disappeared, leaving Tavis to wonder about the brother he never knew.

Mr. Coombes rifled through his pockets—a difficult feat, what with Tavis's iron hold on his jacket—and managed to produce an envelope. Thrusting it under Tavis's nose, he explained, "Your brother's dying wish was for me to find you and give you this."

Eying the letter and the unmistakable seal of the Earl of Stanton, Tavis released the solicitor and took the letter.

"Leave me!" he ordered. Mr. Coombes had been only too happy to oblige as he vacated the tent and left Tavis with his thoughts and his brother's letter.

Tavis had sat for hours staring at the letter in his hands. He didn't want to believe his brother had died and made him earl, and to Tavis's mind, opening the letter would somehow make true everything the twit Coombes had said.

At last, with shaking hands, Tavis broke the seal on the letter and read his brother's last words to him.

Dear Tavis,

If you are reading this letter, then I am dead. Please do not grieve for me. Death will be a sweet release after years of suffering. I never had the chance to know you, Tavis, the difference in our ages being so great. I wasn't there, but it doesn't mean I didn't care for you.

By the time you were born, I was already twelve years of age and well on my way to becoming the future Earl of Stanton. Our parents, as you know, had been older when they conceived me, and Mother's pregnancy was quite difficult. They never thought to have another child. Though Mother was shocked when she found out she was expecting you, she was so happy. I was too, because it meant a baby brother or sister as companion. Father was too worried about Mother to be excited about a new child and frequently predicted Mother would die in childbirth. Well, the old man was right. Her pregnancy was difficult, but she delivered you even though it took all of her strength. Less than a month later, our mother, Lady Janet, passed quietly in the night.

I wish you had known Mother, Tavis. She was a sweet and generous woman, and she brought warmth and laughter into our home. Her death devastated Father and left him a cold, unfeeling man. He wasn't always like that, Brother. Oh, he was serious by nature and very shrewd when it came to business dealings, but he was never without feeling, never cruel. But her death broke something in him, and the old man decided you were to blame.

After Mother died, I didn't see you again until you were six years old. Father couldn't bear to have you anywhere around us, so you were sent to live with Aunt Millie, and I was stuck at home with a temperamental, moody father. I will only say that when I left for boarding school, a year after Mother's death, it was as if the sun finally shined again.

Most holidays I spent with Father in London; Ballywith was too full of lingering memories of Mother. One year Father was occupied with business, so I was given permission to spend the holiday with you and Aunt Millie. I don't know if you will even remember that time, but it was the happiest I had been in years. I taught you to ride your first horse, Legacy, and I even taught you how to shoot a gun. I remember you cried when I had to return to university.

The last time I saw you I was sent to Aunt Millie's after I contracted lung fever at university. You were eight years old at the time. Father didn't want me in London, and he still couldn't bear to travel to Ballywith, so to Aunt Millie's I went. I lingered near death for almost two weeks. Though I was insensible, I remember you wanted to come in to see me but Father refused. Even through the haze of sickness I could hear him yelling at you to stay out. But one night, Tavis, you must have snuck in when Father was asleep. I remember you held my hand and talked to me the whole night. I don't know what you said, but it was you who helped me come back from death. When I awoke, I asked for you, and Father said you had been sent away to school. I was desperate for word of you, Brother, but Father refused to tell me where you had gone.

After that illness, I was never the same again. I was never as strong again or as well again. I eventually married, a lovely young woman named Mary. Unfortunately, we were never blessed with children. She passed away three weeks ago, and I myself am not much longer for this world.

I am ashamed, Tavis, because I was never the brother you deserved. I let Father bully me into ignoring you. He forbade me to speak of you or to find you once you left school. He even threatened to cut off my allowance, and as a young man who had recently married, I foolishly believed money was more important than you. Forgive me my cowardice, Brother, and know that every day since the old man has been dead I have been looking for you, hoping you'll come home to Ballywith.

I know you'll say Ballywith has never been your home. Remember a house is a shell, Tavis. It's not a home until there is love. Mary helped me see that. With her love and strength, I was able to banish all the bad memories from our home for good. We were happy here.

Find a good woman, marry her, and create your own memories at Ballywith. Make your own happiness.

Your loving brother,
John

Long after the last light of day had faded, Tavis sat with his brother's letter clenched in his hands. So many nights he had lain awake wondering why. Why was he sent away? Why did his father hate him? Why did John never come back to see him?

He remembered with clarity those precious moments with his brother at Aunt Millie's. It was true he cried when John went away the first time. He had admired his brother and loved him with all the fierceness and loyalty of a child. When Tavis was sent away at age eight, it had ripped him apart to be separated again from his brother. Tavis had been sure John would find him. Every day he waited for a letter or a message to come from his brother. Every day he grew a little more disillusioned. Then one day about seven months after he was sent to school, he gave up. He closed up that part of his heart and never looked in it again.

This letter, though, changed everything. It told him he was loved. It told him he was wanted by his mother and, for the brief time she lived, she had loved him. It told him John had never forgotten him and had loved him all these years.

Tavis cradled his head in his hands and would have wept had he the strength to do so. Because if this letter was true, it also told him his brother was gone. If not for his stubbornness and pride, he could have reconciled with his brother years ago. His brother's messengers had found him, but Tavis had refused to read any missives sent to him. He wanted his brother to suffer like he had all those years ago.

"What a fool I have been. All the time I wasted, and now I'll never see him again." Downing a hefty amount of Scotch to drown his sorrows, Tavis stumbled to his bed and passed a fitful night's sleep.

On the morning, with heavy heart and a newfound sense of responsibility Tavis McGuire, the fifth Earl of Stanton, packed his belongings and went home.

Chapter 4

Two months after that fateful day, he found himself yelling at Mr. Coombes, his seemingly half-witted solicitor. "What do you mean they've all been sold?" He had come home to find his estate in near ruin and the horses in his brother's stables—*his horses*—sold from under his brother's nose.

Even though Tavis had never contacted his brother since his father sent him away, it didn't mean Tavis wasn't curious about his brother and his interests. Through circuitous routes, he had learned of his brother's interest in breeding race horses. Tavis had recalled how much he had enjoyed riding with John at Aunt Millie's. In fact, it was one of his clearest memories of his childhood and one he still remembered with pleasure. It was those memories of riding horses with his brother which had prompted him to find and buy several horses during his travels. He'd sent them back to Ballywith accompanied by a message that they were "to increase the productivity of the estate." All were sent anonymously, of course. It wouldn't do to appear interested in John's affairs. He was just ensuring the prosperity of the estate should anything untoward happen to John, Tavis had reasoned at the time.

But now it seemed all the trouble he had undertaken in choosing prime breeding stock was for nothing, if what Mr. Coombes said was true. He stared at Mr. Coombes until he swallowed and pulled at the collar of his shirt. "It's just as I said, Lord Stanton. They all were sold shortly before your brother's death."

He jumped from his chair and ran around the desk, carrying the ledger of the estate's expenses. Opening the book, Mr. Coombes cleared his throat and pointed a shaky finger at last year's expenses.

"As you can see, the estate has been rapidly leaching funds. Poor growing seasons resulting in lost crops means lost income. Furthermore, we've had several harsh winters and much of the livestock perished. Your brother did his best to replace the herds, but at considerable cost."

Mr. Coombes turned several more pages to further illustrate the sad state of affairs at Ballywith. "In addition to loss of income, repairs have had to be made on tenant cottages. Additionally, two years ago there was a substantial fire in the servant's quarters here at Ballywith. Extensive repairs were needed."

Tavis studied the ledger for several minutes, thinking, while Coombes droned on with details of the losses to the estate. It was true he knew very little about his holdings, but his aunt had apprised him that, though his father was "an unholy prick," the old earl was a wealthy man.

Despite his indifference toward Tavis, he had sent him to the best schools and seen he always wore the best clothing. When John had visited on those two occasions, he had been well-attired and traveled in a chaise and four. John had even had a trip to the Continent when he turned twenty-two. Tavis remembered his aunt telling him about it when he had been home on holiday that year. The old earl had also provided Aunt Millie with a generous monthly allowance so she was able to live in a modest manor with a handful of servants to care for her.

Which is why when Coombes said the estate had no more money, Tavis questioned it. Because even if everything Coombes had said was true, all those losses would in no way account for the lack of funds which now existed.

"But it was my understanding the estate had enough funds to cover such loss of income and repairs without threatening the monies tied to the estate," Tavis stated. "So where has all the money gone?"

Mr. Coombes was nervous now. His face was flushed, and small dots of perspiration broke out on his forehead. Tavis noted all of this with increasing suspicion.

"Is there something you're not telling me, Coombes?" Tavis asked with deceptive mildness as he rose from his desk to glare at the solicitor.

"Ah, it's just…just…" Coombes stammered, retreating to the other side of the desk, "most of the money was spent before your brother became earl."

"Spent how?" Tavis prompted.

"Spent on repaying debts earned by your father, the third Earl of Stanton. Before he died, he had racked up considerable gaming debts, severely limiting the spending abilities of the estate." Mr. Coombes sank into the chair and fiddled with the buttons on his coat.

"Is there more, Mr. Coombes?" Tavis asked, noting the increased agitation of the solicitor and the sickly pallor on his face.

"Before dying, your father told my father, Mr. Coombes, Senior, who was your father's man of business, that he'd be damned if he left a penny of his money to go to feeding and housing the two most worthless sons in all of Scotland." Mr. Coombes finished in a rush and braced his hands on the arms of the chair almost as if he were ready to push off and run if Tavis showed any signs of displeasure at the news he had just relayed.

Seeing the other man's agitation, Tavis yelled, "Calm down, man! I'm not going to run you through for delivering a message from the old bastard." Mr. Coombes relaxed, though his eyes remained wary.

Raking a hand through his hair, Tavis turned his back on Mr. Coombes to stare out the window. *It figures. Father had to find some way to torment me beyond the grave.*

"I assume John did what he could to regain the funds."

"Yes, my lord." Coombes cleared his throat again. "And I have explained to you the problems plaguing the estate since your brother took over."

"In detail, Mr. Coombes." Tavis moved back to the desk and sank into his chair, where he proceeded to prop his legs on the desktop. Laying his head against the back of the chair, he closed his eyes. With his thumb and forefinger, he pinched the bridge of his nose in a desperate attempt to ward off the pounding headache he felt forming. "Which is why he sold the horses, I presume."

There was a long pause in which Tavis heard the nervous rustling of his solicitor. Tavis cracked open an eye and glared at him.

"Not quite, my lord."

"Explain." Tavis was curt and he knew it, but damn

27

it! Trying to get information out of Coombes was about as painful as running through a briar patch naked. Which he had only ever done once. When he had been drunk. Even now, Tavis winced at the memory.

But Mr. Coombes had begun. "Your brother was approached by a man named Lord Westby about a month before he died. Westby told your brother he was in possession of an outstanding note belonging to your father."

"How much? The note. How much was it for?"

"I believe it was for five thousand pounds," Mr. Coombes stated. "Lord Westby assured your brother he was willing to forgive the note for the top four racers in the stables."

Tavis's legs dropped to the floor, and he jumped up in clear agitation. "What? Any one of those horses would have easily covered the amount of the note plus a healthy amount of interest, too." He began to pace, frustrated by this new turn of events.

"Well, yes, it's what I told your brother, Lord Stanton. Though he was fair gone with grief for his wife and ill himself, your brother realized it too, but Westby was insistent. He said he'd take those horses in exchange for the note and his guaranteed silence on a delicate matter." Coombes trailed off and flushed deeply. If possible, he looked more nervous than he had ever been.

"What delicate matter, Coombes?" Tavis had stopped his pacing to stare at his flustered solicitor.

Though still agitated, the man continued. "Lord Westby told your brother he was in possession of information, sensitive information, damaging to the memory of your father and to the continued legacy of the earldom of Stanton."

"Such as…" Tavis prompted.

"Such as information about some of your father's activities during the war." Coombes started drumming his fingers on the arm of the chair. "Lord Westby claimed he had several pieces of incriminating information that indicated your father had engaged in treasonous activities during the war." By the time he had finished, Coombes's voice was no more than a hoarse whisper.

Tavis stilled and peered at Coombes. "Did he say what kind of activities, Coombes?"

"No, my lord," Coombes replied. "But your brother saw Westby's evidence, and it was damning enough for him to agree to Westby's terms."

Resuming his pacing, Tavis began to think. So the old man had been a traitor, the rat bastard. He smiled humorlessly. *Apparently I was not the only one he betrayed.* It comforted him on some level to know his father's treachery had not been limited to him. No, he had betrayed his family and his country, and now Tavis was left to clean up the mess. God, if Westby were to talk…

"Where are the papers Westby showed my brother, the ones incriminating my father?" Tavis strode to his desk and began rummaging through the mass of papers his brother left him.

He heard Coombes's quiet voice cut through his frantic searching. "There are no papers, my lord."

"What?" Tavis looked up in hope from the pile of papers he had strewn across the desk. "Did John burn them, then?" The solicitor remained silent. "Thank God. Then the only ones who know besides Westby are you and me."

Mr. Coombes shook his head. "I'm afraid you misunderstood me, my lord. When I said there are no papers, I meant your brother never possessed them."

The implications of what his solicitor said began to sink in. "Then if John never had them, then who?"

Mr. Coombes pulled at his collar again and swallowed, but he looked Tavis in the eye when he said, "Westby, my lord."

Tavis sat and lowered his head to the desk contemplating the myriad of problems he had been given upon returning home. He almost wished Mr. Alfred T. Coombes had never found him despite the revelations he'd learned about his family. If only Coombes had been a week later, he would have moved on already, and these problems would belong to someone else and not him.

"My lord?" Coombes's tentative voice interrupted Tavis's dark musings about his untimely arrival in Tavis's life. "There is one more thing. Your brother must have told Westby he was dying and he hoped you would be coming home." Tavis heard Coombes shuffling around for something. Soon a crisp white envelope was shoved under Tavis's nose from where it still lay on his desk.

"Westby found me, right after he left your brother, and gave me this to give to you." Tavis heard the door close, signaling Coombes's departure, and sighed, the harsh sound echoing in the now silent room. Thank God Coombes was gone. Tavis didn't think he could handle any more bad news. He honestly thought he might have needed to kill Coombes if he'd said one more thing in his stuffy lawyer's voice.

Reeling from the news he had just learned about his brother, his finances, and his wretch of a father, Tavis walked to the sideboard with letter in hand and poured himself a generous amount of scotch. Then he chose a comfortable seat near the fire and opened up the missive from Lord Westby.

Two lines were scrawled across the fine paper in a bold, slanted hand.

We have matters to discuss. Come see me when you return.

Westby

Tavis crumpled the letter and threw it into the fire. He watched it until the flames had licked away the last of the paper. Even after the fire burned down, Tavis sat before the cooling embers, thinking late into the night.

At the break of day, Tavis was packed and on the road headed to London.

****

After an arduous four-day trek across Scotland and down to London, Tavis wanted to find Westby as quickly as possible. He stopped at his new London townhouse to change and eat before departing again to begin his search. Throughout the remainder of the day and most of the following one, Tavis wondered what role Westby had actually played in this whole mess. There had to be a reason Westby maintained possession of the incriminating papers that had caused John to give away their horses for the paltry sum of five thousand pounds. Tavis was determined to find out why.

It wasn't too difficult to find Lord Westby with a few questions at the clubs most gentlemen frequented. After a day of inquiries, Tavis had been introduced to Lord Westby at White's. The two of them met for lunch, and it was while dining that Westby's intentions for keeping the documents were revealed.

"I want you to marry my middle daughter, Stanton," Westby stated over drinks.

Tavis spluttered and wiped his face with his napkin. "I beg your pardon?"

"My daughter, I want you to marry her. You do that, and I'll give you the papers about your father."

"What's wrong with her?" Tavis blurted out, more than a little shocked at Westby's daring. Something had to be very wrong with his middle child if he was willing to blackmail a peer of the realm into marrying her.

Lord Westby's face mottled in anger. "I'll have you know there is nothing wrong with my daughter. She's lovely and intelligent and too fine for the likes of you."

"Then why me?" Tavis was truly incredulous. Even though it had been less than a month since he inherited his title, matrimonially minded mothers had been throwing every eligible female under the age of thirty at him. Having Lord Westby do the same was a little surprising, but not out of the realm of normal.

What surprised him was the man felt he had to use blackmail to coerce someone into marrying his daughter. That usually didn't happen. "I repeat, what is wrong with her?"

Westby had calmed himself, and his face no longer appeared to be the deep puce of rage. "I said she is a very lovely young woman, and she is. Accomplished in languages, riding, and household management." He paused, and Tavis swore he saw the man squirm in his seat. "She has a tendency to be a little outspoken, is all." Westby refused to look Tavis in the eye, a sure bet he was hiding something more. "Some people find it off-putting." Westby picked up his glass and swallowed the remainder of his drink.

"So off-putting you need to blackmail someone into marrying her?" Tavis queried.

Westby poured another drink and downed it in one gulp. "She just needs a strong hand. Someone who won't take offense at her odd ways. That's why I thought of you."

Tavis was dumbfounded. He had never met Lord Westby before today, so it was unlikely Westby knew anything about him.

Seeing his confusion, Westby continued, "I knew your father, you understand? He rarely talked about you, but when he did I could tell there was no love lost. One day, about five years ago, he told me you had joined up, sent to the Continent to fight Bonaparte. He was proud of you, though he was reluctant to admit it."

If there was one thing Tavis knew with certainty it was that his father had never been proud of him a day in his life. In fact, he remembered the day he left for the Continent. He had come to London to meet his regiment before sailing off. Deciding to visit his father had been a spur-of-the-moment decision. If he died, he at least wanted the old man to know. Tavis had found him in his offices at Parliament. After he told his father he had bought a commission, the old earl said, "You'll probably screw that up, too, and be sent home in a pine box within a month." That being said, the old earl had waved him out of his office and slammed the door behind him.

The old man must have believed Tavis would be killed within a month, because a batman awaited him at the docks before he shipped out. All his batman had said, a man by the name of Jeremiah Meeks, was that his father thought he could be of service to Tavis during the war. This one act had given Tavis hope his father did not completely hate him. However, he still remained skeptical that at any point the old man came close to admitting pride in him.

His doubt must have shown on his face because Westby held up his hands and crossed his heart.

"It's the truth," he slurred, sounding a little drunk after having downed three glasses of fine whisky in rapid succession. "An' that's when I started to follow you. On the quiet, like, that is." He poured another glass, a little unsteadily this time. "I took note of battles you had led, skirmishes you had won." He leaned in closer to Tavis, his foul breath too close to Tavis's nose. Tavis tried not to pinch his nostrils, so he held his breath instead. "I know people, you understand? People in high places. They would mention your name, casual-like, at White's or in Parliament. They said you were making a name for yourself in the army."

Westby sat back in his chair, taking his foul-smelling breath with him. Tavis let out the breath he had been holding, but Westby wasn't done. "An idea began to form." Westby tapped his temple with his forefinger and leveled a squinty-eyed stare at Tavis. He hissed out in a low voice, "You could help her break the curse."

Tavis straightened and took note of Westby's blathering. "What curse?"

Westby must have realized he had been talking too freely because he backtracked. "No curse. I didn't mean curse. I just meant you would be strong enough to overlook her directness and find the sweet woman inside."

Tavis was intrigued and, if he were honest with himself, a little flattered. It wasn't every day he met someone who had followed his career on the Continent as it appeared Lord Westby had. For him to think Tavis would suit his daughter... Tavis mulled on that. Westby had said she was off-putting and prone to directness. Maybe it wasn't such a compliment, after all, to be thought a suitable mate for his daughter. Still, he reasoned, he needed a wife, and he needed to get his hands on those documents incriminating his father.

"If I agree to meet your daughter"—Tavis paused and Westby perked up, heartened by Tavis's statement—"you would have to guarantee me that upon our marriage you would hand over any and all paperwork concerning my father, the third Earl of Stanton."

"Yes, yes," Westby hurried to assure Tavis. "Of course."

"Also, if we were to marry, I would like to discuss including in your daughter's settlement the horses you took from my stables."

Westby's genial smile disappeared, replaced by a stern line of displeasure. "Absolutely not. Those are my horses, paid for with your father's note."

Tavis's eyes darkened in anger. "You and I both know the horseflesh you stole from my stables that day more than repaid the five thousand pounds my father owed you."

Westby leaned in, his eyes narrowed to obsidian slits. "Listen, Stanton. Those horses were exchanged for the note and for the promise I would not reveal any information about your father until such time as you have married my daughter."

Tavis leaned in too, baring his teeth as he snarled, "It seems, then, we are at an impasse, Lord Westby, because I shall refuse to meet your daughter unless you agree to my terms."

"Are you forgetting the little matter of your father's unfortunate wartime activities?" Tavis felt spittle hit his cheek from Lord Westby's hissed question. With a calm he didn't feel, Tavis removed his handkerchief from his breast pocket and wiped the offending moisture from his cheek.

"Go ahead. Tell everyone." Tavis leaned back and crossed his arms over his chest, meeting the angry glare of Lord Westby. "But when you are brought in and questioned for withholding traitorous materials from the Crown, you very well may be implicated, too."

"Fine. We will discuss the matter of the horses in my daughter's settlement if you agree to marry her."

The two men shook on it, and Westby, with aristocratic grace, staggered out of White's. Tavis remained nursing his glass of whisky.

"McGuire!" A familiar voice hailed him from across the room. Tavis looked up and spied the jovial countenance of his supervising officer, Major-General Wickes, who slid into the chair across from Tavis and signaled the waiter to bring him a drink.

"It's been awhile, Wickes." Tavis greeted his comrade and friend with a smile and a firm handshake. "At least a year."

"I think you're right, McGuire." Wickes thanked the waiter and took a sip. "Ah," he sighed, "I haven't had a good glass of whisky since coming back from the

Continent."

Tavis grimaced into his glass. "This isn't even particularly good." He downed his drink and signaled for another. "You should taste Scotch whisky. Now, that's a smooth drink."

"I had heard rumors you returned to Scotland when your brother died."

"Yes." Tavis brooded into his newly filled glass. "Congratulate me, Wickes. I'm the new Earl of Stanton." He laughed, a sad, bitter sound. "All it took was for my brother to die."

Raising his glass in mock salute, Wickes said, "To you, my friend." Tactfully changing the subject, Wickes asked over his glass, "Was that Lord Westby I saw you talking to?"

"Hmm? Yes." Tavis hesitated for a moment. "He had some information about my father he wanted to give me."

Wickes's eyes took on a hard glint. "Westby is a pig," he spat. "Do you mind me asking what information he had about your father?"

Tavis hedged. "I'd really rather not talk about it."

Grabbing his coat, Wickes suggested, "Let's take a walk, my friend, where there is less noise." He looked around the room at the rapidly filling establishment.

The two men exited and walked toward Hyde Park. Once they had walked a fair distance into the park, Wickes said, "Let me see if I can guess what you two talked about. Westby approached your brother, or maybe you when you returned home, with an offer of some delicate information in return for your cooperation on a matter of import to him. How am I doing so far?"

Tavis jerked back in sudden surprise, wondering how much his old friend actually knew. Deciding it wasn't worth prevaricating to someone who could sniff out a lie like a hound dog could sniff out a fox, Tavis said, "It's true. He approached me with incriminating information about my father, specifically information that detailed illegal wartime activities."

Wickes and Tavis walked in silence while Tavis wondered at the lack of surprise Wickes had shown at the information he had just shared. Most officers of Her Majesty's Royal Army strongly objected to anything smelling of treason, yet Wickes had shown no surprise, which made Tavis wonder what Wickes knew.

"We have suspected Westby of collusion with the enemy for some time."

Tavis started in surprise. "We?" he queried. "Who is we?"

"You're not the only one with a new title, Lord Stanton." Wickes said, emphasizing the new name. "After returning from the Continent, I was named to the War Office, in charge of wartime security."

"What have you suspected Westby of doing?"

"We have long suspected Westby of passing sensitive documents about troop numbers and supplies to English citizens in France. These documents were then passed to French sympathizers, jeopardizing the safety of thousands of English troops."

"But what does my father have to do with any of this?" Tavis asked in frustration. "If Westby is a suspect, then why is he blackmailing me?"

"We have determined Westby has a network of civilians he uses to conduct his business." Wickes blew out a frustrated breath. "This has made it very difficult to pin anything on him. Most of them are peers of the realm, like your father, who owed him a debt. Once the deed is done, usually delivering papers at a designated rendezvous, the debt is considered paid."

"But my father must have died before Westby could collect," Tavis finished, understanding dawning.

Wickes nodded. "That's exactly what we think happened, as well. When he approached your brother about the matter of your father's outstanding debt, Westby must have realized he would not be able to extort your dying brother." Wickes shrugged. "So he waited for you."

Tavis moved off the path they had been walking on to stand with arms crossed before a small pond. "It doesn't make any sense, though, Wickes. He didn't blackmail me into delivering any papers for him." Tavis snorted and turned his head to look at Wickes standing behind him. "Westby wants me to marry his chit of a daughter in return for the information about my father." Tavis stooped down and picked up a smooth rock. With a flick of his wrist, he sent the rock skipping across the pond.

Wickes joined Tavis by the pond. "Tell me what he said." Tavis blinked at Wickes's sudden arrival and at the hard glint Tavis saw in his eyes.

"It's just as I said. Westby sent me a letter requesting that we meet to discuss my father's debt. When we actually sat down to discuss it, he said he would forgive the debt if I married his daughter."

"He said nothing else?"

"I did ask him what was wrong with his daughter that he needed to blackmail a peer to marry her," Tavis mused.

"Did he say why?"

"If you are one to believe the semi-drunken ramblings of a suspected traitor, he said she was 'off-putting and direct.' "

"Think, Tavis," Wickes interjected, oddly agitated. "Did he say anything else about his daughter, anything you found odd?"

He stared unseeing into the pond. "He said I could help her break her curse," he murmured. "Silly, isn't it?" Tavis asked but found Wickes rubbing his hands together in excited anticipation.

"What? What is it?" Tavis demanded. "Was he right?" He looked at his eager friend with astonishment.

Instead of answering him directly, Wickes patted him on the shoulder. "We need you back, McGuire, for one more mission." The light of battle had entered his old friend's eyes, and Tavis could tell he was planning away behind those steely, blue-gray eyes.

Tavis shook off Wickes's hand and rubbed his hands through his hair in disbelief. First he was called home to a crumbling estate on the verge of financial ruin. Then he found out his old man was not just a colossal bastard but a traitor to boot. With Westby's thinly veiled proposition and now Wickes's plea for him to run one more mission, Tavis had had enough.

He took several deep breaths and reminded himself of how much he owed his friend and former supervising officer, one Major-General Thomas Q. Wickes. On more than one occasion Wickes's intervention had prevented him from doing something rash and dangerous.

Hell, without his calm, rational guidance, I would still be digging latrines instead of having become a decorated war hero. Tavis paced as he argued with himself on the potential merits versus dangers of a proposed mission from the War Office. What stopped him was a realization. *You trust him with your life, no?*

"What would you have me do, man?"

A strange light entered Wickes's eyes as he said in all seriousness, "We want you to do as Westby said. Marry the chit."

Chapter 5

The sound of approaching footsteps shook Tavis out of his musings. Not wanting to be found yet, he extinguished his cigar and retreated farther into the shadows on the far side of the barn.

"Oof!" a loud female voice screeched into his ear. As Tavis braced his arms against his unknown visitor to steady himself, he felt a small foot come close to emasculating him. He doubled over and gritted out, "You little minx!"

Tavis's hold on the spitting female weakened due to the pain he was now feeling below the belt. Not wanting to become a eunuch, a distinct possibility the way this hellcat was twisting about, Tavis lurched forward, pushing the woman to the ground. Using the strength and width of his body, he braced her fall before rolling her over and pinning her under his impressive height and weight.

"Get off me!" she screeched again. One of her waving arms managed to clip him under the chin, knocking his teeth together. Tavis swore he saw stars.

"Damn it, woman! Keep still!"

But the woman under him was incensed, flailing her arms and legs in a desperate attempt to escape, making his task that much more difficult. Spitting out several choice words, Tavis grabbed the swinging limbs of the enraged hellcat beneath him and pinned her arms above her head. Her legs were trapped under his weight, and now her arms were, too. She stilled.

"Wh-what are you going to do to me?" she whispered. He heard the nervous tremor in her voice and cursed himself for being so rough.

"Nothing, lass." He sighed. "Hold still until the stars stop spinning around my head."

She remained motionless under him as Tavis pushed back the pounding ache in his head.

At least she could listen.

Once she stilled, he got a good look at her. Frightened green eyes framed by the longest, blackest lashes he had ever seen stared back at him. He took a moment to admire her smooth, creamy skin glowing in the soft moonlight. Ropes of red-blonde curls spilled in a glorious tangle around her head. At last Tavis looked down at her lips. Full, red, and slightly parted, he groaned when he saw her small, red tongue dart out and wet her lower lip.

"Who-who are you?" she whispered.

"Ah, forgive my rudeness, my lady," Tavis grinned. He took one of the woman's imprisoned hands and brought it up to his lips for a gentle kiss.

The lady shivered, and he heard her suck in a breath. "Tavis McGuire, my lady, at your most devoted service." Since she wasn't protesting his liberties, he maintained possession of her hand, keeping it close to his chest while he began to rub the back of it with his thumb. "And you are…?"

Green eyes flashed at him in anger. "Lady Amelia. My family is nearby and shall notice if I have gone missing." She started to squirm again in an attempt to escape. "You will release me at once, or I shall…I shall scream!"

Tavis was reeling from the effects of all of her squirming. In an effort to maintain control, he re-imprisoned both of her hands under his broad chest. Lowering one of his massive hands over her mouth, he glared at her. "You will be quiet, woman, or you will not be released." Her eyes grew wide in fright. "Do you understand me?"

She nodded her head.

Tavis removed his hand from her mouth and saw she kept it closed, though her lips trembled as if she were about to cry.

"Good girl." He patted her head, a move sure to rile her anger, because he hated seeing that spark of fear in her eyes, especially knowing he had put it there. In truth, he'd rather she be a spitting, angry whirlwind, like she had been when they wrestled a few minutes earlier, than this fearful, obedient woman he now held under him.

"There's a good lassie," he crooned for good measure. Her eyes narrowed until they were tiny slits. Oh, he had riled her up all right.

"I'm not a dog, Mr. McGuire," Lady Amelia hissed in a whisper, "so kindly do not speak to me like one."

He chuckled. "I never said you were, my lady, and I apologize if I gave that impression." Aside from her hissed reprimand, Lady Amelia remained silent.

Tavis stared into her eyes. "I am going to remove my weight from your body, and I want your word that once your arms and legs are free you won't start swinging them at me again. You damn near emasculated me with that first kick, lass."

Tavis braced his arms on either side of Lady

Amelia and raised himself onto his knees. When he was sure she had no intention of finishing the job she had started earlier, he rocked back onto his heels and sprang up.

His head still reeled from where she had swiped it, and by the time he had regained his bearings, Lady Amelia was up and had rounded the corner into the stable. When he entered through the stable doors, she had a pitchfork in hand and was pointing it at his chest.

Tavis sucked in a breath. Lady Amelia was stunning. He had already guessed she was a beauty, given the brief glimpses he'd had of her moonlit face, and he had a pretty good idea of what the rest of her looked like, too, based on what he'd felt while lying atop her. *Only a dead man could have ignored those lush, warm curves.*

She was taller than most women, but not tall enough to reach Tavis's shoulders. The ample curves guessed at were now displayed for his hungry eyes, each curve lovingly hugged by the form-fitting blue silk ball gown she wore.

And her breasts. God must have given the most perfect breasts to this woman. They were full and creamy, spilling over her bodice… Tavis's mind blanked for a moment while he marveled at humankind's most perfect breasts. He loved how they moved while her chest heaved…heaved? Tavis tore his eyes away to look up into the spitting eyes of an irritated woman who had just caught him ogling her breasts.

Oh, that's right. The pitchfork.

He backed up, his hands extended in front of him. "Lass. Lady Amelia. I am sorry for scaring you. We had a little misunderstanding out there. I never meant to hurt you." Tears glistened in her mossy green eyes and threatened to spill over onto her rosy cheeks. Tavis groaned.

Sweet Mary! Did I just think that? One look at her comely face and I am turning into a damn poet!

She jabbed the pitchfork in his direction again. "What are you doing here? I don't recognize you." Her voice wobbled, and he knew she was fighting for control of her rioting emotions. "If you were a guest, you would have no need to stable your own horses; you would have a groom do it for you." She circled him until he was pressed flat against the stable wall between a stall and a pile of hay. "And if you were an employee of the stables you would know the most important rule when working with the horses."

He was impressed. When confronted with an unknown person, she fought instead of fleeing. She had also deduced he was an outsider, even if she hadn't quite figured out who he was. And while he was busy ogling her—*and attempting to calm her down*—she'd managed to maneuver him into a corner.

Pretending a casualness he didn't feel with a pitchfork aimed at his chest, he asked, "And what rule is that?"

Her eyes lit with triumph. "The first rule taught to all new groomsmen and stable hands is that no one smokes around the horses." Amelia jabbed again, but this time Tavis was prepared. When she thrust, he reached out and grabbed her by the upper arm and used his other hand to pull the pitchfork out of her hands and toss it far from them. Wrapping his arms about her shoulders, he pulled Lady Amelia into his embrace.

****

Amelia immediately began to struggle in Tavis's grasp. He had not released her after disarming her; instead, he had wrapped his beefy arms around her and pulled her close to his body.

Oh, Lord! If I am caught in this man's arms, my family will be embroiled in a huge scandal.

Her reputation would be destroyed, and she would be a spinster for the rest of her life. Looking into his eyes with wide-eyed fright, she tried to convey this to him, but the words did not form.

"No one is here but the two of us," he reassured her, "and if I hear someone coming, I'll make sure to disappear." He smiled encouragingly, his eyes kind, yet firm. Amelia soon realized she would not escape his embrace. She ceased struggling but remained wary, eyeing him to judge his intentions. It wasn't until he tucked her head under his chin and smoothed his hand along her hair, saying, "Shh, lass, I've got you," that Amelia's thinly held control of her emotions broke.

Amelia's shoulders shook, and the tears she had held in came pouring out while she stayed anchored in the comforting embrace of Tavis McGuire. What a night! It was bad enough to have her plans ruined by Clarisse and Bea, but to be attacked, manhandled, and ogled by Tavis McGuire was too much. Any remaining dignity she possessed came pouring out of her eyes and onto his shirt.

And in the stables, no less.

Through it all, he remained quiet and comforting, a solid rock through the storm of her emotions. Her tears spent, Amelia calmed under his soothing caresses.

For such a big man, he certainly is gentle.

She mulled this information while remembering her first glimpse of Tavis McGuire. In the dark it had been too difficult to make out the finer features of his face or figure. All she really saw was a dark, looming shape. Later, when he had been on top of her (Amelia blushed redder remembering what she had felt during *that*), all she could make out was that he was big and muscled. She remembered the feel of his strong hands grasping her arms and sighed.

"What's that, lass? Did you say something?" Tavis queried, his big hand pausing in the middle of her back.

Too embarrassed to meet his eyes yet, she shook her head and still kept it on his chest. He continued stroking her hair, taking a few silky strands at a time to twirl around his finger. Amelia was at once mortally embarrassed and contented. It was odd, these contrasting emotions she felt, all too similar to the man called Tavis McGuire.

A good head taller than her own father, this man towered over her. When she saw him in the light of the stables for the first time, she had almost dropped her pitchfork because he was so tall, and massive across the chest and shoulders. She had heard of men who used their size to intimidate and coerce a woman into doing what they wanted. Yet aside from her initial fright when they ran into each other and her instincts to defend had kicked in, she had never been in danger from him.

His face was not conventionally handsome, due to the imposing sharp angles of his cheeks and nose, but when he smiled, those sharp angles softened, making him seem less severe. While everything else about him—impressive height, rugged appearance, and obvious strength—screamed masculinity, his eyes, a startling sapphire blue, were pretty and made him appear more approachable.

Oooh, and his hair! She remembered the silky feel of it as it had caressed her cheek when he leaned over her. He kept it longer than was fashionable, and it curled where it touched his jacket collar. In the light from the lanterns, she saw it was a deep brown streaked with red. Amelia shivered at the memory.

He must have felt it, for his embrace tightened, and he asked in a gruff voice near to her ear, "Are ye cold, then, my lady?" His voice had taken on a different timbre, and her toes curled when his breath tickled the side of her face. She also heard a faint brogue.

Amelia stiffened, deciding it was time to end this pleasant and compromising embrace. "No, Mr. McGuire, but I want you to release me, please."

Tavis dropped his arms from around her body and stepped back. Immediately, Amelia missed his warmth. She crossed her arms around her sides to warm herself, and though it embarrassed her to do so, she managed to compose herself long enough to look him in the eyes. "I thank you for your comfort while I was distressed. I now realize you did not intend to manhandle me in such a manner, and I would ask your forgiveness for my part in our altercation."

He seemed uncomfortable too. His face was flushed a dull red, and he kept pulling his shirt away from his neck, almost like his cravat was choking him. Despite his obvious discomfort, he managed a soft chuckle at her words. "Are you referring to when you almost unmanned me, or when you hit my head hard enough to make me see stars?"

She squirmed. "Both."

"I forgive you as long as you promise to never do it to a man again."

"What?" Amelia asked, hands on her hips in irritation. "Defend myself?"

Tavis found a bench on the side of one of the stalls and sank down on to it. "Calm down, my lady," he said. "No, a lass needs to defend herself if needed. I meant the unmanning bit." He patted a spot next to him on the bench, indicating Amelia should join him. "Where did you learn that, anyway? Do they teach it to young misses at finishing school?"

"My sister taught me it." Amelia flushed again but moved to sit by Tavis. "And no, I did not learn it at finishing school. I imagine if they had taught a course called 'How to Unman a Gentleman in Five Simple Moves,' they would have lost all their pupils when irate parents found out." Unable to resist a tease, she added, "Of course for you, it only took two moves."

"I'll have you know, my lady, if you hadn't first kicked me in the…er, where you kicked me, it would have taken at least five moves for you to unman me." He looked so affronted she couldn't help but laugh. Soon he joined in, and their mutual laughter helped to erase the unease and tension of their accidental first meeting.

Amelia hazarded a glance at Tavis out of the corner of her eyes. *He really is a handsome man, especially when he laughs.* She chewed on her bottom lip in thought. *But who is he?*

Even through the haze of fatigue settling over her body and the maelstrom of emotions she had experienced this evening, she was still enough in charge of her senses to maintain her suspicions about Mr.

Tavis McGuire.

"So, Mr. McGuire," Amelia said, "who exactly are you, and what are you doing in the stables alone at this time of night?" Her eyebrows rose, and she stared down her nose at him in what she hoped was a close approximation of her mother's no-nonsense look.

"How about if I tell you why I am here in the stables, and you tell me what you are doing here." He waggled his eyebrows and lowered his voice. "Alone and at this time of night."

"What are you implying, Mr. McGuire?" Her temper sparked, she grew warm at his accusation and jumped up from her perch on the bench to stand in front of him. "Are you saying I came down here alone to conduct some sort of illicit assignation?" As she spoke, she punctuated each word with a poke to his chest.

He grabbed her fingers mid-poke. "I guess it's true what they say about redheads having a foul temper. That's twice you've nearly taken my head off for asking a simple question."

She wrenched her fingers free from his grasp and yelled, "I don't have a foul temper, you big cack-headed buffoon!" He continued to sit there, regarding her with wry amusement until she realized what she said.

Straightening her skirts, she tried to control her raging temper. "Ahem, that is to say, I don't usually have a foul temper." He looked at her, doubt evident in his eyes. "You," she said, "have succeeded in bringing out the worst in me, that's all."

Recapturing her hand, he pulled her down to sit by him once again. "Then I beg your pardon, my lady. I meant no insult." He began running his thumb along the underside of her wrist by her pulse.

Amelia snatched her hand back and mumbled her own apologies. "You're right, Mr. McGuire. I do seem to be ill tempered this evening, and I beg your forgiveness." She turned her head away from the all-too-knowing eyes of Tavis McGuire in embarrassment. *How many times must I apologize to this man?*

"Why do you suppose that is?" he asked.

"I imagine," she replied, "it has something to do with being accosted outside my father's stables by an unknown person." Eyeing him with obvious displeasure, she took her leave of the bench and walked over to the stable door to look up at the night sky.

"Your father's stables?" She whirled around, startled by his sudden nearness, and found herself trapped between a wall and a very tall, very dangerous-looking man. True, he had spoken casually, almost as if he didn't care, but Amelia heard an underlying tone in his voice.

She gulped and looked up. He was so tall she had to crane her neck to look him in the eyes. What she saw caused a shiver to run up her spine. Those bright blue eyes, which had sparkled with laughter moments earlier, were now shadowed by heavy lids, and some indiscernible emotion brewed in their gleaming depths.

"Y-yes," she stammered. "That's why I came down here, to see my horse in my father's stables." Amelia gestured down the row of stalls toward where her horse was stabled. Still, he remained towering over her as he peered into her face.

He was so close to her now she saw a small scar above his left eyebrow. It was no longer than an inch, but it was a silvery trace that only added to his rugged good looks. His warm breath fanned her cheeks and sent pleasant tingles down her spine. Unlike the last time she had been cornered by a man, Tavis's breath was spicy-sweet and held a faint tinge of the cigar he had smoked. He lowered his face until he was eye level with Amelia. Darting her tongue out to wet her lips, she watched as his eyes darkened further.

He's going to kiss me.

Far from being alarmed, a heated anticipation hummed through her veins and curled in her belly. Of their own volition, her eyes closed, and she leaned toward him.

Chapter 6

After several seconds of pursed lips and heated anticipation, Amelia realized no kiss was coming. She shifted into his chest and asked, "Tavis?" When he failed to respond, she opened her eyes to peek up at him from beneath her lashes, and with his face so close to her own, Amelia was able to discern he didn't look like a man who was ready to kiss a woman. Confusion and embarrassment replaced her desire, and she asked, "Is something wrong?"

Though she attempted to pull away, Tavis snaked his arms around her waist and held her fast to him. Bending his head, he nuzzled her neck with his nose.

"No, *mo ghrádh*. I was momentarily stunned by your beauty."

Amelia knew Tavis was keeping something from her. She had seen it in his eyes when he towered over her so dark and brooding before. Yet in spite of her apprehension, she couldn't help the unexpected flare of happiness his compliment brought, even if he wasn't being completely honest with her. "Tavis..." she demurred, blushing a lovely shade of pink.

"It's true. No man has told you that before?"

She lowered her head and shook it. He cupped her chin with his hand and raised her head so she was forced to look him in the eyes. "Men in England must be blind," he whispered. "Because you surely are the prettiest lass this side of Scotland."

Tavis took a blunt finger and stroked her cheek. Helpless to stop, Amelia leaned into his caress as a flower leans toward the sun. "You have such fine skin, soft as silk and the color of fresh cream." He tapped the end of her nose with his finger. "Except for when you blush. Then you turn a lovely shade of pink." She laughed, a breathless nervous sound to her own ears. "And your eyes…" His fingers traced an arched eyebrow. "They are so expressive, showing everything you think and feel." He bent closer so his forehead rested against hers. "A man could lose himself in your eyes."

Drawing in a deep breath, Amelia reveled in the soft seduction of Tavis's words. They flowed like liquid light through her veins, warming her in a way she had never felt before. No man had ever spoken to her in such reverent, adoring tones, and she found she was quite drunk from the experience.

Her arms broke out into goose flesh, and she shivered as she realized how close she was to falling under this man's spell. Tavis was unlike any other man she had ever met, mostly because of how focused he was on her. She had always wondered what it would be like to hold the attention of someone as masculine as Tavis. Now she knew. It was like being bathed in the summer sun—at first the light from gentle rays only kisses delicate skin, but the danger of being burned is much too real to not be cautious.

Too much time with Tavis and I will easily be burned. How can I ever hope to keep my heart safe when his very touch sets me aflame?

Though Tavis had never indicated in either word or

deed he was anything less than a gentleman, Amelia could attest to the unleashed power humming under his smooth façade. She suspected Tavis McGuire could burn her quite badly indeed.

"Dance with me, Amelia," Tavis said breaking into her gloomy thoughts. She looked at him, wondering what had prompted him to suggest a dance in the stables, but Tavis only grinned a slow, seductive smile to her in return. As he unwrapped her hands from around his neck, he laced their fingers together and raised her hand to his lips. Placing gentle kisses on her palm and the inside of her wrist, he urged again, "Dance with me, Amelia. Let me hold you under the stars."

She nodded, not wanting this dream to end. Hand in hand, she allowed Tavis to lead her into the moonlight waiting just outside the stable doors.

"Now, this is a setting worthy of a dance." Tavis motioned around him. Amelia had to agree. He had led them into a small clearing outside the stable doors. It was bordered by a ring of towering oaks and fragrant fruit trees. The exotic smell of gardenia drifted down from the greenhouse, and its heady fragrance permeated the clearing. A small breeze rustled the grass and blew strands of Amelia's curls onto her cheeks. She brushed them away, too overwhelmed by new sensations to fully appreciate the beauty of her surroundings.

High in the sky, the moon bathed the grounds with its muted light. At this location, the music from the ball could be heard loudly enough to dance to. The liquid strains of a waltz floated on the air to Tavis and Amelia.

She looked up at him, too afraid to speak lest the spell of the past few moments be broken. He must have felt it too, because he stared at her for several heartbeats before flashing an endearingly lopsided grin. "With the moonlight to guide us and the stars to accent your beauty, no ballroom could ever compare." He gave a bow and offered her his hand. "My lady?" She curtsied and put her hand in his. With a triumphant smile, he gathered her up into his arms and led her around the clearing.

Dancing with Tavis is like dancing on a cloud.

For such a big man, he was light on his feet. He held her with solid surety in his embrace, the strength of his arms guiding her in the intricate steps of the waltz. Though several inches separated them, as deemed proper by society, she was attuned to the shifting muscles of his legs through the layers of her skirt. Also, dark as it was, she could still make out the glittering intensity of his eyes, which were trained on her with enough force to leave her lightheaded.

He intrigued her as no man ever had before, and, if she were being honest with herself, she was attracted to him. Blushing at the remembrance of her wanton behavior in the stables, Amelia knew had he not stopped her, she would have kissed him.

Amelia sighed. She was disappointed he hadn't kissed her, even if he had shown more restraint and more care for her reputation than she in not doing so.

Because in his arms I would have tossed aside twenty years of carefully bred propriety for one kiss from this man. And more.

Though still a maid, she did understand what happened between a man and a woman. Bea had made sure of that. Amelia giggled to herself, remembering that embarrassing (and revealing) conversation shortly after Beatrice had wed.

"You need to be prepared, Mimi," Bea had said. "Our mother did nothing to prepare me for my wedding night, and it was unpleasant." Bea's nose wrinkled in distaste. "Had she told me anything about what was to happen or how to make it more pleasurable, it could have been better." She thought for a minute and then revised her statement. "Well, less painful at least."

Beatrice had described in excruciating detail exactly what to expect. At first, Amelia was too shocked and embarrassed to think about that aspect of a marriage, but looking at Tavis, Amelia knew in her heart that if he were hers, she would let him do all Beatrice had described and more.

Which brings us back to why Tavis doesn't want to kiss me.

If she had read the situation correctly, and based on Bea's detailed analysis of the male libido she was certain she had, Tavis had wanted to kiss her as much as she had wanted to be kissed. So why had he stopped?

She must have sighed again, because his warm, husky voice filled her ear. "What thoughts have you sighing so, my lady?"

Amelia snapped out of her lust-filled thoughts and blushed hotly, but without time to prepare herself, she blurted out, "I was wondering why you didn't kiss me in the stables."

"Ah, uh, that is to say…" Tavis stammered and faltered on his footing, the first stumble in their otherwise perfect dance. He regained the rhythm of the dance and resumed the steps when she peeked up at him through her lashes. He appeared to be in deep concentration.

"I did want to kiss you, my lady," he said. "However, I did not want to compromise you. You are a lady, and I am a gentleman." He cleared his throat and finished, while avoiding Amelia's eyes, "There are rules."

Though Amelia didn't like his answer, she knew he was right. Out alone under the stars with Tavis it was easy to forget they had not been properly introduced and that she should not be dancing alone with him so far away from the house and any chaperones.

The music from the house stopped, and he ended their dance on a graceful twirl. Bowing over her hand, he kissed it and looked up into her eyes. "Our waltz has ended," he said. When she didn't respond, he added, "It approaches midnight, my lady."

Her eyes snapped to attention from whatever thoughts had been occupying her mind. "What?" she squeaked, scanning the clearing and the house beyond. "Midnight?"

"Yes, I'm afraid it's time to say goodbye. Someone must be looking for you."

Amelia wondered how he knew she had an appointment to keep. "Er, you are right, I guess," she said, startled by the sudden steely light found in his gaze. "I guess I didn't realize how late it was, and I do have someone to meet."

"Who are you meeting?" he demanded. "Do you have a beau you were planning on meeting here when you ran into me?"

"No," she said in confusion, once again surprised by his reaction to her news, especially when moments ago he had told her it was time for them to part. "My mother insists I meet a gentleman at twelve. That's why

I needed to know the time. She'll kill me if I don't show up again."

A strange light entered Tavis's eyes, and the tight lines around his mouth and eyes only seemed to deepen at her words. "Is this a habit of yours, to avoid meeting gentlemen your mother wants you to meet?"

She laughed. "All the time. The last gentleman she introduced me to was seventy if he was a day, and he stank like a distillery."

"Does your mystery man have a name?" he asked.

"Lord Stanton from Scotland. He's new to town, and Mother thought it would be my best chance." Amelia turned her head away from him and began to fiddle with the lace on her sleeves.

"And you?" he asked with sudden interest, his whole body suddenly taut with anticipation. "Do you want to meet him?"

"I did," she whispered. "Now I'm not sure. Men find me...too direct."

"Still," Tavis hedged, "you need to go before your mother starts to worry." He closed the distance between the two of them until they were once again face to face. "Because if you were mine and I couldn't find you," he said, his burr richening his already deep voice, "I'd tear the house and grounds apart until I had you in my arms again."

"But I don't want to say goodbye," Amelia whispered. She swayed toward him, ensnared by his provocative words and enticing nearness.

He seemed to hesitate a moment, perhaps tempted by what he saw written on her face. Shaking his head, he turned to leave, but stopped and faced her again. "Then run away with me, Amelia."

"Wh-what?" she stuttered, backing away from Tavis. She didn't know which of them was more shocked. "We hardly know each other!"

"Many marriages begin on less," Tavis persuaded, crossing his arms over his chest.

"I don't even know who you are. You could be anybody!"

She turned her head to the side and closed her eyes, more tempted by his offer than she was willing to admit to herself. He was giving her a chance to leave behind the solitude and misery her curse had imposed on her from the age of eight. She could leave and start a new life away from London and the gossips of the *ton*. She could finally have a normal life. A husband. A home. A family of her own. She would no longer be the awkward spinster sister of the lovely Beatrice or the bane of her mother's existence. She could be free…

What he is saying is crazy! Respectable gentlemen don't go around offering marriage to near strangers.

Proper young women did not accept offers of marriage from near strangers, either. But, oh, how she was tempted nonetheless to accept and live a life where nobody knew about her curse.

"I could be anybody, 'tis true, lass." Tavis grabbed her chin between his fingers, forcing her to look at him. "But I also could be somebody, Amelia. Somebody you could care for. Somebody you could marry."

She jerked her head away and closed her eyes against the promise she saw on his face. Years of proper upbringing and the ensuing scandal if she eloped were the only things holding her back from saying yes.

Still he continued his pursuit, making her decision to stay strong and refuse him much harder. "Run away with me, Amelia *mia*," he whispered, his face looming over hers. He dropped a kiss on her forehead, and she reveled in the hot, smooth feel of his skin pressed against her own. "Come away with me tonight and be my wife."

Yes, Tavis, she wanted to scream. *Yes, I will be your wife!* But the image of her mother and father's disappointed faces loomed large in her mind. She saw the nosey gossipers of the *ton* snubbing her family, and she saw her family's worry. Most of all, she felt their shame as if it were her own. No, she could not do that to them, no matter how tempted she was.

Amelia shook her head and shuddered as if awakening from a dream. Regardless of her own desires, she could not risk everything for a man she had happened to meet outside her father's stables. When she opened her mouth to explain all this, no words formed. Instead, her face crumpled and tears filled her eyes. Gathering the hems of her skirts, she ran from the clearing, away from Tavis and back to the safety and security of the beckoning house.

Chapter 7

Amelia entered the house and went to the card room to find her sister. Most of the dancers had quit the floor for dinner, so the ballroom was easier to navigate than earlier in the evening.

She entered the room with some haste, repeating, "Bea. Bea. Bea." Spying her sister's blonde head amidst the darker hues of the card dandies who surrounded her, Amelia interrupted her sister's game.

"Bea," she whispered. "I need to talk to you. Now."

"Darling," Bea said in her melodious voice, "can't you see I'm in the middle of a game?" She gestured to the table and the surrounding players.

Amelia huffed out an impatient sigh before she glanced at her sister's cards. "What are you playing?"

"Loo." Bea rolled her eyes dramatically at the interested looks she and her sister were receiving from the other players.

"Trump?" She studied the table with keen eyes and surmised her sister had this game won. As usual, Bea was toying with the other players much like a cat with a mouse before it swallowed the mouse whole. Bea was like that sometimes.

"Spades." Bea's eyes narrowed.

Amelia pulled out the top three trump cards of her sister's hand and laid them on the table.

"Anyone have trump to beat that?" Amelia quizzed the befuddled card players at the table, some of them now muttering their irritation.

"Anyone?" she repeated. "Good." Amelia scooped up Bea's winnings, which were strewn across the table, and threw them into her sister's tiny reticule. "Bea is done for now, boys." Grabbing her sister by the hand, Amelia dragged Beatrice out of the card room and down the hallway, ignoring the muffled shouts of disgruntlement from the card room.

"Will you tell me what is going on?" Bea struggled in Amelia's grasp and managed to successfully pull her hand from Amelia's tight grip.

Beatrice stopped in the middle of the empty hallway, her eyes spitting blue fire at Amelia. It turned to surprise as she assessed Amelia's appearance. Amelia patted her hair in a desperate attempt to secure it into some semblance of what it had been earlier that evening, before…she gulped. *Before I met Tavis.*

Walking away from him was one of the hardest things she'd ever done. She came alive in his presence and felt attractive when she was with him. Usually she was bored to tears with the men of the *ton.* Most were coerced by her father into talking to her, so they were boring, or thought they were doing her a favor by speaking with her. *Or they are Bea's discarded suitors seeking a way to gain favor once more with Queen Bea through me.*

Over time she had come to believe she was a cold, unwanted spinster who was a mere shadow compared to the twin flames of her two brilliant sisters. She was too big and awkward next to them and too unconventional-looking to be called pretty.

When Tavis looked at her, Amelia forgot all that. Tavis liked the way she appeared. He said so, and for some reason she believed him. She felt beautiful and womanly, especially when she saw how he regarded her, like she was a glazed honey ham and he hadn't eaten in years.

Aside from her physical reaction to him, which was strong, he was a true gentleman—thoughtful, solicitous, and kind. Barring his actions during their initial meeting, he behaved with far more decorum than she herself had. And he was content to be with her without asking millions of impolite questions. In their short time together, he appeared to be the perfect man, and she had walked away from it.

More like ran away from.

"If you were mine," he had said in his deep voice.

Oh, if only I were his. But, most likely, he was a poor untitled second son with no prospects. *Mother and Father would never agree to such a match.*

Bea's shrill voice demanded, "What happened to you? Look at your hair! It's completely come undone." Beatrice came forward and shooed Amelia's fluttering hands out of the way. Smoothing the wayward strands together with her hands, Beatrice twisted her sister's hair into a reasonably acceptable coiffure and pinned it with the remaining pins left in the tangled red masses of once stylish hair.

Circling Amelia with a critical eye, Beatrice assessed her costume. "Why are there wrinkles on your dress? And are those"—Beatrice paused as she looked at her sister in shocked amazement—"are those grass stains on the back of your gown? Amelia Jane Westby, what have you been up to?"

"Oh, Bea!" Amelia cried throwing herself into her sister's arms. "I don't know what to do!"

"There, there," Bea soothed, a note of near panic in her cool, cultured voice.

Her tears somewhat quieted, Amelia straightened and caught a glimpse of a familiar pink shape bustling through the hallway.

"Clarisse," Amelia warbled.

Clarisse put her arms around her distraught friend and glared at Beatrice. "What did you do to her?"

"Me? I didn't do anything! This lunatic"—Bea jabbed a finger in Amelia's direction—"attacked me at the tables, pulled me away from the middle of a card game, which I could have won by myself, thank you very much, and dragged me down the hall! Finding her disheveled, I did my best to help repair her hair and costume. And after all that, she throws herself into my arms and starts crying!" Bea ended her tirade on a huff.

"I heard about the ruckus you caused during the card game as I was going in to dinner, so I rushed out to find you two." She squeezed Amelia in a comforting hug. "Are you going to tell us what happened, Mimi?"

Amelia stopped her crying, realizing she had been acting crazily. Taking the handkerchief Clarisse offered her, Amelia wiped her eyes and announced, "We need to find some place private where we can talk."

Amelia saw Beatrice and Clarisse share a look, but they both nodded in agreement. "Come on," Bea said, grabbing Amelia's hand. "I know just the place."

****

"...and then he asked me to dance in the moonlight." Both women listened to Amelia in rapt attention as she described her encounter with Tavis

McGuire by the stables. Sheltered by the cool, comforting walls of the wine cellar, Amelia didn't hesitate to describe the feelings Tavis had aroused in her, his comforting embrace, and her attempt to kiss him.

"What happened next?" Clarisse asked.

Amelia started to fiddle with the folds in her skirt. She turned her head to the side and avoided looking at either her sister or her friend. She mumbled something under her breath, hoping in vain that they didn't hear what she said.

"What?!" shrieked Bea. "He asked you to run away with him?"

"Bloody hell, Bea! I forgot you have ears like a cat."

"He asked you to run away with him?" Clarisse squeaked, too shocked by Amelia's revelation to censure her friend for her bad language. "Did he say why?"

"Since he asked me to be his wife, I assume it was to marry him."

Bea rose from her chair and began to pace. "You mean to tell me a man you just met asked you to marry him…and you left him?"

"What was I supposed to do?" Amelia asked in some confusion. "Had I left with him, I would have caused a terrible scandal, not to mention we had just met, Bea."

"You should have at least tried to kiss him again," Bea replied. "At least, I would have kissed him in spite of his *rules*. Silly man." Bea snorted. "As if gentlemen ever concern themselves with the rules when a pretty woman asks for a kiss."

"He didn't seem to be interested," Amelia muttered under her breath, tugging at the sleeves of her gown.

"Not interested?" Clarisse asked. "If what you say is true, the man obviously wanted to kiss you." She nodded sagely, her large sausage curls bouncing up and down.

"I agree," Bea said. "And I definitely would have stayed to see what could have happened."

"Maybe after kissing him you would have known if you should run away with him or not," Clarisse concurred.

"You seem to be missing the point, ladies. I don't know who he is. He never told me what he was doing in the stables in the first place." She sniffled and threw up her hands. "For all I know, he could be a groomsman, or a…a wandering minstrel, or a gypsy."

"Don't even joke about that, Amelia!" Bea warned.

Amelia cringed and hung her head. The bundle of red curls Bea had pinned up straggled down again to cover Amelia's face. "I'm sorry, Bea."

There was a tense silence for a moment, during which Clarisse cleared her throat and interceded, ticking off the items the ladies knew for sure about the mysterious Mr. McGuire. "I think we can agree Mr. McGuire was raised a gentleman, based on Amelia's descriptions of his dress, his manner of speaking, and his general gentlemanly behaviors." She looked at both sisters, her head swiveling back and forth between the two silent women. "Agreed?"

"Agreed," they mumbled.

"Now, concerning some of Mr. McGuire's phrasings and references throughout your conversation. It would seem he is not a native of England. Perhaps

Scotland?"

"I would concur," Amelia said. With a blush she added, "It also sounded as if he had a slight burr." Amelia remembered those times she had heard his burr come out, the deep rumble in his chest which made her hot and achy.

Bea questioned, "When did that occur?"

"When he held me in his arms in the stables, and while we were dancing under the stars." A knowing look entered Bea's eyes. She glanced at Clarisse, and the two women shared another undecipherable glance. Amelia was really getting tired of those looks. She wished they would say what they were thinking and stop with all this secretive nonsense. She hated being kept in the dark about matters, especially when those matters concerned her.

"Did nothing else unusual happen when the two of you were together?" Bea persisted.

Amelia could tell she had an idea regarding Mr. McGuire, possibly his identity, but she wanted all the information before hazarding a guess.

"No," Amelia said, reviewing her interactions with Tavis. "Well," she amended, "he did seem overly concerned with the time."

"What do you mean?"

"After we finished dancing, he said it was midnight and time for me to go inside." Amelia worried her lower lip with her teeth. "He also said someone was probably looking for me, almost like he knew I had an appointment to keep at midnight."

Jumping up, Amelia swore, "Blast and damn!" Both Bea and Clarisse snapped their heads up from their quiet conversation. "I'm supposed to be meeting

Lord Stanton right now. Mother is going to have my head!"

Amelia raced to the wine cellar door, but before she opened it Bea stopped her and pulled her back.

"Clarisse and I think you should do it," Bea announced.

Amelia looked in confusion at her sister and her best friend. "Do what?"

"Run away with Mr. McGuire," they said in unison.

Of all the advice she expected to receive, running away with a near perfect stranger was not one of them. She staggered over to the chair she had vacated and sank into it. "What? The scandal…"

Clarisse sat next to her and gave her a reassuring smile. She seemed to hesitate for a moment about what to say, but after looking at Bea, she said, "We think, based on what you have said, Mr. McGuire is a gentleman and what he proposed was an earnest offer of marriage."

"You don't think anyone else will ever offer for me, do you? You think my best chance for marriage is with a complete stranger."

"No, Amelia." Clarisse rushed to reassure her. "You obviously are attracted to Mr. McGuire, and from what you said of him, he is interested in you, and many marriages have started with less."

Amelia snorted. "That's what Tavis said, too."

Bea moved to Amelia's other side and took both of her hands. "Mimi," she said in all seriousness, "I want you to listen to me." Amelia studied her sister's face and couldn't recall the last time she had seen her sister so somber.

"You're scaring me, Bea," Amelia whispered. She started to worry about what her sister could possibly say to her. Clarisse squeezed her shoulder and nodded in encouragement at both Amelia and Bea.

"Promise me you'll keep an open mind." Bea took a deep breath and said, "Amelia, since you came out three years ago, I've watched you live your life as a spectator on the sidelines, looking out from the shadows at what could be. It's as if you are too afraid to come out into the light for fear of getting burned."

Amelia started. Bea used the same words she herself had used in thinking of her feelings toward Tavis. She had likened his charisma to the sun, bright and warm and a little bit frightening.

Bea squeezed Amelia's hands. "You gave up on life when it didn't give you what you expected, and you've withdrawn into yourself, disguising your sweetness and goodness with a shield of bitterness and cruelty."

Amelia's eyes filled with tears at her sister's words. Everything she said was true. Amelia had spent the years since her debut waiting and watching from the sidelines. She hadn't taken charge of her life because, after the first rejections she received from the *ton,* the idea of opening herself up to further hurt was too much to bear. So she had hidden herself behind a mask of cool indifference, using her curse as an excuse to push people away.

"I know the curse has held you back; it has for all three of us, but I learned a long time ago the curse has power over you only for as long as you allow it, Mimi." Amelia watched tears run down her sister's face and felt wetness dampen her own cheeks. Grabbing hold of

Amelia's shoulders, Bea enveloped her sister in a tight hug. "It's time to live your life," Bea whispered into Amelia's ears.

For endless moments, Amelia took comfort in her sister's embrace. She gave her sister one final squeeze, wiped her eyes, and announced, "I'll do it. I'll run away with Tavis."

Bea smiled serenely, and behind her, Clarisse squealed in excitement. Amelia gulped and prayed she was making the right choice.

Chapter 8

This night could not possibly get any worse. There had been the shock of discovering Lady Amelia was none other than Lady Amelia Westby, the daughter he was being blackmailed into meeting and possibly marrying, meanwhile needing to seduce her and use her to uncover her father's secrets for his friend in the government. At first, he had not known who Lady Amelia was, never having met her before, but as soon as she said she had come out to visit her horse in her father's stable, he knew.

The enchanting creature with the bright green eyes and curly red hair was Westby's middle daughter. He had reasoned the youngest would be with her betrothed because, after all, the ball was being held in their honor. Also he remembered Meeks telling him she was a petite, fey-like creature with delicate features and fine, white-blonde hair. That eliminated the woman he had been holding in his arms only moments ago. The ample landscape of her curves he had cradled against him would never qualify her as "fairy-like."

No. She was more like a siren, luring men to the promise of heaven with the sway of her wide hips and the temptation of ripe breasts ready for plucking.

She wasn't the eldest, Tavis had rationalized through a hazy fog of lust, as he had stopped himself from burying his face in the thick red hair curling down and around Amelia's shoulders. The eldest, he had recollected, was a stunning blonde. When he first came to Town, they had been introduced over a cutthroat game of cards. She had ice-blue eyes, shrewd and cunning, with a hard edge to them.

Amelia's eyes were the rich green of a field newly carpeted in the springtime. Tavis drew in a deep breath and blew it out. Therefore, the delectable woman he had been lusting after in the stables and squiring about under the stars was the middle daughter, Lady Amelia Westby, the woman he was supposed to be meeting now.

"This is not how tonight was supposed to have gone!" he shouted to the night sky. His mission had been clear. Meet the girl to appease Westby. Break into the study to search for papers on his father and any other papers implicating Westby. Steal the horses Westby had taken from him. (That was not included in his mission, but Tavis reasoned he was owed something for his service to his country.) Leave. That was the mission. Nowhere in his plans did it include falling for the girl.

After everything he had endured these last several months, it was a slap in the face to feel intense attraction for Lady Amelia, the one woman who couldn't tell a lie and who he needed to help bring down her traitorous father. He would do it, though; he would put his attraction for her aside to woo her and to gain the information he needed about her father. If the thought of losing her trust after he betrayed her left him with an uncomfortable feeling of guilt deep in his stomach, Tavis did his best to ignore it. After all, she was just a woman. There were plenty more out there eager for the attentions of a newly titled earl. He didn't need Lady Amelia or her silky skin, pouty lips, or breasts to make a grown man weep.

An unbidden image of Lady Amelia's face came to Tavis's mind, and he remembered how lonely she looked when telling him about her appointment with the unknown Lord Stanton. She had sounded so sad, and Tavis realized how hard it must be for her to be so unusually cursed, to be forced to always tell the truth. He imagined the censure she had received over the years for this unique trait.

What must it be like to always be treated as an outsider by her peers?

Tavis didn't have to think about it for very long. It was pure hell. After years of being treated as the bastard son of his father, he too knew the pain of being an outcast from one's own family and situation in life. How could he even think of using Lady Amelia in such a way when she was so very much like him? No, he needed to consider some way to get the information he needed without using Lady Amelia.

Tavis reviewed his options and found none to fulfill this new requirement. Pulling out his pocket watch, he saw it was five minutes to midnight. A new idea started to form. In less than five minutes, Westby would be waiting for him in the ballroom, and the man's study, the most likely location to look for the information he needed, would be empty. Tavis would find what he needed to complete his mission and be able to return home to begin his life of comfort and ease. Lady Amelia would be safe, and he would just forget her. Yes, it was a brilliant plan.

Enacting his plan immediately, he was unable to

find anything. After a thorough search for hidden compartments in the desk and in the wall, Tavis was about to pry apart the floorboards when he heard someone approaching the main door of the study. Using the side door, Tavis slipped out into the adjoining library and into the main hallway, only to be greeted by Lord Westby.

"Lord Stanton!" boomed the familiar voice of Lord Westby. "How good of you to come to our little soirée!" He pumped Tavis's hand in an enthusiastic greeting, squeezing a little too hard. "I was afraid you weren't coming," he said with a hard edge to his voice. Tavis didn't mistake his meaning.

"Yes, yes," Tavis replied. "I became lost, I'm afraid, in the maze of rooms in your house." He flashed him a cool smile. "But I'm here as requested, Westby."

The two men made their way into the ballroom, and Tavis scanned the room, looking for a glimpse of Amelia's bright red hair amidst the guests who had not yet gone in for dinner. In spite of his reluctance to use Lady Amelia to ferret out her father's secrets, he was oddly excited at the prospect of seeing her again.

"Is she here?" he demanded, turning to address Westby, who had moved off slightly to take the arm of an attractive blonde woman, presumably Westby's wife.

The lady, a petite creature of middling years and regal bearing, regarded him with a frank gaze, startling not for its intensity but because it was the same green he had so admired earlier this evening in the eyes of Lady Amelia Westby.

Westby cleared his throat and announced, "I would like to present to you my wife, Lady Westby." The lady curtsied, and Tavis bowed, murmuring a subdued greeting to the woman whose daughter he had been imagining in many compromising positions.

"We are so pleased you could join us this evening," Lady Westby cooed, holding out her hand for Tavis to kiss. Tavis took the proffered hand and bestowed a perfunctory kiss over her knuckles. She fluttered her lashes and smiled in genuine kindness.

"How could I refuse such an offer?" Tavis asked. "I admit I was reluctant at first. Your husband practically had to blackmail me into coming." He hazarded a sly glance at Westby, who reddened and began to splutter indignantly. "Of course, what gentleman relishes the imminent end of his carefree bachelor days?" Tavis stifled a laugh as Lady Westby patted her husband on the back.

"Yes, I suppose you're right, my lord," she said, though her attention was focused on her husband's unexplained fit of coughing.

"Ha, ha!" Westby clapped Tavis hard on the back. "You're such a kidder, my lord." Westby smiled to reassure his wife while keeping his hand clamped on Tavis's shoulder in silent warning not to make any further allusions to their arrangement.

"What Lord Stanton surely meant was his reluctance to meet our Amelia before I tempted him with her many accomplishments and charms." Westby squeezed Tavis's shoulder and turned his hard, icy eyes toward him. "Isn't that right, Lord Stanton?"

Tavis did not appreciate being manhandled, especially by a middle-aged traitor who bartered his daughter for the reluctant complicity of peers of the realm in his back alley dealings. When he turned to reply to Lord Westby, the light of battle had entered his eyes, and he bared his teeth in a gross imitation of a smile. Removing Westby's hand from his shoulder, he applied more pressure than necessary to the older man's hand. Tavis received not a small amount of satisfaction from the grimace of pain flashing across Westby's face.

"Precisely, my lord," Tavis replied.

Walking over to Lady Westby, who watched the interplay between her husband and Lord Tavis with confusion on her pretty face, Tavis offered his arm to the lady and flashed her a brilliant smile. "Will I have the pleasure of meeting Lady Amelia soon, my lady?"

She fluttered her free hand by her temple, patting the hair there. "Oh, she should be here any moment, my lord," she tittered, her bright eyes scanning the room for signs of her daughter. "She was most anxious to meet you."

Tavis remembered Amelia's downcast eyes and the sad tilt to her mouth when she spoke of her meeting with Lord Stanton. Somehow he doubted she was eager to meet him. He also feared hurting her but saw no way around it.

"Lord Stanton?" a shrill feminine voice demanded, recalling him to his curious hostess on his arm. "I asked if you wanted to go in for dinner."

"I would rather take a turn around the room with you, my lady, while we wait for your daughter. You can tell me all about her." He winked, and Lady Westby tittered, while Lord Westby gritted his teeth in annoyance. "If she is as delightful as you, I shall be most pleased." Arm in arm, Lord Stanton led Lady Westby around the ballroom, with Lord Westby watching from the side.

An hour later, Amelia had yet to appear, much to the aggravation and annoyance of his host and hostess, leaving Tavis to wonder at his role in her disappearance. *Had she been scared off by their encounter in the stables? Had she been planning on meeting someone else all along and had gone off with this other man instead?* Tavis felt his temper rising at that thought, but even in his extreme irritation he recognized it was nothing to the anger Westby displayed when Amelia failed to show. Tavis prayed Amelia was safely hidden away, at least until her father's anger subsided.

Giving his heartfelt regrets and a promise to return on the morrow, Tavis made a hasty departure from the house. He was more than anxious to leave and return home, but since his search of Westby's study had yielded nothing, he needed to use Lady Amelia as originally planned. With any luck, she would be available tomorrow so he could begin the exciting yet distasteful business of seducing her. She would capitulate; they all did. It was not conceit; Tavis was simply good at his job. The question remaining was whether he could avoid falling further under her spell in the process.

He was rounding a corner to take the path back to the stables when he heard a commotion, almost as if someone were rattling branches against the side of the house. His ears perked, and he scanned the area for any disturbances. Aside from a cool breeze rustling the trees and bushes, there was nothing out of the ordinary to indicate any foul play, yet the noise continued.

"Bollocks!" He heard the soft whisper coming from...above? Tavis whipped his head back, and his jaw hung open in astonishment. For coming down the trellis was a nicely rounded arse that from this angle he could only surmise belonged to a woman. He watched her make her way down the trellis, using the open latticework like the rungs of a ladder. She had descended about three quarters of the way down when he saw her foot falter on one of the rungs. The woman grasped at the twining vines growing up the side of the house in a desperate attempt to regain her balance and stop her fall, but her hands slipped off the vines, and she pitched backwards.

Tavis had only a second to reach out his arms to break her fall before she crashed on top of him. They both landed with a thud on the hard earth. That is to say, Tavis landed on the hard earth, and the woman landed on his chest, the rounded flesh of her skirt-clad buttocks obstructing his breath.

"Are you unharmed?" a woman's voice whispered, oddly enough not the voice of the woman who was sitting on him.

"Yes," the mystery woman atop him whispered back, wiggling her buttocks over his face. "Something soft broke my fall."

"Oh, good," the other woman replied. Tavis heard a large thunk and felt a slight vibration in the ground next to him like something had been thrown out of the window to land there.

"Good luck, darling!" He heard a far-off click and assumed the other woman had leaned back in and closed the window behind her, because now all was silent. Except the pounding in his head from it hitting the ground.

He felt the woman moving around again,

attempting to stand. She braced her hands on his chest, giving it an exploratory squeeze. And then she paused.

"Uh-oh." She gulped. Her hands fluttered down his chest, over his stomach, and into dangerous areas below his waist.

"Good lord," she whispered, now stroking the flesh on his thighs. "I think I've killed someone!" He felt her scramble off his body, and for the first time since she landed on him, he was able to take in a deep breath.

Tavis propped himself up on his elbows and tried to get a look at his assailant, but there was no light on this side of the house, and the moon was hiding behind a grove of trees. He sensed her near his left side and imagined she was working up the nerve to see if she had actually killed him or not.

Maybe wondering, too, how to finish the job.

Moving with a swiftness belying the pain he was in, he grabbed the woman by her arms and rolled her under him.

He tried to ascertain her features, but she must have had a cloak or other dark garment over her head concealing her face. "Who are you and what do you mean by nearly killing me?" Tavis growled to the struggling woman in his grasp.

She stilled. "T-Tavis?" a familiar voice whispered to him. "Is that you?"

He immediately released her arms and jumped away from her. She stood, too, and he watched in growing alarm as she pushed aside the hood that concealed her face. Now that she was uncovered, Tavis recognized the familiar red curls and pale features of the woman he had been struggling to put out of his mind.

"Amelia?" He stepped back to her. His hand seemed to take on a mind of its own, and he watched his fingers trace the smooth lines of her cheek. She turned her head to nuzzle into his hand, and when she placed a soft kiss there, he noticed an odd ache near the vicinity of his heart.

It was Amelia. The mystery woman who had nearly killed him when she landed on him was his Amelia. Tavis chuckled to himself. *Twice in one night the damn chit has nearly killed me.*

"It's lucky I was there to break your fall, my lady. I would hate to think what would have happened if I hadn't been here." It was only then he took in her appearance. Unlike earlier this evening, when she had been bedecked in soft blue silk, she wore a dark, sturdy dress covered by a heavy traveling cloak. Tall leather boots completed her ensemble. And next to her on the ground was a medium-sized carpet bag.

That must be what I heard hit the ground.

An uneasy suspicion took root in his mind.

She nodded and smiled shyly up at him. "I am glad it was you who found me, Tavis. Otherwise it might have been…awkward, explaining what I am doing here."

"What *are* you doing here, my lady?" he asked, though he had a good idea he knew exactly what she was up to. Sneaking down the trellis in sturdy traveling clothes with a packed bag usually meant one thing, but he needed to hear her say it.

"I've come to run away with you, Mr. McGuire." Her voice was soft but clear. There was no hesitation or embarrassment in her voice, and despite the darkness they were in, the whites of her eyes were trained unwaveringly on his face.

He blew out a big breath and cursed the Tavis of an hour ago who had blurted out his ill-conceived plan to have Amelia run away with him instead of meeting with Lord Stanton. His blood-deprived brain had most likely compromised his mission and the safety of Lady Amelia.

Tavis thought for a moment. *But since Lord Stanton is actually me, she would still be marrying Lord Stanton if she runs away with Tavis McGuire, which was the original plan all along.*

Brilliant! I didn't compromise the mission after all. He would take Amelia away from Westby, find out what she knew, and locate the information he needed to complete his mission. Yes, it would work.

He thought a little bit more about the muddle he had created and decided he might have made things worse after all. *However, if she runs away with Tavis McGuire, eventually she'll discover he is Lord Stanton, er, I mean me. And then she'll want to know why Tavis lied to her about who he, Lord Stanton, ah, I mean me, and he, uh, we were.*

Good Christ, but his head hurt! Absently, he scrubbed his fingers through his hair. He felt a soft touch on his wrist and looked down in amazement at the slender fingers resting there, momentarily having forgotten Amelia's presence before him.

"Tavis? Do you not want me to come away with you anymore?"

The moon chose this moment to peek out from behind the grove of trees, shedding enough light for Tavis to see the hurt swimming in Amelia's wide, green eyes.

"No, Amelia. I do want you." His throbbing body echoed that sentiment, but his conscience demanded he try one last time to dissuade her from coming with him. "But you know nothing of me. I could be anyone!"

She said not a word but only stood there with a wry expression on her face, and he realized he used the same words on her she had tried to use on him earlier in the evening when he had proposed the very same thing.

"I'll take my chances, Tavis. I know enough to know I'll be safe with you."

The little chit thinks herself safe, does she? Tavis grabbed her around the waist and pulled her against his body. He leaned his head down for his lips to graze the sensitive flesh of her neck. Nibbling up the graceful column, he whispered in her ear, "You never know. I could be dangerous." He felt her shiver and hoped he had succeeded in intimidating her enough that she would return to her room.

But she was bolder than he had given her credit for. Amelia twined her hands around his neck and pulled his head nearer her own. "I am not afraid of you, Tavis McGuire," Amelia whispered. "And I already know you're dangerous," she said in a stronger voice meeting his hot, wicked gaze with her own.

Tavis groaned when plump lips clamped around the sensitive flesh of his earlobes. The sharp bite of her teeth as they grazed his flesh had him taut and hard within seconds, and when she nibbled her way down the corded muscles of his neck, he was helpless to stop the thick swelling of his flesh pushing against the tight confines of his breeches.

As he debated the merits of pushing her away from him versus rushing her back to the stables to finish what they had started earlier in the evening, her warm breath fanned his ear.

"In fact, I'm planning on it."

Chapter 9

Several things became abundantly clear to Amelia the farther she and Tavis traveled from London. For one, she was not as good an equestrian as she had thought. Every muscle in her body ached, and she groaned as her bottom jostled about in her saddle. Since their late night escape from London, Tavis had ridden hard, insisting he wanted as much distance as possible between him and her father. Shifting on her saddle, she winced as tender muscles protested. "When I envisioned running away with you, Tavis McGuire," she muttered under her breath, "it did not involve spending our days riding as if the hounds of hell were chasing us halfway across England."

Secondly, Tavis had taken to treating her more like a soldier in the army than like his affianced bride, a fact that particularly rankled with her. For over four days and nights they had ridden north, barely stopping to eat and sleep. When they did finally quit for the day, was it ever to enter one of those quaint little villages she had seen that looked like it boasted an inn with hot food and a bed softer than a slab of granite?

"I wouldn't know, since I've been eating cold biscuits and cheese and sleeping on a bedroll out under the stars." She shot a murderous glance at Tavis, who was, as usual, riding several lengths in front of her. "Cold and alone," she gritted out.

"And your conversation, Mr. McGuire," Amelia continued in a high sing-song voice while batting her eyelashes. "So sparing with your words. So terse in your commands." She waved her hands in front of her face as though she were near to swooning. "Why, I positively went loose in the knees last night when you grunted at me to quit my yapping and go to sleep." That made her smile, and she thought wickedly on how that little altercation ended when she had refused to stop talking.

"What are you grinning at?" Tavis asked, startling her out of her thoughts. Somewhere during her musings he had slowed his mount and now was trotting next to her.

"How's your hand?" she asked, unable to resist poking fun at him, especially when all day he had been treating her like she had the plague.

He flexed his right hand and glowered at Amelia, who was doing her best not to laugh out loud. "It hurts like the devil, you wee hellion."

At Tavis's outraged expression, she gave up and laughed loud and long for the first time in days. "You big bully. Serves you right."

"Weren't you ever taught any manners?" he wondered in exasperation. "Didn't anyone ever tell you it's very unladylike to bite someone?"

"I must have been sick the day my governess was reviewing that particular lesson." She thought he would ride ahead again and leave her alone to stew by herself, but this time he stayed.

"Besides," she added, unable to resist adding her own jab at his expense, "I didn't see evidence of your gentlemanly behavior when you tossed me around like a sack of flour and clamped your hand over my mouth so I would 'stop my yapping.' "

There was an awkward silence next to her, and when she peeked over at Tavis, his entire face had gone alarmingly red, and there was a tiny tic jumping in his jaw.

"I wonder, are you embarrassed because I called attention to your lack of manners toward me during our journey, or are you simply resisting the urge to throttle me?"

When he uttered a short bark of laughter, she jumped in surprise and offered him a rueful smile, remembering she had become accustomed to speaking her unfiltered thoughts aloud. She flushed red herself and thanked God silently that Tavis hadn't been around to hear her earlier rant about him.

"Both," he admitted. She watched him pull his collar away from his neck.

"You do that a lot," she observed.

When he looked at her in blank confusion, she continued, "Pull on your collar, I mean." She demonstrated by pulling the neck of her own bodice away from her skin, grimacing in as near an imitation as she could of the tight face he made while he did it. "It makes you look nervous and jumpy."

Tavis muttered something under his breath, and he started to pull at his collar again, only to stop when he realized what he was doing. "It's my solicitor. He always does it when he's nervous." He let out a loud sigh. "It seems I have adopted his habit for myself."

"Does that mean I make you nervous?"

He avoided looking at her, and she wondered if he would even answer. Then he noticeably straightened in his saddle and gestured off into the distance. If Amelia squinted, she could make out the shape of a small hut nestled amidst a grove of trees.

"Up ahead is where we'll rest tonight. It's been abandoned for years, but the last time I was through here it still had all four walls, a solid roof, and a working fireplace."

Amelia yawned, the fatigue from their long journey catching up to her. She looked at the small, rundown crofter's hut through hungry eyes.

"An actual house? Does it have a bed, too?" she whipped her head around to look at him in eager anticipation. He coughed and pulled his collar away from his neck again.

"Are you ill, Tavis? You've got that look again."

"No, just something stuck in my throat." He thumped his chest and coughed again, giving her a weak smile.

She narrowed her eyes, not believing his overdramatic cough, but soon ignored him in favor of studying her surroundings. Though the journey had been rough, Amelia had to admit she enjoyed watching the ever-changing scenery. From the urban streets of London, across the rolling plains of England, to the rugged landscape where they now rested, she had been enchanted by the sprawling vistas and the wild beauty all around her. She breathed in the fresh, woodsy air from the nearby forest and was content.

"Where are we now, Tavis?" she asked, her curiosity aroused by the imposing peaks towering above them.

He hesitated for a moment. "A half day's ride to Gretna Green."

Amelia resisted the urge to pepper him with more questions. He had been tight-lipped about their final destination the entire way, so hearing they were so close to Gretna Green made her lightheaded.

By tomorrow evening I will be a bride.

Suddenly the events of the last four days caught up to her in a rush, and it was all she could do to tamp down her rising panic as he continued talking.

"I'll prepare us our dinner, once I've arrived at the hut, and wait for you within." He flashed her that lopsided smile of his, the one she had seen a lifetime ago in her father's stable, and with a mock salute, he rode ahead with the other horses, leaving her to follow behind.

Amelia, once again left alone with her thoughts, was powerless to stop her mind from revisiting her list of things that had gone wrong since leaving her home. Strangely enough, hearing they were so close to Gretna Green did little to ease her anxieties about Tavis and this whole situation. While it was true she had been most anxious to be wed to him, there were other concerns overshadowing the immediacy of needing to be married. She nibbled on her lower lip and fretted to herself as she watched him ride on ahead of her, leading a string of horses behind him. Because in spite of the hectic pace and the uncertainty of her future, one other thing remained crystal clear. Tavis McGuire was a horse thief.

Four nights ago, she had seen him leading a string of horses from her father's stables and knew in that instant that her suspicions about him had been correct all along. He was a horse thief and had been planning all evening on stealing her father's horses. Amelia had been torn, in that moment, as to what to do. If she had gone back inside, her father's horses would have been saved but Tavis would probably have hanged. Running away with him meant betraying her family's trust by aiding a thief. No matter how she looked at it, someone was going to be hurt.

Then he had turned to her and asked in a low urgent whisper, "Do you trust me?" It was the last thing she expected to hear from him. She had been hoping for an explanation of what she was seeing, at the very least, or perhaps an idea of what his plans were for them, but he had asked her if she trusted him. Twice.

He had looked vulnerable in that moment, sitting beside her on his horse and asking that question. Amelia was helpless to deny him any reassurance she could give. Knowing somehow her fate and this man's were tied together, Amelia made her decision. Offering him her hand, she laced their fingers together and nodded, "Yes, Tavis, with my life."

He had kissed her, a quick brush of the lips across her mouth in silent thanks, and the two had ridden off into the waning night.

Now, four days later, Amelia wondered not for the first time if she had been too rash in her decision to leave with Tavis, especially in light of his recent treatment of her. He had not been acting like a fiancé should, though she had no previous knowledge to compare his actions to. "But one would think a fiancé would show more tender concern for his betrothed than what Tavis has shown me. Idiotic, hare-brained man," she muttered. "What does he think he's about, stealing my father's horses and trifling with my emotions?" She wanted to know who Tavis McGuire really was. On first impression, she found him to be a thoughtful and courteous gentleman. He had charmed her when they met, with his reverent words of praise and courtly charm, leading her about in a magical moonlit dance. She hugged those memories to her late at night as she tried to sleep on the cold, hard ground across the fire from him.

Other times, though, he was aloof and commanding, like last night when he had barked at her to be quiet and go to sleep when she had wanted to share in his company. She couldn't quite make out his character, which was frustrating, as they were soon to be man and wife. She missed the easy camaraderie they had shared within the comforting embrace of the cozy stables.

Something else is missing, too. Amelia blew out a frustrated breath. There were no more "almost" kisses or longing looks that made her toes curl and her skin steam. In that respect, he remained every bit a gentleman. On more than one occasion she had made it clear she would gladly accept more intimacies. Despite the ample opportunities she had given him to defile her person, *blast the man*, he hadn't. He was always polite, if not a touch cool.

"He must be a man of very firm morals, or at the very least not experienced with women."

Legacy's Daughter nickered beneath her as she ambled to another area of tender grass. Amelia held the reins in her lap and reminded herself why she had run off with him in spite of her worries.

Had Tavis been a common thief, he wouldn't have given her a chance to change her mind about running away with him. But he did offer that possibility when he asked if she trusted him. She knew if she had objected to the horse stealing and had insisted on remaining with her parents, he would not have stopped her even though it surely would have meant the gallows. But when Tavis took those horses, he must have had a good reason to do so.

"That still doesn't mean he doesn't owe me an explanation, girl," Amelia whispered into the soft hair of her horse's neck.

Having arrived at the small crofter's cottage, she dismounted and looked around. Tavis's massive horse was hobbled at the side of the cottage along with the other horses. Taking Legacy's Daughter by the reins, she led her horse to the side of the hut. Seeing the other horses, the mare nickered and nudged Amelia with her nose.

"All right. I'll get on with it." Amelia smiled at her horse and removed the saddle. She rubbed her down with tufts of soft grass and then tied her next to the others already hobbled and enjoying the plentiful spring shoots found near the hut.

Tavis had been busy inside. Already a fire was crackling in the fireplace and what looked like a rabbit was roasting on a spit, filling the interior of the hut with its mouthwatering aroma. Several small candles were scattered about the room, shedding a comforting light into the dreary corners.

He had done his best to set the table with an oddly shaped cloth that looked to be an old yet clean undershirt or perhaps a handkerchief. From out of his pack bag, he pulled a wedge of cheese and a loaf of bread and placed them on the table. Her stomach growled, reminding Amelia how long ago breakfast had been.

"Here." He broke off some bread and handed it to her. She snatched it up and devoured it, watching him as he tended the fire and turned the spit with the roasting meat.

"I want to apologize for how hard I've been riding you these last couple of days," he said and then paled once he realized what he had said.

"I beg your pardon?"

"Oh, Jesus! I mean, how hard we've been riding," he amended.

She watched in amazement as his face flushed a deep red. "Christ, that's not what I meant either," he blurted out. Running his hands through his hair, he let out a deep breath. "I'm just sorry, Amelia."

He looked so miserable that even though she really wanted to see him squirm, she took pity on him. "Thank you." *It would serve him right if I did make him work a little harder for my forgiveness.* But once she saw his shoulders relax, she knew she had done the right thing. In spite of how angry he made her, it wasn't in her to be vengeful.

Besides, she reasoned, the way he kept insulting her, she would have plenty of practice forgiving him. She hid a smile while biting into her chunk of bread as she thought of all the ways he had misstepped with her over the last several days. It was impossible for her to understand how she had mistaken his earlier behavior with her for the courtly charm of a sophisticated gentleman, when he clearly was quite clueless about how to deal with women.

Tavis pulled the meat off the spit and served Amelia and himself. Once he was seated and they were eating, she decided to find out if what she suspected was true. "Do you come from a large family, Tavis? Many brothers and sisters?"

"No, not really. My mother died when I was a month old, and my Aunt Millie raised me until I was sent to school at eight."

"Eight? Isn't that a bit young to be sent away from home?"

"Is it?" He paused mid-bite to consider her question. "I guess I thought all boys were sent off to school at such an age. Surely there must have been one or two boys at school who were as young as I was."

She didn't like the frown that had appeared to mar his handsome features. Offering him a tentative smile, she rushed to concur. "I'm sure you are right. I only thought, well, if I were to ever have children..." She looked down at the table in embarrassment to avoid meeting his eyes. "That is, if *we* were ever to have children, I wouldn't want them to be sent away from home so early."

She waited in awkward silence for him to say something, but all she heard was the quiet crackling of the fire. Eventually, he cleared his throat, and she persuaded herself to peek up at him from underneath her lashes. Seeing he was at least as disconcerted as she was, if not more, she gave him a shy smile and asked, "Wouldn't you agree?"

He took a deep swallow of wine before he answered. "Yes, I imagine so. I had never given it consideration before, but I suppose that's because after my mother's death my father never wanted me around. Obviously your feelings and needs would have to be taken into consideration as well." He grimaced, and she had to stifle an amused giggle when she saw his hand move to tug at his collar.

At his ridiculous glower, Amelia tried to stifle the inappropriate smile threatening to break out on her face. It soon faded when she contemplated a young Tavis being sent away to school having no mother and a father who detested him. She pictured an eight-year-old Tavis dropped into the middle of an all-male boarding school, surrounded by older, more mature companions. There would have been no one to listen to his thoughts or to tuck him in at night. *No one to kiss away his fears and fix his problems with some milk and a biscuit.*

No, he had grown up quickly without the tender guidance of a loving female.

While he had taken holidays with his aunt, those times apparently were not frequent enough to smooth out his rough edges. At least she was beginning to understand why Tavis, a handsome, confident man in the prime of his life, had been acting as if she were a male companion instead of the lady she was. Before she could stop herself or even think about what she was saying, she blurted out, "So you really don't know much about women, do you?"

He choked on the bite of meat in his mouth and started coughing. She watched as his face reddened before he downed a sip of wine to clear his throat.

"Of course I know about women!" he insisted, his manly pride pricked by her frank assessment of his character.

"There goes my theory, then," she mumbled, picking at the meat of her rabbit's leg.

"And what theory was that?"

"That perhaps the reason you have pushed me so

hard is that you are more accustomed to the habits of men rather than those of women." She knew he was processing her statement by the shrewd way his blue eyes observed her. He had ceased eating, and she found herself the recipient of his full attention, so she plunged ahead with the next idea that had been floating around in her head all day. "And that perhaps the reason you have overlooked my blatant attempts to, er, compromise my virtue is you yourself are equally inexperienced in matters of love and do not know how to"—she made a vague gesture with her hand—"to mmphh." Her eyes flitted between his face, which had gone an alarming shade of red, and her unfinished meal on the table before her. "If you take my meaning."

"I understand you clearly, madam." He regarded her through narrowed eyes and leaned his elbows on the table so his face loomed closer to her own. "Why, I'll have you know I have had relations, that is to say, I have known many a woman…"

Amelia resumed eating her meal. "If I may offer you some advice, Tavis? When alone with a lady who is your betrothed, it would serve you well to avoid talking about any and all past relationships." She popped a bite of bread into her mouth. "You may take my advice or leave it, as you see fit."

"Fine." He shoved back his chair, prowled the short distance around the table to where she sat, and braced his arms on either side of her chair to box her in. The muscles of his arms bunched and shimmied in front of her hungry eyes, and she gulped at the raw masculinity of the man before her.

"Perhaps I might offer you some advice, as well?"

"But of course."

"When alone with a man who is your betrothed, it would serve you well to avoid questioning his manhood or implying in any way that he is incapable of pleasing you." He hauled her up and ensnared her in the iron bands of his arms. She didn't miss the fierce light that had entered his eyes or the way his hands roamed over her back and down to the firm curves of her buttocks.

"You will take my advice, my lady, because I will say it only this one time." He pulled her closer to him, and she gasped at the hardness she felt pressing into her belly. "And trust me when I say you will be pleased." The rumble of his voice sent tingles racing up and down her spine.

Her arms wound themselves around his neck in a tight embrace, and she lifted her eyes, capturing his gaze with her own in a hot, bold stare of naked desire. "Then kiss me, Tavis," she pleaded. "Show me."

He muttered a strangled curse and lowered his mouth to her eagerly awaiting one.

With as much tension as there was humming between the two of them, she had expected him to claim her lips in a rough, demanding kiss. Instead, his mouth brushed her cheeks with featherlike kisses and then proceeded to caress every inch of her face, bestowing soft kisses on her closed eyes, her nose, down the sides of her neck, and then—finally!—she felt his firm lips tease the corners of her mouth before possessing them with his on a low growl.

So this is what it's like to be kissed.

Tavis had ceased being gentle, and now his tongue impatiently tested the seam of her mouth, which opened on a gasp of surprise. He took the opportunity to thrust within the warm caverns of her mouth. Tentatively she moved her own tongue against his and was rewarded by a throaty moan and an increase of pressure from his lips.

She was surrounded by him. His musky scent. The way he tasted, dark and spicy and hot. The feeling of his muscled frame pressed against her flesh. He pushed her past the limits of her control. Anchoring her fingers in his hair, she held him to her while he moved his hands to grasp her hips, which allowed her to better feel how the thrusting of his hips mirrored the motion of his tongue in her mouth.

Pulling away with a gasp, she tried to fill her lungs with air. Tavis continued his assault on her senses by pressing passionate humid kisses down her neck and onto the trembling white flesh above her bodice. She shuddered when he slid his nose along her cleavage, and almost crumpled into a heap when his hot tongue slid in and out of her generous cleft.

Without warning, he pushed her away, and she stayed upright only by clinging to the back of the chair.

"Tavis? Is something wrong?" He looked as dazed as she felt, which, given her limited experience, she guessed was a good sign, yet he had stopped and shoved her aside.

She took a tentative step toward him only to stop when he held up a hand to halt her advance. Confusion and hurt warred within her, and she wanted to scream. "I promised myself...I wasn't going to do that...until we were wed," he said between labored pants.

"I don't understand. We're to be married tomorrow. What harm is there in one kiss?" She reached out to touch him. When he shied away, she retracted her hand as if it had been burned.

"We have much to discuss before we wed."

"What…?" But his eyes were shuttered, and she could no longer see the bright flame of passion that had illuminated them moments ago.

"It's late. You should go to bed."

"But…"

"I'll be sleeping out by the horses. Good night, Amelia." Turning abruptly, he walked out into the night, leaving her to wonder what had happened.

Chapter 10

"Good Christ but she makes me nervous," Tavis swore once he was outside and away from the siren's call that was Amelia. In fact, he had been nervous ever since they left her father's grounds. He would be happy when this mission was over and he could go back to being plain Tavis McGuire, decorated war hero and the fifth Earl of Stanton. All of this secrecy and lying didn't sit well with him or his conscience.

Making his way to the side of the hut, he pulled his jacket closer around his ears as he settled in near his horse under the makeshift lean-to that housed them for the evening. He wasn't fit company for anyone this night, but at least the horses wouldn't look at him with hurt green eyes and tempt him with plump, red lips begging to be kissed. As it was, it had taken all his will power to leave Amelia standing there with her clothes on when all he really wanted to do was bury himself in her for several weeks and only come up for air when they needed to eat.

"That was a close one, Magnus," he said to his horse, who had reached down to nibble at the top of his head. He swatted his horse away and scooted off to a far corner, away from the curious mouths of the assembled equines.

"What a mess I've made of everything," he sighed. Between the botched mission, his unfortunate attempt at horse thievery, and his ill-treatment of Amelia, this trip had been a catastrophe. His intentions had been noble, he reasoned, but the results nothing short of disastrous.

When he realized he couldn't use Amelia to spy on her father, he had suggested the elopement. Never in a million years did he think she would agree. At most, he figured he'd spend a couple of weeks more in London seducing her to get what he needed. Then he would be on his way with what was rightfully his. But when she agreed to his foolish plan, everything turned upside down, and he knew they needed to escape or else be found out by her father.

Once on the road, though, it became apparent escaping was the easy part of his plan. Spending his days on a horse only gave him plenty of time to stew and torment himself about how he had probably jeopardized his mission and put in peril thousands of good, brave men. He had labeled that particular torment "Reasons Why I'll Likely Hang."

Nighttime was a completely different type of agony he simply called "Amelia." During the day, it was easier to forget she was with him, but at night, under the quiet of the evening sky, it was an impossible task. He couldn't ignore her even if he wanted to, so attuned he was to her every movement and nuance of her countenance. Whether it was her quiet conversation around the campfire or watching the way the firelight flickered off her hair and skin, casting her eyes in mysterious shadows, she overwhelmed his senses. Even when she slept she called to him. Her tiny sighs and murmurs as she drifted off to sleep stirred his blood and the dormant emotions he had thought long buried.

The sooner they wed, the better for both of them.

Because he knew if he had to spend one more night with her, he was not going to be able to help himself, and she would be compromised before they married. He had nearly lost control and ruined everything between them tonight when he kissed her. True, she had asked him to show her what it could be like between them, but he didn't want to continue until she knew everything there was to know about him.

And that's why he was sleeping with the horses. Better a cold, uncomfortable night outside with the snoring, farting horses than being warmed in front of a fire embraced by a sexy, bold redhead with breasts he couldn't wait to bury his face in.

"Yeah," he said from his corner of the lean-to to the lolling horses, "this is infinitely better." He tugged the collar of his jacket higher onto his neck and petulantly crossed his arms over his chest.

"At least she still seems to want to be with me," he said aloud after a moment, surprised at how comforting the thought was. Even after all he had put her through these past four days, she was still there by his side. It was baffling, to say the least. But since he had very limited experience with women, maybe this was how women preferred to be treated. Like equals, not cosseted like some porcelain doll only meant to be taken out and admired on special occasions.

He thought back to the one and only female in his life, his Aunt Millie, and pondered how she would have taken to riding nonstop for four days across rugged terrain on horseback with only the ground for a bed and the stars for a blanket. He tried to reconcile those two ideas in his head, but failed to make his thoughts fit with what he knew about his aunt. It wasn't until he heard his aunt's unmistakable brogue filling his head with, "Yer a daft idjut, me lad, for treatin' that wee lassie like she were no more than one of yer soldiers," when Tavis perceived how badly he had messed up with Amelia.

"And that brings me to the third anguish of this journey which I like to call, 'Reasons why I am an ass.' "

Tavis rose and walked over to the comforting presence of his horse. Looping his arms around the beast's neck, he laid his head on the furry warmth of the great barrel chest. "Even knowing next to nothing about women as I do, Magnus," he said to his horse with a note of self-disgust in his voice, "I should never have treated her as I've done."

He recalled the hectic pace of the last several days and ticked off the ways in which he had wronged her: the insufficient meals, the uncomfortable lodgings, and the tireless pace he had insisted on. He rubbed his hand where she had bitten him.

The less than gentlemanly way in which I have handled her.

Tavis groaned and smacked himself on the forehead. "I've treated her like she was one of my soldiers!" He shook his head in disgust and leaned into his horse's neck. "God, I've been such a dimwitted idiot!" Magnus must have agreed, or he might have been irritated at being woken up, because he swung his head at Tavis and nipped at his arm.

"You're right, Magnus. I've treated her worse than a common foot soldier." His horse nickered in response, and he gave him a final pat. Looking around the cozy interior of the lean-to at the drowsy heads of the horses, he steeled himself for a long evening.

"I don't belong out here with the horses, either." Dejected and miserable, he left the lean-to.

****

Tavis thought he was going to die. It was as if he had been thrown into a raging fire and had no way to escape. He was desperate to pull in a cleansing breath of air, but every time he inhaled he breathed in more of that burning heat. His entire body was now aflame, heat seared his skin, and sweat dampened his clothing. *I'm going to die,* he thought hazily, *for this heat will surely kill me.*

But upon looking down at his body, he discovered the heat wasn't his only worry, for climbing up his limbs and torso were millions of grasping vines curling up his sides and threatening to engulf his head. Immediately he started pushing at the vines in an attempt to break them off his body, but it seemed the more he struggled the tighter the vines held him. He was going to lose feeling in his body before he suffocated to death from the heat, he decided. Already he couldn't feel sensation in his left arm. He struggled, thrashing to and fro, trying to free himself from the soft, clingy vines.

"Tavis." A soft, whispered voice floated to his ear. "Hmm." Though he still felt he was likely going to die from suffocation, or worse, strangulation, the quiet voice whispering his name soothed him. Realizing suddenly the voice had come from outside his dream and not in it, he awakened with a jolt and cracked a tired eye.

The fire had long since died, but there was enough light left in the sky coming in through the dingy windows that he was able to assess the rustic hut and his pack splayed out on the old table where he had unpacked it last night. His boots, he saw, were crumpled on the floor where he had kicked them off before lying down. And then he remembered exactly where he was.

Inside the hut. With Amelia. Sometime in the middle of the night, after several guilt-ridden hours spent talking to the horses and walking about in the cold evening air, Tavis had given up his struggle to stay away from her. Yes, it had been a foolish lapse of judgment to kiss her before telling her the truth about himself. At least he hadn't actually bedded her like he wanted. Once he had come to terms with his actions, he snuck back into the house and climbed onto the bed behind Amelia, arranging the cloak she was using as a blanket to cover both of them. She had turned in her sleep, snuggling her curvy bottom into the crook of his legs. With her warm body tucked against his, he had fallen asleep.

Only after remembering all this did he hazard a glance at his body. Amelia was wrapped around him much like the clinging vine of his dream. Pressed into his side, her legs intertwined with his, and her arms draped across his chest, she had him in a tight embrace. Her fiery red hair, lightly gilded by the faint rays of the rising sun through the window, tumbled about her shoulders. In his fists he held tendrils of her silken red strands. He must have grabbed onto it during the night and in his dream wound it around himself like the clinging vine he had imagined it to be.

Releasing his hold on her hair, he tried to extricate himself from her possessive hold. She stirred restlessly before letting go. Turning onto her other side, she curled away from him, dragging the cloak with her. His sense of relief at her leaving was great, for he now realized the blazing inferno in his dream was Amelia. Cool air brushed his skin, and he sucked in several refreshing breaths.

The relief did not last long, though, as pins and needles shot through his arm, a sure sign he was regaining sensation in the place where Amelia had rested for most of the night. He gritted his teeth manfully while he tried to shake the feeling back into his arm without disturbing Amelia's slumber. Carefully, he scooted down to the edge of the bed and made his way to the fireplace. In no time, he had built a small but steadily rising fire.

"Tavis, what are you doing?" her sleepy voice asked. "Come here and warm me up. I'm cold."

He snorted. No woman was less cold than Amelia. She radiated sultry heat, and he had been the unwitting recipient of it for the better part of the evening. Besides, if he climbed back into bed with her, there was no guarantee he could continue to call himself a gentleman.

"The fire will be blazing and warming you up soon enough." He made the mistake of looking behind him at Amelia lounging in the bed.

"Fine." She pouted, pushing out her plump lower lip. While he stared, entranced, at her glistening red mouth, she let go of her hold on the cloak to pinch her lower lip between her two fingers before readjusting the collar of her loosened bodice. It slipped off her shoulder to reveal creamy expanses of neck and collarbone.

He turned back to the fire and shoved more tinder

onto the burgeoning blaze. There were soft rustling sounds coming from the bed behind him as she resettled herself on the bed, followed by a deep sigh and then silence.

"Only a couple more hours, man," he said to reassure himself. "Only a couple more hours." Repeating those words like a prayer, he tore his gaze away from her supine form, pulled on his boots, and stepped out of the hut to tend the horses.

Chapter 11

Sometime later, Amelia reawakened to find herself in an empty room. Tavis was nowhere to be seen, and the fire he had started last night had since died down. Rising from the bed, she smoothed out her costume and pulled on her boots. With her fingers, she managed to brush through the thick mane of her curls and pull the wayward strands into a simple bun.

She stepped outside into the cool morning air to look for Tavis. The sun was just rising, and she was surprised to discover that, despite her troubled mind upon going to bed last evening, she had slept the night through. At one point it seemed Tavis was in bed with her, too. It had been lovely to curl up with him, the warmth of his body against hers. When she had awakened, he was gone, and she knew it must have been a dream.

The horses were still tied a little distance away from the hut, including the reassuring sight of Tavis's huge stallion, Magnus. Though she didn't think he would leave her, she couldn't be too sure after last night. Even after pondering his reaction to their kiss, she still didn't understand why he had reacted the way he did.

"No Tavis," she muttered, scanning the area around the hut. The horses nickered in response, and she felt a sudden urge to take a walk. Recalling a small path located near the horses, she set out to see where it led. She hoped it would help clear her confused mind.

Amelia allowed the heady scent of the evergreens to soothe her frazzled nerves. All too soon, though, the anxieties she had tried to put aside crept to the forefront of her mind.

"Run away with him, Mimi," she muttered, imitating her sister's cool, cultured voice. "You need to live life in the light, not in the shadows." She continued walking at a faster pace as her anger and agitation increased.

"Don't worry about the scandal, Mimi. Everyone will think it is terribly romantic." This time, she spoke in the earnest, bubbly qualities of Clarisse, even adding her friend's emphatic head bobs and clasped hands for good measure.

She was running down the path now, her boots crunching in the still of the morning. In her careless flight, her foot caught on a raised tree root, and she fell onto the path. Rolling over to glare at the lightening sky, she shouted, "I've run away with him, and the dimwitted oaf of a man is nowhere to be found!" The only answer she received was the muted squawking of birds she had disturbed in her heated exclamation.

Amelia picked herself up and brushed off the dirt and debris from her skirt. Hugging her knees with her arms, she put her head down toward her lap. "You never said what to do if he didn't want me anymore." She sniffled and was ready to enjoy a healthy, self-indulgent cry when she heard a rustling on the path. Lifting her head in alarm, she demanded, "Who's there?"

"Amelia, is that you?"

Swiping at the tears on her face, she stood up. "Yes. It's me. Where are you?" She looked ahead of her and behind.

There were more rustling and crunching sounds, and Tavis appeared in front of her, about three feet from where she stood.

"Are you injured?" he asked with a note of concern in his voice. "I heard some loud yelling, so I rushed up the path, worried you were in danger." He took her arms and began to assess her person for any injuries.

"I-I was walking down the path, and I fell," she explained.

He knelt in front of her and continued to check her for injuries, skimming his hands up her legs and down again to feel her ankles. She wobbled in his grasp.

"You are hurt," he said, coming to stand in front of her once again. Lifting her in his arms, he held her close to his chest and strode down the path in the direction from which he had come.

"There's a small lake ahead, with a pretty view," he explained to her. "You'll rest there for a bit while we talk." She nodded and settled her head on his chest, taking comfort in his strong arms and the steady beat of his heart. Too soon, they arrived at their destination and he set her down on the soft earth by the lake. He moved off behind her, only to return with his pack bag.

"I thought you'd be hungry, so I rode into the nearest town and bought us some food from the local inn." He shrugged in self-conscious embarrassment. "I had planned on coming to get you soon to break our fast by the lake. I thought you'd like looking at the view."

Her heart melted a little at his gesture. She patted

the spot next to her. "Thank you, Tavis." He ambled over to her and lowered his tall frame to the ground. Opening the pack, he served their meal of cold meat pies, bread, cheese, and fruit. "It was a very kind thought."

In companionable silence, they ate the meal Tavis had procured. When the last crumb was licked away, he lay back, cupping his head with his hands clasped behind his neck.

"It was always on mornings like these, with the sun peeking over the horizon and the sound of birds stirring in the treetops, I could almost imagine myself at home again." Watching him as closely as she was, she did not miss the wistful expression on his face. "Home again in the comforting green hills of Scotland instead of on a bloody battlefield in France."

"You were in the army?" After the last four days with him, she had expected as much.

"Oh, aye. And a captain, to boot."

"Did you sell your commission, or are you on leave?" She tried sounding nonchalant, but it was difficult to do. Because if Tavis had a career as a soldier, she didn't know how she would bear it if she had to let him go.

"I did sell my commission," he admitted, though the way he said it left Amelia to infer there was a *but* coming.

"But not because I wanted to. About three months ago, I learned my brother and his wife had died, leaving my father's estate without an heir."

Amelia felt a rush of compassion for him, thinking of the grief he must have experienced upon learning of the death of his family. "Oh, I'm so sorry for your loss,

Tavis." Laying her hand on his taut bicep, she squeezed it in sympathy. "I don't know what I would do if I lost one of my sisters."

"Thank you, Amelia, for your kindness." He had looked so sad when he told her about his deceased brother, and she thought he might say more to her, but the anguish she had seen on his face was replaced by a genial mask of good humor.

"We had been estranged, in fact, for several years, and John—my brother—had been looking for me for some time. When my brother's solicitor found me and informed me of his death, I sold my commission and went home to assume my responsibilities."

She had been right in her first assessment of him. He had been a second son. And as most second sons, he had bought a commission in the military. But because of several unfortunate incidents he was now... Amelia paused, coming back to the question that had plagued her since leaving with him. *Who was he?*

He eyed her with caution, and she became uneasy at his expression. "What aren't you telling me, Tavis? Who are you really?" she whispered.

"I am Tavis McGuire, my lady, formerly Captain McGuire of Her Majesty's Royal Army, and now the fifth Earl of Stanton."

Amelia's eyes widened in stunned surprised. "You're Stanton?" she squeaked. "Y-You lied to me!"

She jumped up from the ground and stood above him with her hands on her hips, shaking in rage.

"No, Amelia, I never lied." He rose and backed away, using his hands to shield himself from attack. "I didn't tell you all of my names."

"You knew I was supposed to meet Lord Stanton,

and yet you played the fool at my expense, letting me ramble on and on about him." She was furious with him, trembling in uncontrolled rage.

"I did not know who you were until right before we went out to dance."

"Don't lie to me again!" she screamed. "You knew who I was, and you decided to play with the freak, see if you wanted to waste your precious time meeting me."

"That's not what happened. If you'd only listen to me, Amelia, I can explain."

Amelia was done listening. There was no Clarisse telling her to count to ten before acting in anger, and no one was there to restrain her actions. So when Tavis stepped toward her, she didn't count or stop to think. She lunged.

****

Though it had taken her some time, Amelia calmed herself down and was sitting on a log near the lake, while her companion washed his wounds in the lake. Even from where she sat, she heard him grumbling under his breath. "Serves you right, Tavis, or should I say *Lord Stanton,*" she muttered.

"What?" he demanded. He stopped washing and was now glaring at her, water dripping from his hair and onto the once-dry linen of his shirt. She took a strangled breath as the wet shirt clung to his broad chest. *Drat the man! After everything, I still want him.*

To cover her growing unease at her uncheckable desires, she waved and responded with false gaiety, "I said it serves you right. What a shame if your wounds turned putrid and you were to lose a limb, or better yet, die."

He doused his head with water one more time and

stomped out of the lake. "You little hellcat," he growled. "If you had listened to me before attacking, I could have told you what happened."

"Like I would believe anything you would have to tell me now."

A dark shadow loomed over her. Looking up, she was confronted with the imposing figure of a very wet and very large man. He stared down at her with teeth gritted and panting in restrained anger.

"You are dripping water on me," she said, dismissing him with a flick of her wrist. "If you were any sort of a gentleman, you would kindly step back." She pushed at him, but her efforts were ineffectual. The man was like a stone wall.

"Oh, no," he said with grim satisfaction, capturing her hands in his. "You can't cast me as the devil one moment and then expect me to behave as the gentleman the next."

"Fine," she said on a huff. "I'm leaving." She stood but was shoved down by Tavis's blunt fingers.

"You'll stay, and you'll listen to me, or so help me God, I will turn you over my knee and give you the spanking you so richly deserve."

Her pulse beat faster in alarm at the thought of Tavis laying hands to her. Or maybe it was beating faster from the thought of him touching her in so intimate a place. Either way, she shivered and decided to stay put.

After several moments in which she remained mute, he broke their tense silence by saying, "I didn't know who you were, Amelia, when you ran into me at the stables. I was not expecting anyone to venture there that time of night."

He blew out a large breath and started to pace. "It wasn't until you said you were visiting your father's stables I began to ken who you were. You asked me what I was doing in the stables, Amelia, and by the end of the night, you had figured it out for yourself." He stopped his pacing in front of her. "I was planning all along to steal those horses you saw me take."

"But why?" she asked. "You are the Earl of Stanton and can buy anything you want."

"It all started with a bet."

At her interested look, he continued his story. "Are you familiar with the betting book at White's?"

"You mean the one listing ridiculous wagers placed by silly men so they can prove they are better than other silly men?" She arched a red brow. "*That* betting book at White's?"

"Er, yes. Well, as it turns out, my father and your father had a bet that was placed in the books when they were both at university together. I think my father must have been two or three years older than yours. One day, after classes, they were boasting about who was the better horseman and who would have the better stables when they each took over their respective estates. Each, of course, thought it would be himself, and that's when the idea for the bet was born."

"I don't understand," she said shaking her head. "What does a bet at White's have to do with you stealing my father's horses?"

He held up his hand to stop her inquiry. "I'm coming to that, my lady. While our fathers were vehemently arguing for their own talent, all the other lads at the school had gathered round and were keenly interested in determining who the better horseman was.

Several ideas were tossed back and forth, but one young gentleman suggested a truly good horseman would be able to whisk away several horses from someone's stables without anyone being the wiser. When questioned as to how that proved superiority in horsemanship, the gentleman replied only a truly superior horseman would be able to persuade a high-strung team of horses to willingly depart from their comfortable lodgings. And so the bet was struck."

"What was the bet?"

"The gentleman who was able to steal the other gentleman's horses from underneath his very nose would be declared the superior horseman. But since both of our fathers were highly competitive, it didn't stop there. Once the first team of horses was stolen, and I believe it was by your father, well, my father had to get even, you see. He stole those horses right back and had them in their stalls before the week's end. Soon after, those horses and others throughout the years were traveling across the countryside on a regular basis."

"How odd I didn't know that about my father. All these years, and he never let on." She gave Tavis a puzzled look. "Funny, isn't it? How we can live with someone all of our lives and still know nothing about them?"

Tavis gulped and pulled at his collar, his face flushing a dull red. "Er, yes." Clearing his throat, Tavis said, "After my father died, the tradition seemed to die with him. Except your father must have decided to try once more to prove he was the better horseman, even though his rival had been dead for years. He succeeded again in taking those horses, and I imagine he thought my brother would continue the tradition he had had with my father. Unfortunately, your father didn't know my brother was on his deathbed and therefore unable to act. At some point, your father must have discovered John's death, because on my arrival home a note was waiting for me from your father."

"What did it say?" she asked, more than a little excited from hearing about such intrigues happening at her home.

"He invited me to your sister's ball, where he said he would divulge his little game and I could have my horses back if I were horseman enough to take them. It's where he also invited me to meet you."

"So when I ran into you in the stables you were…?"

"I couldn't very well let your father get away with taking my horses, now, could I?" He smiled mischievously, bringing her in on his little secret. "I was looking for them when we ran into each other, so I could make a hasty getaway after the ball was over."

"Did you even want to meet me?" She felt her old anxieties returning, always feeling like she was not good enough.

"At first I was reluctant, I admit, but your father was most persistent. He told me of your many accomplishments and your shining beauty. Aye, after that I was a little more eager to meet you than I had been."

"Yet you knew how I felt about meeting Lord Stanton, er, you." She flushed when she met his gaze.

"I did, except you failed to meet me, my lady," Tavis reminded her. "I spent an hour in your mother's company, delightful as it was, but it did not allow us to formally meet in the eyes of your parents."

"I am sorry, Tavis, but you had just asked me to run away with you. I needed to think." A suspicious thought entered her mind, and before she had time to consider her words she blurted, "Why did you ask me, if you knew we were to meet so soon? Was this a game to you?"

"Never, Amelia. As soon as I learned who you were and how you felt about meeting Lord Stanton, I didn't want you believing I had been forced to meet you. After what you shared about your experiences with the gentlemen of the *ton,* I knew you weren't keen on meeting me. But we also shared an easy camaraderie and a mutual attraction for each other. That's the reason I asked you to run away with me as Tavis McGuire and not as Lord Stanton."

"What if I had showed and had met you as Lord Stanton?"

"I don't know. Maybe I would have taken you into the gardens and kissed you until you were no longer angry at me." Tavis wiggled his eyebrows at Amelia, who rolled her eyes at his antics.

"You are all talk, Lord Stanton. Kiss me until I wasn't angry. Humph! You have had plenty of chances to kiss me—at the stables, outside my window, under the stars—and last night. And when you finally do, you push me away and sleep with the horses. I am beginning to think you don't want me anymore."

"You can believe me or not, but I knew we had things to discuss. If you objected to what I had to say, I wanted you to be free to leave. Had I compromised you and then told you the truth, you might have felt compelled to stay even though you had come to hate me for lying. I couldn't do that to either of us." He reached his hand up to ease her hair behind her ear. "As you so perceptively pointed out, I may not know a lot about women, Amelia *mia*, but I do know in a marriage it's the wife who rules the roost, and if she isn't happy, no one is happy."

Taking her hands and kissing each one on the palm, he asked, "Not want you, you foolish woman? I burn for you, Amelia. Never doubt that."

She frowned and nibbled on her lower lip. "What if you change your mind after I tell you my secret?"

"About what?"

"I'm cursed," she whispered, once again hanging her head, but this time in shame.

Gentle fingers caressed her chin, pulling her head up. "Aye, lass, I already knew that."

"You did? And it doesn't frighten you?"

"No, *mo chroí*, your wee curse doesna scare a big, bad Scot like me," he said in a thick Scots burr. "I want to know how it works, though, so I can be prepared in any case."

She let out a breath she didn't even know she'd been holding. On the rare occasions she had revealed she was cursed, people treated her as if she had the plague. Even though she asked for her secret to remain one, it soon spread. Before long, everyone in town knew her family's wretched plight. By the end of her first season, more than half the *ton* reviled her as an unholy spawn of Satan while the other half thought she was a ridiculous liar hoping to draw attention to herself by inventing ludicrous stories about a gypsy curse. It had been several lonely years since her come out.

Tavis not only accepted her curse, he wanted to know more. A warm, happy glow began to chip away at the shield around her heart, giving her a warmth she usually found only with her family and Clarisse.

"I'd like you to know, too."

Tavis dug out a blanket from his pack and spread it on the ground. Pulling her down with him, the two leaned up against the log as Amelia told Tavis how she came to be cursed all those years ago.

"So, if someone were to ask you a question, you can't tell a lie?" he asked, startling Amelia with his deep voice. He had remained silent throughout her lengthy story and explanation of how the curse worked, and she had almost forgotten he was there next to her.

Almost, but not quite. His warm body pressed by her side was reminder enough he was near. "Yes, that's right."

"What happens if you don't answer someone honestly?"

"I get very ill to my stomach, and sometimes I even faint." Amelia shrugged. "Over the years, I've developed several tricks for delaying the inevitable truth I must tell."

"Like what?"

"I speak over half a dozen languages. Did you know that?"

"Aye, well, not that it was so many. Your father told me you were an accomplished linguist. How can speaking so many languages help you?"

"If someone asks me a question and I don't want to hurt their feelings, I reply in a different language. They usually find it charming and forget all about the fact I didn't answer them in a language they understand."

"Clever girl," he praised.

"I can stall, or ask people to repeat, but in the end I

have to answer or I'll be sick."

A speculative gleam entered Tavis's eyes. "Then if I were to ask you a personal question, you would have to answer honestly?"

She gulped and nodded, loving the rich way he rolled the "r" in the word personal. Tiny tremors of excitement began to form in her spine, and as they spread throughout her body she became lightheaded and giddy.

"Did you ever have any serious suitors before me?" Tavis asked.

Amelia was disappointed. She had hoped for a much more personal question than one about her past suitors.

"What? Why do you ask?"

"Just curious."

"No, not really. My first year out, I had several suitors, but most did not linger past an initial outing together. After that, word went around I was rude, and soon it was rumored I was cold. Suitors stopped calling after that." She fidgeted with her hands and then laughed, a rather derisive, lonely sound.

"Mother and Father never gave up, though, despite lack of interest. Mother especially took it as her personal mission to find me a husband, and Father even went so far as to pay gentlemen to dance with me. I can't tell you how many of their friends they've thrown at me over the years."

"Was it very terrible, lass?"

"Not at first, no. Some of the gentlemen were very kind and charming. I would be lying if I said I didn't enjoy the attention." Her eyes flitted downwards to stare at her fingers clenched in her lap. "But then, well, the men after that weren't so kind or charming. Most were older than my father and several..." She trailed off and swallowed to hold back her tears.

Tavis reached over to hold her hand. Giving it a squeeze, he prompted, "Several were what, Amelia?"

She flushed and turned her head away, refusing to look at Tavis, his kind face so near her own. Amelia couldn't bear to see his disgust when he found out. "Several tried to compromise me," she whispered. "One would have, if my sister hadn't happened to come along and found me. He...Jeremy was—and still is, I imagine—a house guest. My father took his side instead of mine. M-my father told me if I continued to wear such revealing clothing then I was just asking for male attention."

"Were you hurt very badly?" Tavis asked with deathly calm, his glittering sapphire eyes having turned hard as steel at her stammered confession of near rape.

Amelia shrugged as if almost being raped was of no consequence. If it weren't for the trembling of her hands no one would know how much it still affected her. "Some scratches and some bruising but otherwise intact." She gifted Tavis with a coy look. "It was after that incident Bea taught me how to defend myself. She said every woman should know how to take care of herself. Just in case."

"Your sister is very wise," Tavis said, never once taking his eyes off her. The pressure of his hands on hers increased, and Amelia began to feel an intense rush of warmth pooling low in her stomach. Her mouth dried, and her breath came in unexpected bursts from her lungs.

She cleared her throat and smoothed her hair back

from her face. "Was there something else you wanted to ask me, Tavis? Another personal question?" she asked, swallowing hard. Amelia allowed her eyes to roam over the taut lines of Tavis's neck and shoulders and down to the burgeoning hardness swelling beneath her hot gaze. She gasped and licked her lips.

He spread his legs a little bit wider, and Amelia's gasp turned to a low, throaty moan at the delicious ridge caused by hard male flesh, on display for her eager perusal. His dark chuckle recalled her to herself, and she pulled her wanton gaze up to look into Tavis's dark, glittering eyes. "I think I'll save that personal question for later tonight. After we're married."

Chapter 12

He was already five minutes late. Closing the lid of his watch, Tavis placed it in his breast pocket and resumed his pacing in the private sitting room of the inn where he and Amelia were staying in Gretna Green. He smoothed back his still damp hair and ran a hand over the fabric of his already wrinkle-free coat.

"Good lord," he muttered. "I haven't been this nervous since I was sixteen." Then, he had been a green lad, inexperienced with women but eager to learn. His first was a fine French whore named Giselle. She was a birthday present from his father, the one and only gift he had ever received from the old man. Though she had been much older than he, Tavis had worshiped her, and she in turn had taught him everything she knew about the fine art of making love. They had passed two glorious months together before his father's money ran out and she returned to London, leaving young Tavis heartbroken and once again alone.

There had been other women after Giselle, but none who mattered, and certainly none to whom he had ever proposed marriage.

Tavis stopped mid-pace and scrubbed at his face. "Married!" he said to the empty room, that one word sticking in his throat and causing dots of perspiration to break out on his forehead.

A bachelor one minute and a husband the next.

Tavis still couldn't believe all that had happened since leaving the hut at the lake. After they returned to pack their belongings, it was a short half-day's ride to Gretna Green. They had arrived by one, eaten a quick lunch, and were married by two. Tavis had given Amelia his ring with the Stanton family crest on it. Though it was too big and Tavis had assured his new wife he would buy her a new one once they were settled, Amelia had ignored him and looped it onto a gold chain around her neck, where it nestled in the warm valley of her breasts.

The thought of his ring belonging to Amelia, *his wife,* did strange things to him. He felt at once happy and also ill. Frankly, this whole business of courtship and marriage made him queasy.

In the past, he'd never had time to form an attachment with a gentlewoman. After university, he bought a commission and left to fight on the Continent. That left little time for paying court to young misses and learning their unique and mysterious ways. Before Amelia, he had never cared. What did it matter if he knew how to treat a gentlewoman or how to talk to one? All he needed to know was how to lead a battalion of soldiers and to not get killed. Now, it was the only thing that mattered.

Tavis had mishandled things so badly since meeting Amelia, and he wanted everything to be perfect this evening. He wanted Amelia to see he knew how to treat a lady. He wanted her to not regret her decision to elope with him. So much depended on how this first night as man and wife passed, which scared the hell out of Tavis.

Once again he pulled his watch out to check the time. He was now ten minutes late, and it was past time for him to join his wife in their room. Here he was having a fit of the vapors to rival any young miss of the *ton*, while his lovely, passionate wife waited above.

"You faced thousands of French soldiers, McGuire. You're a damned national hero. A wee redheaded lass will be easy in comparison." With a grim nod of determination at the conclusion of his less than rousing speech, Tavis straightened his shoulders, ascended the stairs, and knocked on the door.

Amelia's rosy-cheeked face greeted him from behind the door, and he swallowed upon entering. The room was dark, lit only by a few candles and a low fire in the fireplace, yet when Tavis entered the room he was struck dumb by the beauty of his wife. All of his anxieties and fears quieted, moving to the background while he stared in awe.

She stood near the bed with the firelight illuminating her from behind and highlighting the simple elegance of the nightgown she wore. Made of some kind of shimmery, sheer confection of lace and satin, the soft green brought out the rich tint of her hair and accented the gold flecks in her green eyes. Her cheeks looked flushed, and he wondered if it was from the heat of the room or from her excitement.

"What are you wearing, Amelia *mia?*"

She ran her hands down the smooth fabric and up again. "Do you like it?" she asked shyly. "I bought it today in town to surprise you."

It took him a moment to respond, his mouth having gone dry of a sudden, and his mind more agreeably occupied in ogling his new wife. "Aye, I like it." He prowled forward and grabbed her around the waist. "But I wonder if you realized that while you were standing there with the fire behind you I could see all of you. Each. Luscious. Curve." He emphasized his point by running his hands up and down her backside. Finding the firm flesh of her bottom, he squeezed.

"Really?" she asked and wound her own arms around his neck. "What did I look like?"

He leaned over so his mouth was next to her ear. "Like an angel." He started spreading soft kisses along her neck and over her face. Remembering how lush and full she had looked standing there before the fire in the scrap of lace, with all of her curves outlined for his ravenous gaze, he amended, "Well, maybe a fallen angel."

"If you stood in front of the fire would I be able to see everything of you?" Her hands found their way to his chest, where her fingers smoothed over the hard planes under the fabric of his shirt.

Tavis grunted in amusement. "I'm not going to wear your damn nightdress, Amelia, so you can find out. I don't care how tempting you look in it and what it is currently doing to my reasoning. There is absolutely no way."

He was rewarded with a sweet giggle. "I wasn't suggesting you wear my gown, Tavis. I was just wondering what you would look like…you know." She trailed off in embarrassment and peeked up at him shyly.

"You would like to see me without my clothes on?" He couldn't help the pleased grin that broke out on his face at her eager nod. He wasn't vain about his body. It was well muscled and lean and did what he wanted it to do. That's all a man could really expect. That and to still have a full head of hair at forty, he supposed.

Other women said he had a fine form, but hearing his wife was eager to discover what he looked like under his clothing made him feel oddly anxious. *Maybe she won't like what she sees.* Or maybe she would think he was too muscled and too hard. Some women didn't like all those muscles, preferring a softer and leaner male form. He couldn't think why, but apparently the sallow, half-fed weakling look was appealing to some ladies.

When he looked down, Amelia had already discarded his tie, and her nimble fingers were at work pulling his shirt free from his waistband. Almost before he realized what was happening, she had helped him remove his shirt. With her fingers spread apart, she caressed the smooth skin of his chest, the delicate padding of her fingers passing over his now hardened nipples. It wasn't until she raked her nails up and down his abdomen he knew if he didn't take some control of this situation he would embarrass himself before he even got Amelia out of her nightgown.

He tried to grab her hands, but the slippery temptress was too quick for him. Both hands snaked down across his stomach to the waistband of his breeches. He looked down in hazy desire at her small fingers grasping the fabric at his waist. She hesitated for several seconds, and Tavis guessed she was warring with her maidenly modesty.

"Would you like me to finish disrobing, my lady wife?" he asked. She swallowed and nodded.

Once he sank onto the bed, he motioned for Amelia to come over as he implored, "Help me with my boots."

Amelia sauntered until she nestled between Tavis's

Sara Ackerman

outstretched legs. "Show me what to do," she whispered her face a mere breath away from his.

Using his hands, he positioned her so she faced away from him, straddling one of his thighs. With only a slight pressure from him on her lower back, she soon bent over his foot, first wriggling a boot off one foot and then the other. He dimly heard his boots hit the floor, too entranced by the sight of Amelia's wiggling arse while she straddled his thighs. All sorts of lewd ideas entered his mind, seeing her bent over in front of him, the thin fabric of her nightdress doing nothing to disguise the roundness of her bottom. It was only sheer force of will and an iron grip on the counterpane preventing him from grabbing her hips, lifting her nightgown, and taking his wife while she straddled his lap. Tavis was strung too tightly, and at the moment he was unsure how gentle he was going to be with his tender new bride.

Tavis patted the bed in invitation for Amelia to join him. Her catlike green eyes watched him while he reached down to his breeches and flicked open the buttons, a task made more difficult by the tight press of his swelling erection against the front flap. Finally, his stiff cock pushed free, and Tavis breathed a sigh of relief.

"What do you think, lass?" Tavis stood and shed his breeches to the floor. "Do I please you?"

"Oh, my," she gasped her hand going to cover her mouth. Her eyes had gone as wide as saucers.

"What's wrong?" He looked down his body to make sure he wasn't covered in dirt or hadn't grown an extra limb since he had dressed earlier that morning.

"You're too big," she whispered gesturing down

130

toward his thrusting manhood.

He smiled indulgently at her, realizing she was just nervous about what was to come. "No, don't worry, Amelia sweet. Everything will work out."

"No, you're too big." A mulish line of determination was set on her sweet face. "Put it back."

"What? Are you serious?" At her vehement nod, he snapped, "It won't go back so easily, Amelia."

He tried to be sympathetic, really he did. Once he had seen her reaction, he had even willed his erection to begin to abate. Just a little so she wouldn't be so scared. Amelia wasn't making it easy, though. In her agitation, she had begun to gesture about, and all that gesturing and moving was causing her lovely breasts to jiggle and bounce. No matter what he tried to think of so he would become less aroused, all that came to mind were those big, bouncing breasts right in front of his face.

"What? You have to! Just pull up your breeches and...shove it back in there." She made a pushing motion with her hands.

"I assure you, even if I wanted to shove it back in there, which I don't, like this I don't think I could. As it is, I am so hard with wanting you I don't think I'll be able to button my breeches for a solid week, if not longer."

She tapped her chin. "Maybe you could fold it? You know, bend it under and then....mmph? In it goes?"

"Madam, in this condition, or any condition, mind you, it does not bend." He was starting to get a little irritated. When he had imagined his wedding night, it had not included ways to put his male part back in his breeches. His imaginings had been more along the line of how to put it someplace else much more warm and inviting.

"Here, let me try. I bet I could do it." He didn't like the purposeful look in her eyes.

He backed away from her. "No, keep your…" Before he could stop her, his girth was encircled by slender, warm fingers.

From out of her mouth came a different sort of "oh, my." This one was laced with breathless awe.

Tavis hissed out a breath between his gritted teeth. "Amelia," he warned.

"Am I hurting you, Tavis?" she asked in concern, her clever hands ceasing to caress his hardness.

"No, *lass*, not how you think, at least." He took her hands in his, lest she take it into her head to start up her torturous caresses again, and held them close to his heart. Lowering his mouth to hers, he took her lips in a soft, lingering kiss.

She kissed him back, at first tentatively, but then with increasing ardor. When he deepened the kiss, slanting his mouth over hers, her tongue darted out and flicked over his lips. He sucked in a breath, surprised at her daring.

Amelia shifted in his embrace, apparently not content to be idle, for somehow she had managed to wriggle her hands free from his embrace where they now glided over the taut skin of his biceps and lower onto the firm flesh of his buttocks. When she squeezed, he tore his mouth away from hers and let out a shaky laugh.

What a unique combination of innocence and seduction! She flushed, perhaps in embarrassment at the forwardness of her actions, but Tavis didn't mind. He liked her boldness, liked the way her body became soft and pliant in his embrace. Even now with her red curls hanging in disarray on the ivory expanse of her shoulders, he found her delightful.

Desire thrummed through his body. He wanted her. That didn't surprise him; he had wanted her since that night in the stables when he'd first seen her. No, this wanting was something more. He wanted to please her, an unfamiliar notion to a man accustomed to pleasing himself.

"I want to show you such pleasure, Amelia. Will you let me?" He brushed a soft kiss over her still glistening lips.

"Yes."

Picking her up in his arms, he carried her back to the bed and set her down.

"Do you trust me?" he asked, more for his peace of mind than hers.

She stared steadfastly into his eyes, not a glimmer of doubt in their emerald depths. "With my life, Tavis."

Perspiration dotted his brow at such absolute trust, and an uneasy lump filled his throat, constricting his breathing. Something akin to panic lodged in his chest when his subconscious whispered, *You don't deserve her.*

He didn't want those harsh words to be true, but they were. Amelia was a good person and warranted more than the outcast son of a traitor. What did he have to give her besides his name? Thanks to his father's duplicity, even that was tarnished. He had nothing to offer but himself.

And what if that's not good enough?

He had to leave now before anything else happened

133

between them. Tomorrow he would petition for an annulment and return Amelia to London. He would tell Wickes to find someone else to complete the mission, and he'd go home where it was safe. Everything would be back to normal and he'd no longer….this horrible, clawing panic would just…

Tavis stumbled backwards, his eyes squeezed shut against his own inadequacies, but warm hands encircled his arm, halting his retreat.

Amelia rose on her knees and placed her small hands on his bare chest. "It's all right if you're scared, Tavis," she said laying her head on his shoulder. "I'm scared, too."

She comforted him, her cool, slim arms wrapped around his heated flesh. His racing heart slowed, and the tight grip of fear loosened its hold on his throat, allowing him to admit, "I don't know what to do. It never mattered before…no one else mattered. What if I'm not enough?" he whispered, finally voicing his fear to his wife.

Raising her head from his chest, she said, "You have me to lean on now. Those times you doubt yourself, I will be there to be enough for both of us."

He pulled her into a tight embrace and buried his face in her hair. "I don't know what to do," he repeated, though it embarrassed him to admit it. "You are no paid consort, but my wife. I would treat you as the lady you are."

Lacing their fingers together, she said, "Then we'll learn together and forge a new path tonight."

She was offering him a new beginning, a chance to bury his past and create something new, something precious. Tavis joined her on the bed, humbled by her gift of innocence and trust. He was determined to put aside everything he had known before—costly lessons bought by a younger and less compassionate man—to learn alongside his wife.

With shaking hands and gentle touches he set out to discover what pleased her, what caused her to thrash her head to and fro, what made her arch into his hands and moan his name. He reveled in the silky feel of her skin under the rough padding of his fingers, of her breathy pants as they fanned across his flesh. Every tremble and sigh seared through his blood and had him aching to claim her for his own. When at last they joined in a heated rush of flesh melding with flesh, he could no longer tell where he left off and she began.

Later, when the fire had receded from his blood and his skin began to cool, he nestled his sleepy wife into the sheltering embrace of his body. He pulled the counterpane over their bodies and listened as her breathing evened out and slowed. Eventually he drifted off to sleep with a smile on his face, the first time he had been happy in years.

Chapter 13

Staring out the carriage window at the changing landscape, Amelia sighed, not wishing to disturb Tavis, who appeared to be deep in thought. Once they left Gretna to head north for his home, he had immersed himself in some papers his solicitor sent with him two weeks before. He'd apologized and admitted he hadn't even given them a thought in all this time, but since they were traveling more comfortably now would she mind if he looked them over? So here she sat in a carriage taking her to a new life, with nothing but her thoughts to distract her.

Instead of examining that particular anxiety, she reviewed the events of her honeymoon, taking the time to linger over the pleasurable details. She squirmed in her seat at the arousal coursing through her body and knew she needed to redirect her thoughts soon or it was going to be a long and uncomfortable ride. Glancing over at her husband, she noticed his large hands holding those papers from his blasted solicitor, and Amelia remembered what else his hands had been holding a few hours earlier...

Amelia gave up. It was hopeless to avoid thinking about her handsome new husband, and if she wanted to fantasize about him, there was nothing wrong with that. After all, he *was* her husband, a point he took pride in mentioning every morning after awakening her with slow, languid kisses. Many times, they hadn't left bed until late morning.

While mornings were passed in exploring their mutual passion, their afternoons were filled with intimate outings in which they had spent much time in deep conversation. At first, the two exchanged small parts of their lives in halting conversation. She had revealed parts of herself never before shared. She suspected the same was true for Tavis, as well.

Now she was going to be mistress of Ballywith, an estate she knew nothing about. The one time she asked Tavis about it she distracted him in the most pleasurable way possible.

Darn it all! Her attempt to redirect her thoughts from her husband only led to more of the same. She sighed again, but this time in complete annoyance at her wayward thoughts.

"If you sigh like that again, Wife, you'll likely blow all my papers out the window."

Startled, Amelia looked up to find her husband regarding her over the papers he held in his hand.

"Care to tell me what's on your mind?"

"I was actually wondering what Ballywith was like. If you recall, the last time we tried to discuss your home, other things came up." Amelia couldn't resist aiming a pointed stare at his groin.

"Ah, yes. You distracted me quite shamelessly from my husbandly duty to inform you of what awaits at Ballywith." Tavis set aside his papers in his valise, which he stowed on the seat next to her. Patting the now empty seat next to him, he said, "Let me remedy that, Wife."

Amelia joined her husband, having mourned the

loss of his touch since they left that morning and he became immersed in his papers. He wrapped his arm around her waist and pulled her into his side, where she snuggled her head into the crook of his arm.

"What do you wish to know?" he asked as he placed his chin comfortably atop her head.

"Tell me how big it is and what it looks like and how many servants you have," she rattled off.

"Ballywith…"

"Oh, and the history of it, too, and how many tenants you have, and…"

"Peace, woman! I will stop your words with a kiss!"

Amelia turned her head and pursed her lips in expectation, but when no kiss was forthcoming, she cracked an eye and saw Tavis watching her with amusement. "What? No kiss?" she asked through her puckered lips.

"You'll not distract me again, woman, with your witchy ways!" At her disgruntled pout, he laughed. "I'll make it up to you tonight when we arrive home."

"Promises, promises," she sniffed, resettling her head on his arm.

"As I was saying, Ballywith is really an old castle, quite small, actually, built in the valley of Ballywith Mountain, so named by my illustrious forefathers. I imagine since Ballywith was built in front of the ben, they decided to name it the same. Not very imaginative, my ancestors."

"And the castle itself? How many rooms are there?"

"Several hundred, I believe, but I could be off by a dozen or so."

"Several hundred? That's what you call small?"

"By most people's standards it would be considered small, petite."

"Your definition of small and mine are obviously different. Why, a castle of one hundred rooms in England would be considered quite large for most ancestral homes."

"Aye, I noticed what you English consider large"—here he placed his hands a small distance from each other—"we Scots would call small, even tiny." Now he held his thumb and forefinger together to indicate a much tinier size.

Amelia stifled a snort at Tavis's estimation of English sizes, knowing full well what he was comparing. "Yes, well things must simply be larger in Scotland." She felt Tavis shifting under her. When she looked, he had widened the spread of his legs and was grinning at her in smug male satisfaction.

Covering a grin with the back of her hand, she smoothed out her features and looked at him in wide-eyed amazement. "Your horses are positively monstrous! I've never seen horses so large before."

"There are certainly large beasties in Scotland," he said with pride. "Our mammoth horses being only one of them."

"Oh, I would agree. One could even say the horses are bred to fit the men, you all being so very large." She let the back of her hand brush over the largeness she knew lurked behind that flap in his breeches. If he took notice, he didn't let on he had felt her casual caress.

With her hand resting on his thigh, she pretended to ponder something before saying, "But now I understand from whence that expression came."

"And what expression would that be?"

"Why to be hung like a horse." Amelia held back her laughter as he blustered about.

"Amelia, that's not exactly—"

"I didn't realize what a compliment it was until now, Husband, but knowing how highly such largesse is valued in Scotland, especially that of horseflesh, I am sure everyone I meet will be pleased to learn I have acquired such a well hu-hung hu-husband…" Her voice warbled as her attempt to hold back her fit of giggles failed. "They will consider me the lu-luckiest of women and will be positively green with envy." She burst out into peals of laughter at Tavis's incredulous look.

All of a sudden his blustering stopped, and he grabbed her around the waist. Hauling her up on his lap, he attacked her ribs in ticklish retribution for her apt tease about his size. "You little wretch!" He laughed. "I'll teach you to joke about your husband!"

"Wait until I write my sister and let her know her pre-marital talk was for naught and I would have been better prepared had I gone to the stables and watched the stallions service the mares."

Tavis flashed her a wicked smile. "You weren't complaining last night, Amelia *mia*, when I had you on your knees and your plump arse in my hands as I serviced you like the stallion I am."

She curved her arms around his neck and inhaled deeply, loving the musky scent wafting off his skin. "Hmm. I never said I minded, Tavis, and fortunate woman I am, I'll be the only one who ever knows." Taking his mouth in a deep kiss, she reassured him how much his size didn't bother her in the least.

"Aye, well, I suppose I shouldn't have teased you

so about your home," he said when they broke apart. "Are you very sad to be leaving England? In all the rush, I never thought to ask you if you minded much."

"A little. Nervous, too, and when I get nervous my tongue tends to run away with itself. It's an old habit and a bad one that I am trying to change. I am sorry, too, Tavis, for my tease." She wound her arms around his neck and asked in a little-girl voice, "Forgive me?"

He nodded, and she rested her head on his chest, nestling there in contentment.

"I'm almost afraid to ask, but wherever did you hear such language? I imagine it's not something most young ladies are privy to."

"I often heard my father's associates use language like that. Often much worse, actually."

"What? Your father allowed them to speak like that in front of you?"

"Oh, no, Father would not have allowed that."

"Then how did you come to hear it?"

She squirmed a little on his lap, an uncomfortable feeling of shame settling over her.

"Do you not want to tell me? You don't have to if you don't want to."

"No, it's all right. I was just embarrassed because I probably shouldn't have been listening in the first place. Next to my father's study is a smaller room, not much bigger than a changing room, really. It's comfortably furnished with a small desk and a chair, and it's lined with books from floor to ceiling. Aside from the stables, it was my favorite spot at home."

"And you could hear your father speaking to his associates through the walls?"

"Usually, yes. Sometimes they spoke too quietly

for me to hear, but other times their voices carried clearly through the thin walls to my little nook."

"Is your room hidden?"

"Not hidden exactly, but yes, I could see how someone might mistake it for another section of wall. If you don't know where to look for the latch to open it, I imagine it could easily be overlooked. As far as I know, no one except me ever entered it."

****

Upon hearing Amelia had been privy to her father's private conversations with his business associates, Tavis's mind raced at the possibilities of what she had heard. He wished he had known about the little room when he searched the study. It was odd that Meeks hadn't said anything to him about it when they had debriefed the night of the ball, but if it was as small as Amelia claimed, then it was possible Meeks had missed it also. It sounded like the type of room known only to those intimately familiar with the house.

"And that's where you heard them speaking in such vulgar terms?"

She nodded and laughed. "When I could hear them, they only ever talked about horses. They always talked about this one horse called Big Harry. On more than one occasion I heard them laughing loudly about how the females always liked Big Harry because he was hung like a horse, and I remembered thinking to myself how odd it was for them to laugh about Harry being hung like a horse when he obviously was a horse, so how else could he be hung? It didn't make any sense to me. I asked Bea about it, and she laughed and said I would understand once I was married." Amelia lifted her head off his chest to give him a mischievous look.

"And now I've seen you, I completely understand what they were talking about. I blush at how naive I was, for it is clear to me now they must have been speaking of a man." Her expression turned to one of absolute befuddlement. "Though why gentlemen discuss another man's appendages is beyond me."

He chuckled. "Yes, well, we gentleman are a strange lot, and luckily for mankind, you women are willing to put up with us."

"Hmpf, you most certainly are!" She gave him a quick peck to the mouth and resettled on his chest. Tavis stretched out his leg on the seat bench to better accommodate holding her. While he stroked her hair, his mind reeled in excitement.

Could Harry the Horse be Westby's contact? Is it possible this man had been to Westby's house? What about the men Amelia heard in Westby's office, his associates? Were they always the same men she heard? And how many were there?

"Amelia," he said, touching her shoulder to rouse her. When she remained still, he tried again. "Amelia, sweet, are you awake?"

Her deep breathing and sleepy murmur were his only response. Tavis blew out a frustrated breath. He needed answers, and the sooner the better. He couldn't keep up this charade with Amelia much longer. She was too perceptive by half and would soon discover what he was hiding before he was ready for her to know, potentially endangering her, a risk he was not willing to take.

Leaning his head against the seat back, Tavis mulled over the letters he had been reading, particularly the one from Wickes, which had awaited him at the inn in Gretna Green. Before he and Amelia left London, he had made sure to inform Wickes of his change of plans. Unsurprisingly, Wickes was not pleased by his elopement, but he said they would discuss further in two weeks when he traveled to Ballywith. Tavis was not looking forward to their discussion and would rather have it done and over with. He recalled Wickes's strongly worded censure and recalled his own experiences with Wickes when he was angered. Tavis shuddered. *Then again, maybe not.* Though he hated to do so, this time he could wait.

At times like these, he questioned whether his decision to disobey direct orders was worth the impatience he'd had in making Amelia his bride. Had he waited and followed the plan, they would be engaged and he would be able to investigate Amelia's secret room for himself at his leisure, a fact that rankled more as the miles increased between him and Amelia's London home. Looking at his sleeping wife, Tavis pushed aside his guilt and decided the risk was worth it. This first week of marriage had been the most rewarding of his entire life. Every day he learned something new about her, and every day she burrowed more deeply into his heart.

To his great joy, he found she enjoyed being in the outdoors, something he had never deemed important until they discussed it. Amelia was also an avid reader, and he discovered they had read many of the same books, the works of Shakespeare being a favorite for both of them. Through their talks regarding some of their reading, Tavis was delighted to find she possessed a keen and assessing mind and looked forward to testing that mind, during the long winter months, over many a competitive game of chess.

It was also a time of great peace for him. In Amelia he found a kindred spirit, someone who because of her unique curse was also familiar with loneliness and feeling out of step with society. Being with her and knowing she was his filled an empty hollow inside him with warm contentment and belonging. It was a heady experience for a solitary man, and one which brought him fits of anxiety, especially when so many things remained unresolved.

Tavis stared out the window, worrying about what the future held, until he spied the familiar jagged peaks of Ballywith and the densely wooded forests surrounding the estate. He looked down to Amelia to awaken her and marveled yet again that this beautiful passionate woman was his. Forever.

Quite suddenly, a heavy weight settled in Tavis's stomach. His insides churned and went hollow all at once, and the foreign emotion that struggled up from all that riotous churning had him queasy, lightheaded, and elated, all at once. It was only through intense concentration he was able to push away whatever it was and regain his equilibrium. Or so he hoped.

With a little trepidation at triggering a repeat of those emotions, he shook Amelia's shoulders to rouse her. "We're home."

Amelia yawned and stretched. Wiping the sleep from her eyes, she pressed her nose to the window and admired the beauty of her new home. After several moments of silent delight, in which Amelia gazed at the rolling hills, towering peaks and wooded forests of Ballywith, all softly illuminated for her wondering eyes by the amber light of the fading day, she finally turned to him with shining eyes. "Oh, Tavis! How wonderful to be starting our lives together in such a magical place!"

He had felt fine watching Amelia take pleasure in seeing her new home, had again thanked his lucky stars for giving him such a woman, but as soon as she flashed those sparkling eyes in his direction and smiled at him, that unfamiliar sensation rose up again, threatening to choke the air from his lungs. His stomach clenched, and he briefly questioned if he had contracted some sort of fatal illness.

Swallowing through the tightness constricting his throat, he croaked, "How wonderful."

She turned away and continued to gaze out the window, exclaiming at everything she found to be interesting or beautiful.

He thought it was odd how he only felt ill when looking upon his wife. With her back turned to him, he felt peaceful and comfortable. The moment she looked at him and he saw the vibrancy of her very soul staring back at him with such honest intensity, well, it was as though he were drowning with no promise of survival. *It is almost as if…*

The carriage hit a large bump as it pulled around a curve, and the castle was visible in all its glory. Whatever was struggling to surface in his mind was lost, and the moment was gone.

The Earl and Countess of Stanton were home.

Chapter 14

Walking to the windows of her new master suite, Amelia gazed out onto the grounds, hoping the serene beauty of her new home would help lift her flagging spirits. But as she watched, dark clouds covered the sun and plunged everything into deep shadows. More depressed than ever, she turned away from the window to wander about the room, bemoaning Tavis's absence.

Ever since arriving at Ballywith over a week ago, Amelia had felt a chilly reserve from Tavis that hadn't existed since their marriage. In fact, they had only just arrived at Ballywith when he made his apologies to her and left to attend to some business while she remained behind to rest and get settled in by herself. She wanted to spend some time with him, had in fact asked him to stay, but he placed a chaste kiss on the top of her head and told her his business could not be delayed.

She hoped once he had settled his immediate business on the estate he would be able to spend more time with her, yet each day he seemed to have more and more work to do. Sometimes she awakened to find him gone for the day and it wasn't until the evening meal that she saw him for the first time. Tavis was always apologetic, yet he still remained distant. The passionate spontaneity of their honeymoon had disappeared. Amelia missed the loss of their intimacy, but she mourned the loss of his company also and wondered if her honeymoon was well and truly over.

Shaking her head to dispel her gloomy mood, she thought perhaps a nap would help clear her head. Remembering her new dressing room had a cozy fire already built up and a comfortable chaise to relax on, Amelia went into her dressing room and stopped in surprise.

Upon entering, she noticed several large changes to the room. Previously, only a few of her meager belongings were present, only those things she had been able to carry with her, yet now she saw all her familiar items lining the lavish vanity. On the walls were other of her possessions, including a beloved painting her sister Evie had done for her as a present on her last birthday. She spied her own silky dressing gown and matching slippers, as well as other clothing she had left behind.

"Margaret!" Amelia gasped when the plump, brown-haired figure of her longtime maid appeared before her in her dressing room. "Whatever are you doing here? Why aren't you still in London?" Amelia sank down into the chair in front of her vanity and regarded her maid with undisguised shock and curiosity.

The little maid smiled at her frazzled mistress and handed her the cup of hot tea she had brought in with her on a silver tray. "I left London the night you did, my lady, and was sent here to wait for you to come home with the master. Been at my sister's visiting, since then, and would have been here upon your arrival, but she took ill and there was no one else to nurse her, so I had to stay. I'm so sorry, my lady, I wasn't here when you arrived."

Amelia drank the hot tea, its familiar taste easing her sudden surprise. She waved off her maid's apology. "But how did you know where to find me? I don't understand how you could be here, especially since when I left I didn't even know this was where I would end up."

"It's an exciting story, my lady, at least exciting for me." She turned Amelia around to face the mirror of her vanity. Picking up the hairbrush, Margaret began to work through the snarls Amelia had been unable to untangle herself, having refused to let anyone else in the household attend her hair. Margaret tugged on a stubborn knot and smiled in apology at Amelia's sharp wince of pain. "I'd say it's a good thing I came when I did, my lady, as it's obvious you're in need of a little caring after."

"Your story, Margaret." She set the teacup aside on the tray next to her. "If you please."

"Right you are, my lady. It was the night of the ball, and I was awaiting your return in your dressing room. It were only an hour or so past midnight, but seeing as how you don't like them balls, I knew you would be coming in soon to go to bed. Well, imagine my surprise when at half one the door opens and in comes Her Majesty Queen Bea and Clarisse!" She stopped her brushing to throw her hands over her chest.

Amelia smothered a frustrated sigh, knowing there was no hurrying Margaret, who would get around to telling her story in her own time. She might as well be comfortable while she waited. Grabbing a hot scone from her tea tray, Amelia devoured it while waiting for Margaret to continue.

"I says to them, 'Where is my lady Amelia? Is she

ill?' Because, truth be told, both of them were acting a little queerly, and I thought for sure you had taken ill or maybe broken your leg, but then the Queen starts giving me orders, telling me, 'Pack Amelia's trunks and be quick about it.' When I tried to ask where you were going, she just shooed me off and told me to hurry."

"What happened then?" Amelia asked.

"The three of us packed your trunks. Cleaned out your room, we did. Then she says, 'We must hurry. Help me move these across the hall to my room.' So the three of us pushed and shoved those trunks across the hall and hid them in your sister's old room. I thought it was all rather strange, but then something stranger still happened." Margaret put down the brush and looked at Amelia through the mirror in wide-eyed excitement. "I was peeking out the door and saw your father come running up those stairs like the very devil himself was a-chasing him, and Mr. Jeremy hard on his heels. The two men stormed into your room, ripped the door right off its hinges, they did. I didn't see anything more, but it was a good thing we were all over in the Queen Bea's room, because from the sounds coming from yours, all holy hell was being unleashed."

Amelia winced, knowing her father must have been uncommonly angry with her for having missed her appointment with Lord Stanton. She couldn't even imagine how he must have felt when she failed to appear. And Jeremy? It wasn't like they had an understanding or even affection between the two of them. She couldn't imagine why he would be so upset by her leaving.

I hope Father will be pleased when he finds out everything worked out for the best.

"And when we went over there after everything had calmed down, it was like a storm had been unleashed in your room," Margaret continued. "Someone had ripped apart your bed and torn apart your dressing table. All of your drawers were opened and some lay broken on the floor. Even your favorite rocking chair was mangled in a heap in the corner."

"Oh, my!" Amelia pressed her hand over her mouth in patent disbelief. How could he have done something like that? What if she or Margaret had still been in the room? How would they have fared in the face of such anger?

"Oh, too right, my lady. It was then I knew something was going on, so I turn to the Queen and demand, 'Where is my lady? What has happened to her?' I thought for sure she was going to tell me you had died, or maybe been kidnapped." Margaret paused and contemplated this sad fate with a hint of maudlin glee in her deep brown eyes. Amelia stifled a laugh. She loved her maid dearly, had done so since she ceased being her nurse and took the post of maid when Amelia turned fourteen, but oh, she was bloodthirsty.

Margaret shook her head and smiled at Amelia. "Then an amazing thing happened. Bea smiles, a real smile, not one of those fake society things she plasters on her face most of the time, mind you, and she tells me, 'Amelia has eloped with Lord Stanton.' "

"What? Beatrice said those exact words?" Amelia demanded of her maid.

"I remember it clearly because of how happy I was for you, my lady, to have finally found someone you cared for so much that you would run away with him."

How did she know? Amelia hadn't even known

until right before their wedding, so what did Bea know that evening that she didn't?

"And then your sister says to me, 'You must go and wait for her in her new home. It isn't safe for you to be here when Father is still so upset.' While I can tell you I didn't much enjoy the thought of leaving London, I knew it was probably for the best. Just in case." She winked at Amelia and resumed brushing Amelia's hair.

"And so?"

"And so what, my lady?"

"And so how did you get here, Margaret? That can't be the end of it!"

"Your sister left and hired a carriage to take me and your trunks to Lord Stanton's house. We sneaked everything out of the house, and I was out of London before the sun rose. I stopped by my sister's, like I told you, and here I am."

"Bea left nothing for me? No note or a message from her to me?" Amelia thought for sure that if her sister had already been aware of who she was running away with, she would have at least sent a letter along with her maid.

"So she did, my lady, so she did."

"Margaret!" Amelia yelled. "Where is it?"

"Are you wanting to read it now, then, my lady? I thought perhaps you would be wanting to take a nap, since I can see as how you got some real dark circles under your eyes like you haven't been sleeping all that well." Margaret winked at Amelia, who blushed at the insinuation. *If only.* But Amelia knew the real reason she hadn't been sleeping was due to her husband's sudden distance.

Amelia allowed Margaret to help her out of her

dress and into her familiar dressing robe and slippers. Once settled onto the chaise with a warm blanket wrapped about her legs, she closed her eyes, though sleep eluded her. Too much had happened in the last three weeks, and while most of it was wonderful, this last week had been eye-opening for her. Where once she was convinced she had done the right thing in eloping with Tavis, his cool reticence had her worrying whether perhaps she had moved too hastily.

Because now we are actually married and settled, he seems to want nothing to do with me!

Silent tears flowed down her cheeks, and Amelia covered her sobs with her hands, hoping Margaret wouldn't notice.

Margaret, though, had keen eyes and even keener ears. "What's this, my lady?" She bustled over from the vanity to Amelia and offered her a handkerchief.

Knowing there was no use trying to hide anything from Margaret, Amelia took the handkerchief to wipe her face and said, "I…I think I made a mistake in marrying Lord Stanton."

Margaret's eyes narrowed to two dark little slits of vexation. "Has he hurt you, my lady? Is that it?"

"No, no," she rushed to reassure, "nothing like that. But ever since we've arrived at Ballywith, he's been so very distant and cool. I don't know what happened, Margaret. He doesn't seem to want me anymore. When we arrived, he introduced me to the servants, and then he…he left me in the hallway soon after. He didn't even bother showing me to my rooms." Amelia wiped at her eyes again. "Said he had business to attend to. Every day since then has been the same. I've barely seen him, and I don't know what I did!" Amelia started sobbing in earnest into the comforting arms of Margaret.

Margaret clucked and patted Amelia on the back. "Let me tell you something about menfolk, Amelia. They get scared real easy when it comes to women and marriage. Don't even try to get them to talk about their feelings, because more than likely they won't know the difference between a tender emotion like love or indigestion from eating too quickly." Margaret chuckled to herself at her own wit and shook her head. "Probably your man got a little scared about bringing home a new wife, especially when he hasn't figured out for himself that he cares for you."

"He doesn't care for me," Amelia protested. "How can you even think that or even know that? You just arrived." Nonetheless, she was helpless to stop the nervous hope fluttering about in her belly.

"Because you haven't talked to the servants and heard what I've heard about how his eyes fairly glowed with pride and affection when he introduced you to the staff. Everyone saw and was so happy for the master finding someone he obviously cared for. That man has got tender feelings for you, Amelia. He's just terrified, poor man, because he's been caught, and he doesn't know what to do about it."

"Really?"

"You mark my words, my lady. That man is smitten. Why, when he left you in the hall, the servants saw him steal a glance at you over his shoulder. They said he looked like a dying man, and you were his only chance at salvation. Looked right sorrowful, he did, when he finally turned away and marched down that hall, his shoulders all slumped over. Kind of like you did when I found you in here, moping about, looking all sad." Margaret unstopped a bottle of lavender water and applied it to the back of Amelia's neck and behind her ears.

"There, now," she said as she re-stopped the bottle. "That'll help you relax some so you can get some sleep. Don't you worry any about that man of yours. He'll come around. Give him some time."

With a final pat on Amelia's back, Margaret left Amelia, who fell into a fitful slumber.

****

Amelia awoke with a start and looked around her dressing room. Since she had lain down for her nap the afternoon sun had disappeared beyond the horizon, plunging the dressing room into muted twilight. The fire had long since died, and deep shadows hugged the walls, giving Amelia the vague, uneasy feeling someone else was in the room with her.

Peering into the darkness, she demanded, "Who's there? Is that you, Margaret?"

Instead of her maid, though, the tall, handsome figure of her husband stepped away from the doorway and into the waning light from the window. "It's just me, Amelia," he said, clearing his throat. "I didn't mean to awaken you."

The thudding of Amelia's heart sped up at the appearance of her husband. "Oh," she said and fiddled with the edges of her blanket. "It's you."

Tavis walked to the fireplace and stoked the fire. Soon a warm blaze crackled in the hearth and illuminated the room. Amelia watched with wide curious eyes as he proceeded to light several candles on the mantelpiece. When he was done, the room was alight with a soft glow, and Tavis stood to the side, almost as if he were unsure of his welcome.

Amelia wasn't sure, either. After the events of the previous week, she didn't know how to talk to her husband anymore. "What do you want, Tavis?" she asked in a meaner tone than she had intended.

His face fell, and Amelia felt horrible. "I wanted to see you," he stammered, "and to talk to you, if you weren't busy." He shuffled his feet and turned to leave. "But I see I've interrupted you, so I will leave."

That's when she realized this was as hard for him as it was for her. Whatever had happened between them to cause such tension, she knew they could not continue living in the same house under these circumstances.

"Wait, Tavis," she implored. "I'd like to talk to you, too."

He hesitated at the door, and Amelia knew he was hurt. If he was as scared as Margaret had said he was, she needed to meet him more than half way. Jumping up from the settee, she crossed the room to stop his departure. "Please, Tavis. Stay."

He turned and stood, gathering her hands in his. "As you wish, my lady wife."

She led him by the hand to her settee and patted the seat next to her. He sat down and leaned onto the seat back, looking tired and worn. They sat there holding hands while the fire filled in the silence with its crackles and pops.

"I'm sorry, Amelia," he said after a lengthy silence. "I've been a complete ass this week."

He glanced at her, but she held her tongue.

"Aren't you going to say something?"

"Yes, Tavis."

"Yes, Tavis, what?"

"Yes, Tavis, you have been a complete ass this week."

"You don't need to so readily agree, Amelia."

She smiled sweetly at him, enjoying the sight of him squirming just a bit. "My mother told me to never contradict my husband, and so if you say you are an ass, then an ass you shall be."

"Amelia!" he thundered. "You're not making this any easier on me!"

Her own temper pricked, her sweet smile turned into a frown as she yelled, "And why should I make it any easier on you when you've been nothing but beastly to me this whole week? It's bad enough you abandoned me on our first night here, but I've scarcely seen you since we arrived. How do you think that makes me feel?"

Tavis started to speak, but Amelia was much too angry to let him interrupt her. "I'll tell you how it feels, Tavis McGuire! It feels awful!" Her voice began to wobble, and Amelia knew she was close to losing her composure, so she jumped up from the settee and moved to the window to hide her face from him. Staring out through the glass panes at the deepening night, she whispered her deepest fear to the silent grounds below. "It feels like I made a mistake in coming here with you, that you never wanted me in the first place."

"No!" Tavis shouted in dismay. Tavis's strong arms enfolded her. "Don't ever think that, Amelia. Marrying you was the best thing I have ever done."

She looked up into his dear eyes, wanting to believe him, yet years of rejection and hurt made it difficult to do. "I want to believe you, Tavis, but what am I to think when you shut me out of your life and ignore me? I can't continue in this manner."

He buried his head in the hollow of her neck before saying, "I was scared."

So Margaret was right after all! Does this mean he cares for me? She ran her fingers through his hair, petting him much like a mother with a small, fractious child, attempting to soothe him. "Scared of what, Tavis?"

"I don't know. We came home and I…panicked." He lifted his head from her shoulder and regarded her with intense focus. "I had never thought to marry, Amelia. Not that I regret the decision, but it was something I had never dreamed of for myself. Bringing you here, to our home, made everything that had happened very real to me, and I reacted poorly."

She resisted the urge to sigh. He had not said he loved her. "I forgive you, Tavis, as long as you promise to not keep me out of your life again."

"I promise, Amelia. Never again."

Tavis led her back to the settee and settled her on his lap so he could wrap his arms about her waist. Nestling her into the crook of his arm, he sighed in contentment and rested his head against hers.

Soon she heard deep, even breathing from him, and a gentle snore. She tried to extricate herself from his embrace, but as soon as she moved, he tightened his hold on her so it was impossible to move.

Poor Tavis. He's never had anyone to love. Yet she knew he cared for her. Perhaps he didn't recognize it, but it didn't mean he was incapable of loving.

It was up to her to show him how.

Chapter 15

It was early morning still, and the sun had not made an appearance above the horizon, yet Tavis was awake and trying to dress without disturbing Amelia. Unlike the last week, this time he wanted to stay and linger in bed with her, which is why he had his back to the bed while he pulled on his shirt and gathered his pants, all the while consciously fighting the urge to glance back at the bed where his wife lay in delightful dishevelment.

With a firm push, he set aside all thoughts of their passionate night together. After awakening refreshed in body and spirit from his nap, he had led Amelia to their bed and spent the rest of the evening showing his wife how grateful he was to her for being so forgiving and understanding. It was one of the best nights of his life, even rivaling the night he'd made Amelia his.

Put it out of your mind, Tavis! There is work to do this morning.

Hastily donning his boots lest she awaken before he could leave, he crept out of the room and down the stairs. This early in the morning, not many servants were about, so he passed unnoticed through the house. Tavis snuck out of the back door, walked down past the stables, and entered a small hunting shack he had stumbled upon in his explorations of the grounds. He allowed his eyes to adjust to the dim interior.

"I didn't think you were coming," a dry voice said from the shadows.

"Jesus, Wickes!" Tavis exclaimed, looking at his friend and supervisor emerging from a corner. "I wasn't expecting you for another twenty minutes at least."

"And here I was expecting you twenty minutes ago."

Tavis pulled out his pocket watch and winced when he realized he was indeed late for their meeting. "I was unavoidably detained," he said.

"I'm sure your lovely new wife wouldn't have had anything to do with that, would she?" Wickes queried in a mild voice.

"About that—"

"Damn it, Tavis!" Wickes exploded and began to pace the small confines of the shack. "What were you thinking?"

Tavis tried to reply but was not given a chance to speak. Wickes rounded on him and grabbed him by the front of his shirt. Though Tavis was a tall man, Wickes towered over him by several inches, and he used every bit of that advantage as he expressed his extreme displeasure.

"You were supposed to get engaged to the chit and stay in London so you had time to conduct your own reconnaissance, not elope with her to the wilds of Scotland! That shouldn't have been too hard even for you to handle, considering she was an unmarried woman allegedly plagued by a gypsy curse," Wickes hissed. He released Tavis and stepped back. "Do you realize what kind of danger you have placed your new wife in? She cannot tell a lie, Tavis! Did you even think of the implications of that?"

"Of course I did, Tom," Tavis snapped. "Despite your obvious doubts, I am not a complete idiot. Her safety is my primary concern!"

"Then explain to me what happened. Why would a man, a decorated officer and a goddamned national hero, no less, ignore direct orders from his chief officer and run off with some chit?" Wickes sneered and spit out, "I don't care how plump her tits are rumored to be or how wide her arse, what possible reason can there be to explain your actions? Unless you were only thinking with your cock, that is. From all I have heard, in spite of her oddities she sounds like she'd be a willing partner in the bedroom."

A red haze filled Tavis's vision, and he lunged at Wickes, crossing the room in one stride and pinning him to the wall. His hands circled Wickes's neck and squeezed. "Don't you ever speak of my wife in those terms again, you bastard! She is a good and honest woman, better than any other woman I've ever known. More importantly, she is my wife, Lady Stanton, and you will speak of her and treat her as the lady she is, or I will kill you with my bare hands. Do you understand me?" Wickes's face had turned an alarming shade of purple in his struggle to take in air, but he managed to nod.

Tavis released him, and Wickes beat on his chest, straining to fill his lungs with air.

"Christ, Tavis, you nearly killed me!"

"Had I wanted to kill you, you would already be dead." Tavis retreated to the opposite side of the room, the pulsing anger slow to recede.

"At least now I know why you did it."

"What do you mean?"

"It's obvious you care for her, if not already love her." Wickes ran his fingers through his hair, clearly ignoring Tavis's sputtering over the unexpected assessment. With a huge sigh, Wickes said, "This, of course, changes everything."

Tavis was still too busy processing what Wickes had suggested to understand what his friend meant.

Exasperated, Wickes shook his head and began to explain his reasoning to Tavis as though he were a child. "If you care for her, Tavis, then it wouldn't be ethical for us to use her as we had originally planned to get the information we need to implicate her father. And now you are married to her, well, I'm afraid you are done with this mission, old friend. I suppose we could target the older sister, or perhaps set up a new servant in the household, since Meeks has discovered nothing in all this time. Perhaps Blake would work. He's quite unobtrusive."

"I don't love her," Tavis said. "We've…we've only known each other two weeks."

"Glad you finally rejoined the conversation, Tavis. I was tiring of my monologue," Wickes replied, amusement lacing his voice. "But, yes, Tavis, whether you've realized it yet or not, you do love the woman, and as I said, that changes everything."

"I love her?" Tavis's mind raced, thinking of all the little ways his life had changed since Amelia had become a part of it. For once, he was no longer alone and had found himself a witty, good-humored companion to share his life. It didn't hurt she was also a beautiful, intelligent woman who shared his passions and, if asked, would share his burdens and his struggles, too. She soothed his fears and filled him with such a feeling of joy at times his heart felt…

Oh, God! This was what I've been trying to run away from since coming home… This is what I was fleeing from.

All of a sudden, his knees felt a little weak, and he sank to the floor, leaning his head against the rough wall. He stared at the empty space in front of him as he came to terms with this new epiphany. When he felt a hand on his shoulder, he looked up in surprise, having forgotten Wickes was still in the room with him.

"I love her," he said in a panic. "Oh, God! I love her! What did I do? How am I going to keep her safe now?"

Wickes put his hand on Tavis's head and pushed it forward, so it rested between his knees. "Come on, man, breathe in through your nose and out through your mouth."

Tavis sucked in a deep breath of air and blew it out in unsteady bursts.

"I feel like my stomach has been ripped out my ear and shoved back in through my nose."

"I've heard love can do that to a man," Wickes said. "Knocks a body flat on their arse, it does. Though I can't say as how I've ever experienced it. Looks like nasty business to me."

Tavis pulled up his head and glared at his friend. "You're not being particularly helpful, Wickes, so shove it in your hole, would you?"

His friend laughed long and hard. "To see your expression, Tavis! You look like a stag who knows it's been targeted and is about to be killed. I never thought you'd succumb to Cupid's arrow, but it seems I was wrong." Wickes offered his hand to Tavis and pulled him up.

"Now, how about you take me to the house for some breakfast, so I can meet this lovely wife of yours?" Wickes clapped a still dazed Tavis on the back. "I don't know about you, but all this talk of love has really worked up my appetite."

****

When Amelia failed to show for breakfast, Wickes suggested they get in a spot of hunting before the day grew too much longer. Unfortunately, it didn't take his old friend long to recognize how distracted Tavis was, and he sent him back to the castle to Amelia.

Sprinting up the stairs, he opened the door with some haste. Amelia was not there. Hearing the unmistakable sound of splashing coming from her dressing room, he bounded across the room and opened the door.

"I'm not ready yet, Margaret. I'll call you if I need you," Amelia said.

Tavis stopped in his tracks. With her back to him, he wasn't able to see as much of his bathing wife as he would have liked, but the parts he could see were enough to cloud his vision and fire his blood. Large expanses of ivory skin peeked over the top of the bathtub, exposing clusters of tiny freckles on her shoulder blades. Large tendrils of hair drooped down the back of her neck, and tiny pink ears peeked out from beneath the mass of curls she had pinned atop her head. On silent feet, he crept up behind her, hoping his presence would be a welcome surprise.

"Margaret!" Amelia snapped. "I said I'd call you when I was ready."

He placed a large hand on her shoulder and

squeezed. When she turned her head, presumably to give the persistent Margaret a scolding, he smiled charmingly at her, telling her with his smile what he could not yet say in words.

"Tavis!" she exclaimed, her expression changing from stormy frustration to sunny delight. "I thought you were away until later this afternoon. My maid informed me you have an old friend calling."

"I was planning on being gone most of the day, when I left," he explained, "but once we were out, thoughts of you distracted me until I had to come home."

Unable to resist any longer the urge to touch her fragrant skin, he took a bar of soap in his hands and worked up a sudsy lather. Reaching into the tub, he took her arm and began to smooth the fragrant bubbles over it.

Amelia sighed and sank a little lower in the tub at his relaxing caress.

Tavis finished with the one arm and moved on to the other. "I missed you this morning for breakfast," he whispered into the tight curls at the base of Amelia's neck.

"Don't you mean *at* breakfast?"

Grabbing an ear between his teeth, he bit her before caressing the sensitive flesh behind her ears with his tongue. "No. I meant for breakfast."

A flash of ivory on the floor caught his attention. "What's this?" He bent to retrieve the fallen paper and held it up, unable to disguise his curiosity regarding the crumpled letter. Though he wanted nothing more than to smooth it out to better read the content, he resisted until Amelia gave him permission.

Sara Ackerman

"It's from Bea." At his questioning look, she urged, "Go ahead and read it."

Smoothing out the paper the best he could, he read the letter from Amelia's sister:

Dear Mimi,

Everyone has secrets, Sister. Me, Evie, Father, Mother, you, and yes, even your new husband. When you finally find out his secret, don't condemn him for it. Remember what made you go off with him in the first place, and above all, trust him. He's a good man.

Bea

"Who exactly is your sister?" Tavis asked. "How can she claim to know my secrets when I've only ever met the woman once?"

He was worried. He knew what secrets Amelia's sister referenced, but for the life of him he had no idea how she knew. Her knowledge was a danger to his mission, putting Amelia into harm's way. That was unacceptable.

"You've met her once?" Amelia asked, excitement in her green eyes.

He didn't understand his wife's excitement, either. Why did Amelia care if he knew her sister? Did she know his secret? That did not explain her happiness. Like last time, she'd be angry if she knew he'd been lying to her.

To cover his growing unease, he asked, "Is your sister some kind of a...a witch?" He turned to look at Amelia. "What are you grinning at?"

She rose from the tub and dried off with a towel before slipping her arms into the sleeves of her dressing gown. "I thought..." But then she stopped herself, as if she were unsure what to say.

A hint of alarm entered her eyes, but before Tavis began to worry what was going on, she asked, "Do you...do you speak..."

Tavis grew worried. Amelia was pale and trembling, and he didn't understand why. When she turned to the wall and reached a hand out to steady herself, panic replaced worry, and Tavis sprang to action. He reached his wife as her body slid down the wall and landed in a heap on the floor. Tavis leaned over her and shook her loose body. Amelia's eyes opened only a little and she slurred, "D'you speak Greek?" before they closed again and she passed out.

"Amelia," he shouted. "Amelia!" He shook her by the shoulders again, hoping to rouse her from whatever illness had caused her stupor.

He pressed his ear to his chest. When he heard the reassuring thud of her heartbeat, he sat back on his haunches, trying to figure out what to do, a difficult feat considering all of his blood had drained from his head the moment he saw her falling.

The door opened, and a small woman with a plump frame bustled into the room. She spied Amelia lying still and pale on the floor and rushed over to her.

"What did you do to her?" she demanded, shooting a furious glare at Tavis. "Why is she on the floor? Did she faint?"

"We were just... I was saying..." Tavis spluttered, too taken aback by this small whirlwind of a woman who was, if he weren't mistaken, eviscerating him with her eyes. *Who does she think she is?* He was lord and master of this house, and she would do well to learn her place now. "Madam," he said in his loftiest voice, "I am Stanton, lord of this house and this lady's husband.

Who are you to accuse me of wrongdoing toward my wife in my home?" He finished his speech by crossing his arms over his chest and leveling his own cool stare at the woman.

The little termagant didn't back down, though, as he had expected. What she did do was to push him out of the way and kneel by Amelia's side. Taking Amelia's hand in her own, she put two of her fingers on the inside of her wrist, all the while muttering under her breath. Then the nervy she-troll took out a small vial of liquid and unstopped it. Placing several drops on her fingers, she massaged the liquid at the base of Amelia's wrists and at the back of her neck. Those ministrations accomplished, she stood and went to the chair by the fire. Over it was draped a fine, woven blanket, which she snatched and spread over Amelia's still form.

Her immediate care of Amelia complete, she acknowledged Tavis, who had grown only angrier at Margaret's silence. "I am Margaret, my lord, Lady Amelia's maid and servant since she was no more than eight years old." Margaret tilted her head to meet Tavis's gaze. "I figure I've been more of a mother to her than her own was, and weren't I the one who always nursed her since she were young?"

Though he knew it was a rhetorical question, Tavis felt compelled to answer, given Margaret's intense, steely-eyed stare. As though he were a naughty schoolboy being scolded by his governess, he mumbled, "But of course," feeling that much more the fool for being cowed by his wife's lady's maid.

Margaret nodded. "And seeing as how I was her nurse and maid, I know the only times my lady ever takes ill like this is if she has told a lie. Now I ask you again, my lord, what did you ask my lady that she would rather make herself ill and faint than to answer it?"

The tension in Tavis's body eased somewhat as he realized the cause of his wife's unexplained sickness. Of course it was the curse! Because he had not seen it in their two weeks together, he did not know what to expect. Now he knew it was a lie that had brought on her faint, he felt more at ease.

Yet if she fainted, it must mean my question upset her in some way. Otherwise she would have answered it honestly and not be unconscious on the floor.

He tried to recall what they had been talking about before she fainted.

"I had asked her why she was smiling," he responded after replaying their conversation in his head.

"That doesn't make much sense." Margaret looked as confused as he. She tapped her finger on her chin in thought. "Maybe there was something before that? There's got to be something else to make her clamp up and refuse to tell the truth."

"We were discussing the letter her sister sent her, which was disturbing in and of itself." Tavis felt the anger returning as he wondered again what it was his new sister-in-law knew about him.

"Bea certainly knows how to disturb a body. What did she say in her letter?"

Tavis glared at Margaret and debated whether or not to call her out for her impertinence. Chances were if he did reprimand her she'd only stare at him with those beady little eyes of hers until he broke down and answered her.

Might as well save her the effort of glaring, at

least.

"In her letter, she told Amelia I had secrets. She urged Amelia not to condemn me for them when she found out."

He refused to squirm under Margaret's steady gaze while she contemplated what he said. They passed several moments that way, the two locked in an intense battle of wills, until she spoke.

"I won't be asking you if you do have secrets, because in my experience most men do." She held up her hand in defense when Tavis began to protest. "You know I speak true, my lord. No sense in denying it."

Motioning to the floor where Amelia still lay unconscious, she said, "You might as well pick her up and bring her to bed. It could be hours before she awakens again."

Tavis lifted his wife into his arms, being mindful to protect her head as he walked through the door into the master chambers. Laying her under the counterpane, he was struck at how fragile she looked and realized he had never thought of her in those terms before. She was normally so vibrant and full of life it was difficult for him to reconcile the woman he had come to know with this pale, delicate creature on the bed before him.

"You can go about your day if you wish, my lord," Margaret stated as she moved a chair closer to the bedside to better tend Amelia. "I'll sit with her until she awakens. Don't you worry." She went to sit in the chair, but Tavis's hand on her upper arm stopped her.

"I will watch her, Margaret. She is my wife, and I will care for her." For a moment, it seemed like Margaret would protest, but she must have noted the determined set of Tavis's jaw and realized it was useless to argue with him.

"Right you are, my lord." Going into the adjoining room, she returned moments later carrying a small basin of water and a dry cloth. "If she gets hot, you can wipe her brow with a damp cloth. Sometimes it helps to put the cloth on the back of her neck, too."

"What about the liquid I saw you put on her wrists and neck? Should I do that again?"

"I shouldn't think so. It was just a bit of lavender oil to calm her down, you see. Every time she has one of these spells, her heart gets to racing so fast I worry it will pump clean out of her chest. I've found a little lavender oil on her wrist and neck helps to calm her, even while unconscious." She took the small vial out of her apron pocket and put it next to the basin. "Here. I'll leave it with you just in case she starts getting restless again."

"Thank you, Margaret. I will call if I have need of you."

Margaret curtsied and walked to the door. "My lord? I know you will have your secrets. It's only natural." She paused and seemed to be searching for what to say, something he doubted she had to do very often. "I would only hope…when she does find out what it is, she won't be hurt too bad." Margaret glanced at Amelia lying on the bed and smiled a tender, sweet smile. "She's a special person, my lord, so kind and trusting." Her voice wobbled a bit, and she curtsied again before reaching for the doorknob. "Ring for me if I am needed."

Tavis looked back to Amelia and lifted her small hand to his mouth to bestow a soft kiss on it. He heard the unmistakable sound of the door opening and then

Margaret's voice from the doorway imploring, "Please don't hurt her, my lord."

When he turned to tell her he didn't plan to, the door had already closed and Margaret was gone.

Chapter 16

Amelia slept the entire day and night through, which sometimes happened after she had an episode, but the next morning she made it downstairs to breakfast. Though Tavis wasn't there when she awakened, she knew he had been with her throughout the day and evening. There was a chair next to the bed and a Tavis-sized impression on the bed next to her, testament to his sickbed vigil.

About halfway down the stairs, she realized she didn't even know where the breakfast room was, having only taken her breakfast in her room since arriving at Ballywith. With no footmen in sight, Amelia wandered on the lower level, poking her nose into rooms, praying one of them led to breakfast.

Upon opening the third door, she thought she heard the low timbre of her husband's voice. Following it through one room and into another, she had her hand on the knob when an unfamiliar voice spoke.

"Have you found out anything more from her?"

"No." Tavis sighed. "I've told you everything she's told me already. Aside from the name Harry the Horse, she has not said anything else of what she overheard from her small nook. Besides, I thought you no longer wanted to use her for information."

Amelia was confused. Why was Tavis sharing with his friend the information she'd told him about her secret nook? Of what importance could it be to Tavis or his friend? She pressed her ear to the door. Perhaps one of them would say something to give her an idea of what secret her husband was keeping from her.

"Have you heard of anyone who goes by that name, Wickes?"

"I thought perhaps there was someone..." The stranger's voice trailed off. "But it can't be him because he's been dead for years."

A chair scraped on the floor, making it difficult for Amelia to hear what Tavis said next. She caught the tail end of the other man's reply.

"...and there was no one by that name at Westby's house."

"Who did we send in?"

"I said that no one knew the name Jeremiah Meeks, but when I described Meeks to them, they knew exactly who I was talking about. Do you remember Amelia discussing her father's houseguest?"

"Yes. Vividly."

"No one knew who Jeremiah Meeks was, but from the description I gave them, they all recognized him as one Jeremy Michelson, the Westbys' long-time houseguest."

"That bastard!" Tavis's furious shout echoed throughout the room, startling Amelia in the process.

Jeremy! She slapped her hand over her mouth to quiet her surprised gasp. *Why are they talking about him?* Pressing her ear once more to the door, she heard Tavis yell, "He lied to me!"

"He lied to all of us, Tavis. No one knew of his other identity or of the game he was playing." Wickes sighed, and Amelia wondered how her husband and this

Mr. Wickes knew Jeremy and why they were so upset he had lied to them.

Wickes was speaking again. "But now that we know, we can search for him. It's obvious Westby planted Meeks with you to act as courier between you and your father when you were both stationed in France. Think, Tavis," Wickes demanded. "Did you ever receive any correspondence from home in all the time you were on the Continent?"

My father? Why are they talking about my father like this? What is going on? Amelia chewed her nails and waited to hear more from Tavis. Yet nothing made any sense! The more she heard, the more confused she became.

"No, never, Tom." Amelia heard Tavis pacing across the floor, his step already familiar to her ears. "You know my father hated me. I never…" The pacing stopped.

Wickes pounced at Tavis's falter. "What? What is it, Tavis?"

"Once." His voice had become so low and hoarse Amelia had to strain to hear. "I received one letter from my father in all the time I was stationed in France." There was a pause in which Amelia heard the pounding of her own blood in her veins. "I…I didn't even look at it when Meeks brought it to me. I told him to get rid of it, and he obviously did. I never saw it again."

"Your father was probably betting on the fact you wouldn't read anything from him, which gave Meeks the perfect opportunity to read the letter and pass on whatever information was written within it."

"I don't understand. Surely the War Department was reading letters before they were sent abroad. I've heard how they blocked any incriminating information and discovered many traitors through this practice. How did my father get away with it?"

The War Department? What is Tavis doing involved with the War Department?

"An encoded message. It had to be. Otherwise you are right; it would have been stopped. That's why Meeks showed up out of nowhere to be your batman. Once your father realized you were going abroad, he and Westby must have arranged to send Meeks along to intercept it and carry it on to their contact in France."

"Do you know where Meeks has gone, Tom?"

"When I asked, none of the servants knew. All they told me was that he left a week ago Friday, but no one knew where."

"Which means he could be anywhere, including here in Stanton."

This time Amelia did gasp out loud. *Jeremy here in Stanton? Near Ballywith?* She backed away from the door, and in the process knocked into a side table, sending a vase crashing to the floor. The talking from the other room stopped. Afraid of being caught, Amelia hiked up her skirts and ran out the door.

"Stupid, stubborn man!" Amelia yelled. She stomped into the gardens at the side of the house and kicked a small bush near the main path. When her foot connected with its solid trunk, she cried out in pain.

"Ouch!" Amelia hopped on one foot down the path to where a small wrought iron bench waited underneath a flowering tree. Sinking onto the seat, she took off her slipper, now stained from its contact with the plant, and lifted her foot to examine it for any injuries. Aside from a small bruise, she was in fine physical shape. It was her emotional state she questioned.

It was obvious her husband was keeping something from her, but what his secret entailed was no longer clear. If it had been a simple affair with her sister, as she had thought upon reading Bea's letter, why involve Mr. Wickes? Amelia now knew he was involved, and according to Mr. Wickes, this secret could prove dangerous to…Tavis? To her?

"If only Tavis would trust me with his burdens, I could help him."

"Men do tend to keep things close to themselves, don't they? And yours especially."

"Who's there?" Amelia demanded, rubbing her arms against the sudden chill in the air.

From out of the dark shadows of a sheltering grove of trees stepped an old woman. Despite age, her posture remained proud and erect. Her hair was thick but gray, making it impossible for Amelia to tell what color it might have been when she was younger. Fine lines adorned the woman's face around her eyes and mouth, a testament to the joys and sorrows she had lived through. Dressed in a simple gown of fine, silver cloth, she wore no other accessories save for a magnificent hand-woven shawl of startling green, the same shade as her eyes, draped around her shoulders.

"Who are you?" Amelia asked.

The old woman walked regally over to Amelia, who sat clutching her dirty slipper in a white-knuckled grip, and seated herself. "I'm just an old woman passing through, but you can call me Jane, if you'd like." Jane had an amused smile on her face, and Amelia wondered what could possibly be making her smile in such a manner.

"I'm Lady Amelia Stanton," Amelia said. She was still too taken aback by the sudden appearance of this woman to truly credit what was happening.

"I thought you might be," Jane said again, that same amused smile gracing her face.

"How did you know that?" For a moment, Amelia feared Jane might be a gypsy. The last time she had been spoken to by an elderly woman alone in the outdoors had not turned out well for her or her family. She prayed Jane was not a gypsy.

Jane patted her on the arm in a familiar, grandmotherly fashion. "Oh, you know how word gets around. People love to gossip, especially when it involves a young, handsome earl marrying a beautiful titian-haired woman from London. I made an educated guess when I saw you sitting here."

Said like that, Amelia guessed Jane was a local woman who had wandered up toward Ballywith on her daily walk to see the new Countess of Stanton for herself. "Do you know my husband or his family well, Jane?"

This time, Jane outright laughed. "You could say that, my dear!" Amelia waited to see if Jane would elaborate, but the perplexing woman remained silent, her laughing eyes trained on Amelia.

"What did you mean about my husband keeping things closely to himself? Do you know what he's keeping from me?" Amelia needed to discover what her husband was hiding, and she wasn't going to overlook any scrap of information, even if it were given by a stranger with questionable sanity.

Jane's eyes sobered and misted over as she stared off into the distance, lost in her memories of the past.

"Yes, yes, I believe I do know what he is hiding from you, and no, my dear, I cannot tell you what it is."

Amelia balled up her fists tighter until the hard sole of her shoe cut into the tender flesh of her palm. "Why won't he trust me?"

Jane took the shoe from Amelia's hand and smoothed out the creases made in anger and frustration. Setting it on her lap, Jane rubbed the palm of her own hand in the exact location where Amelia was now wrapping a handkerchief over hers to stanch the bleeding from the cut on her palm. "Careful," Jane said as she massaged her palm. "You'll leave a mark."

"Can you tell me anything useful?" Amelia demanded, growing frustrated with Jane's cryptic comments and unanswered questions. She tied off the handkerchief and re-balled her fist. "Such as how I'm supposed to help my husband when he won't tell me what's going on?"

"I think you already know the answer to that question, Amelia."

"No, Jane! No, I don't know the answer. That's why I'm asking you!"

Once again, Jane's eyes grew misty, as if she were looking back through the veils of time. "I had forgotten…" she said. Placing Amelia's shoe on the bench, she rose and stepped away from Amelia toward the dark shadows of the trees. "I had forgotten how passionate youth is."

"Amelia!" Tavis's shouted voice echoed in the distance. Amelia suspected Tavis had seen her hurried flight from the house and guessed she had overheard his conversation with his friend, Mr. Wickes. He would want to know what she had heard, but right now, she needed to know what Jane knew, and she needed to know now.

Jane turned and took Amelia's hands in her own. "It is time for me to leave."

"But...but you haven't answered any of my questions." Amelia knew she sounded desperate, but she was. Jane had only raised more questions than she had answered, and Amelia was more confused now than she was before their talk. "How am I going to make him trust me?"

"You're not asking the right question, Amelia. Instead of asking how you can get your husband to trust you, you need to ask yourself why he doesn't."

"Fine, then. Why doesn't he trust me?"

"I think you know the answer to that, Amelia."

Amelia knew. She had known all along if Tavis were keeping something from her it had to be something big, something that could endanger either one or both of them. He didn't tell her because it was too risky to involve her. No one confided in Amelia, not unless they wanted to run the risk of having their innermost thoughts and feelings shared with the world should someone ask the right question. And she hated that. Hated not being trustworthy, and that's why Tavis refused to divulge whatever it was he was keeping from her.

"The curse," she whispered. "He can't trust me because he can't be sure I won't be forced to tell the truth."

"Amelia!" Tavis shouted, his voice louder than before. He was getting closer.

"What do I do, Jane?" Amelia clutched Jane's hands.

"It's time for me to leave," the woman repeated, removing her hands from Amelia's tight hold. Jane moved back toward the awaiting darkness in the tree grove.

"Please!" Amelia begged. "Tell me! What should I do?"

Jane stopped and looked over her shoulder at Amelia, who was hugging herself about the middle, as if her arms were the only things holding her emotions together.

"Break the curse, Amelia. That's the only way." Jane turned around again and stepped into the darkness on the other side of the path.

"I've tried! I don't know how, Jane," Amelia cried to the darkness which enfolded the old woman in its ghostly embrace.

From a distance, as if traveling through time itself, came the faint echo of Jane's parting words. "The curse has power over you only for as long as you allow it, Mimi." Amelia blanched and took an unsteady step back until her knees hit the edge of the wrought iron bench. Sinking onto it, she asked herself how Jane knew the exact words her sister Bea had said to her weeks ago when she told Amelia to stop letting her curse take over her life. How had Jane known?

A cold lick of fear shivered up and down her spine, and Amelia rubbed her chilled arms. As she contemplated returning to the house, Jane's voice once again reached her ears, not faint as it had been for her last message but clear and strong, a forceful cry slicing through the turmoil in Amelia's mind.

"Hurry and break it, Amelia! You are going to be tested sooner than he thinks!"

Amelia jumped and looked next to her, expecting to see Jane once more sitting beside her, but she was alone. The inky darkness in the tree grove into which Jane had disappeared was gone, and faint rays of sunlight filtered through the branches.

Wasting no time in replacing her shoe, Amelia sprang up from the bench and ran along the main path back to the house.

"Amelia!" Tavis shouted again, but closer this time. Hiking up her green skirts, she raced faster up the path. Spying him, she picked up speed and ran straight into his arms.

"Amelia!" he exclaimed. "You're trembling!"

She buried her head on his chest and took in several shaky breaths to slow her pounding heart. "Do you believe in ghosts, Tavis?" she asked.

"Ghosts?" he asked. "Don't tell me you saw one wandering the gardens, Amelia, *mia.*" He laughed but stopped when she nodded her head yes.

"I…I think I saw one."

"You aren't hurt, are you?" he asked with true concern in his voice.

"No, just a little shaken."

"As long as you're unhurt, then there's nothing to worry about." He kissed her on the lips, and as always, her passions quickly began to rise. Wrapping her arms around his neck, she pulled herself flush against Tavis's solid, reassuring body and tangled her fingers in his hair. Darting her tongue into his mouth, she reveled at the dark, salty flavor of his mouth. When she sucked on his lower lip, he rewarded her with a throaty growl from deep in his chest. He grabbed her around the waist and trailed kisses on her neck and shoulders.

"I heard you talking to your friend Mr. Wickes this morning," Amelia accused, her breath coming in rapid pants because her husband's gentle kisses had turned more lingering and intimate.

His kisses stopped, and he raised his head to look at Amelia with a mixture of suspicion and dread on his face. "What did you hear?"

"A lot of things," she responded, "but mostly you and he share a secret you are unwilling to tell me."

"That's true. Are you angry with me?"

"I was, mind you, but not anymore," she replied, pleased when he resumed his attentions to her neck and collarbone.

"Did your conversation with the ghost change your mind?" he teased, his gentle laughter tickling the tops of her breasts.

"Joke all you want, Tavis," Amelia retorted as she leaned her head back to allow him better access to her throat and chest, "but she made me understand why you can't tell me what I want to know. I understand now, and I want you to know it's all right."

"She?" he asked straightening from where he had been engaged in tormenting her trembling breasts from their perch over her bodice.

Amelia related what had happened to her with Jane. When she was done, he looked more worried than when she had first told him she had seen a ghost.

He grabbed her hand and pulled her down the path she had come from. She sat on the bench and watched him walk to the tree grove and back. "Find anything?"

"Nothing. I guess you were right; it must have been a ghost."

Amelia shivered again, and he joined her on the

bench. Wrapping his arm around her shoulders, he pulled her close. "I am curious. What did she help you figure out?"

"That what is preventing you from trusting me fully is me. You want to trust me, but my curse makes it difficult for you to confide in me."

"I want to, lass, more than anything, but not all of the secret is mine to tell."

"Then how is it that Bea knows?" she asked. "Did you have an affair with her? Is that how she knows?"

"What? God, no! What gave you that idea?"

"Her letter. I thought she must know because of what she wrote."

"You concluded that, did you?" he asked. "I told you yesterday I only ever met your sister one time, and it's not an occasion I am keen on remembering. She took me for a hundred pounds at the tables, and was most unladylike about it, too."

"I remember you saying that, but I needed to be sure. It's what I was trying to avoid saying yesterday when I fainted."

"You were going to ask me if I'd had an affair with your sister? Why didn't you say so in the first place? You could have avoided all the pain you caused yourself."

Amelia fiddled with the folds of her skirt, avoiding Tavis's gaze. "I didn't know how to say it without upsetting you."

"So instead of risking my anger, you'd rather make yourself sick?"

Amelia rose and walked over to a hydrangea bush to bury her nose in a fragrant bloom before she nodded, still refusing to meet Tavis's eye. She'd rather not talk about this particular aspect of her curse; she had hoped it would never come up.

Tavis followed and wrapped her in his embrace. "You don't have to worry about telling the truth, lass. I won't run away if you tell me something you think I won't like." She flinched at his words, knowing his perceptive eyes missed nothing. He'd found the truth behind her evasive actions.

"That's what you say now," she said, pulling away from his arms. She sidled to the other side of the bush to keep some distance between her and Tavis, using it as a shield to protect her fragile and exposed emotions. "Everyone thinks they want the truth until confronted with it."

Swallowing hard, Amelia's eyes skittered away from her husband's face, knowing if she looked there she would feel compelled to promise him something she wasn't sure she was capable of giving.

"I'm not like everyone else, Amelia. If you make me angry with your truth, I won't take offense and leave you to yourself. It must have been lonely for you, all those years, telling a truth no one wanted to hear. I can imagine people didn't take too kindly to your candor, did they?"

Tears filled her eyes because everything Tavis said was true. It was a lonely life being the voice of truth.

"You never have to be alone again, lass, not as long as I am with you. I'm begging you, please, tell me the truth. I don't know that I'm strong enough to watch you become ill. I was never so scared as I was when I watched you fall to the floor unconscious." He looked haggard and pale, almost as if he were reliving the events of yesterday as they spoke. "Please, Amelia, trust me to care for you and your curse. I promise I won't let you down."

Several silent moments passed as Amelia mulled over Tavis's words and his plea for her to trust him. She had asked him as much the other night. Now it was her turn to decide whether to trust her new husband with the enormity of her curse and all of its consequences.

Amelia turned her gaze back to Tavis, and what she saw staring back at her made her catch her breath. Tavis, the man who shied away from tender emotions like love, was looking at her with such earnest devotion she knew in that instant she could trust him with any of her burdens.

"Mother always said my curse was the easiest to bear. I could speak, unlike Evie, who was mostly mute, and every other word out of my mouth wasn't a lie, like Bea's. Mother said telling the truth was refreshing, and it would endear me to those in my acquaintance."

"It must have been hard not to have anyone who understood."

"Bea and Evie did, to an extent. We were always close, but after that day we became even closer. We learned to cope, but it never became any easier." Amelia looked up from the flowers she had been staring at, tears streaming down her face. "She was wrong, you know. People don't want the truth. They want to hear a version of the truth that fits with their narrow view of the world. I found this to be true early on, when my light revealed the ugliness in people's souls. People prefer the dark, Tavis, because coming out into the light hurts too much."

Tavis engulfed Amelia's stiff body into the sure solidity of his embrace and held on, a steady rock in the swirling waters of her emotions. "I wish I could make you believe me, Amelia, but only time will prove my words are sincere. I promise to never take offense and run away when you tell me the truth."

She allowed him to hold her, letting his strength bolster her confidence and lay her fears to rest. Amelia wanted to believe Tavis, she truly did, but more than that, she wanted Tavis to believe in her. She wanted to be the one Tavis confided in, the one he turned to with his secrets and his thoughts. Until her curse was broken, though, how could she ask him to trust her when she didn't even trust herself?

Chapter 17

Over the next several days, Amelia became acquainted with her new home under the watchful eye of Mrs. Tuddle, the housekeeper. A short, gray-haired woman of indeterminate age, Mrs. Tuddle had run the estate for years, hired on to the staff when Tavis's mother was a new bride. She was loyal to the former Lady Stanton, and those loyalties extended over time to include Tavis's deceased brother John and now to Tavis himself.

It soon became clear Mrs. Tuddle had been in full charge of the household for the last several years as John and Mary's health worsened and the two died. Mrs. Tuddle was efficient and organized, a fact Amelia appreciated; she learned more with Mrs. Tuddle in two days about running a household as large as Ballywith than she had ever learned from her mother in all the years she had instructed the girls on managing a large estate.

The household was efficient, and there was not much for Amelia to do but approve expenses and oversee the care of the servants and the tenants. Mrs. Tuddle was also blunt in her honesty with Amelia and informed her that without a large influx of money the estate would be operating with a deficit by the end of the year. Throughout the morning, the two women pored over the household ledgers to find some way to squeeze any extra funds from existing resources.

Between the two of them, they came up with several ways to further slash expenses, though Mrs. Tuddle was reluctant to cut so deeply. Amelia had little desire to do so either, but something needed to be done to rectify the bleakness of the situation at Ballywith. Mrs. Tuddle explained the various expenses that had cropped up over the years and how they had depleted the resources of the estate. Ballywith was definitely in dire financial straits, and Amelia knew something that might help their situation.

As she went down the hallway to her husband's study, Gerard, the butler, stopped her. When informed Tavis was in the stables, Amelia went to her room to gather her shawl, as the days still remained cool, something she hadn't quite grown accustomed to.

Amelia had otherwise settled into her new home, loving the raw power of the rugged landscape of Ballywith and the surrounding land. Towering peaks still dusted with the last remnants of winter reached proudly to the sky, while the deep valleys around those peaks burst forth with the first hardy shoots of pale green, spring grass interspersed with the faint violet of the heather soon to carpet the valleys with its rich, vibrant hues. Spring had arrived—Amelia had only to look outside at the bowers of blossoms on the trees dotting the grounds or at the triumphant flowers bursting through the ground over the course of these past weeks to know it. She just wished it weren't so cold!

Wrapping up in her warm woolen shawl, Amelia left her room to find Tavis in the stables and to have this particular piece of business past her. No matter how idyllic and content she had been this past month, her elopement and the way she had disappeared without a word to her parents made her uncomfortable. She needed to see her parents, if only to explain to them what had happened to her. While there, she would talk to her father about her dowry, a source of much needed funds to help restore the estate. It wouldn't be an easy trip down to London and back via carriage, she considered, but it was important she go to secure the necessary resources for Ballywith. In all, it was a well-thought-out plan.

Amelia chewed on her lower lip, thinking how she was going to convince her husband to let her go. Ever since the incident with Jane, Tavis had been cautious about her safety. Though he claimed to have found nothing out of the ordinary amongst the grove of trees, his actions indicated otherwise. He wanted to know where she was at all times and insisted on escorting her if she ventured outdoors. In fact, she was surprised he hadn't arranged for one of the footmen to walk her to the stables to meet him. Maybe he thought she couldn't get into too much trouble on the path from the house to the stables.

Pausing on the landing, she spied the young footman William, her constant shadow when Tavis was unavailable, waiting for her at the front entrance. She sighed. "Then again maybe not."

"Lady Stanton?" William looked up to Amelia as she stood on the first-floor landing. "Might I accompany you to his lordship?"

Stifling the urge to curse, she smiled at the boy. "But of course, William. I would appreciate the escort."

Really, she fumed, but she reminded herself it

wasn't his fault. Young William was following orders, and he took his role as guardian seriously. Over the past several days William had been always present whenever she decided to take a walk around the grounds or sit in the gardens outside the kitchen. He was always polite, never once insisting he accompany her. Instead, he asked her for permission to attend her should a need arise. When stated in such a manner, how could she refuse? It would look churlish and ill-mannered to decline such gentlemanly solicitousness, especially when it was for her benefit.

Somehow she needed to convince her husband to either confide in her his worries or to allow her more latitude in her movements. But how to convince him?

"My lady?" William's worried voice brought her to attention, and she realized she had been staring at William for several minutes while she considered her predicament.

Amelia hurried down the stairs and took William's arm. "Before you escort me to his lordship, William, I'd like to stop by the kitchens and see the cook."

The kitchen, Amelia had learned, was one of the only remaining structures of the castle from the original edifice erected several hundred years ago. Built into the side of a large rock formation, the kitchen was a sturdy room. It had survived through war, the vagaries of the weather, and several fires which had plagued the castle over the centuries. Constructed of sturdy stone, it preserved the warmth during the long, cold days of winter, and it kept the room cool in those rare hot days of summer. Only two narrow windows had been built into the original foundation, both of which faced south to catch any feeble rays of sun brave enough to shine in the dead of winter. Down that same small hallway to the rear of the huge fireplace, there was a sturdy wooden door for servants to enter and exit into the walled kitchen garden and courtyard.

Despite its age, it was an efficient, well-lit room run under the watchful eye of Mrs. Dowling, the robust cook who had served the family since she herself was a young girl hired on to be a kitchen maid.

"Mrs. Dowling?" Amelia inquired as she descended the remaining steps into the warm kitchen. "Are you here, Mrs. Dowling?" She peered around the open door with caution. The last time she'd made an unscheduled visit to the kitchen, the woman nearly ripped her in two at the intrusion during one of her busiest times. Upon learning it was the new mistress, the cook apologized but was no less irritated by the unwelcome visit. Amelia was advised the next time she visited she needed to give warning or call down ahead.

Since no one answered her, Amelia walked into the kitchen with William close behind. The fire blazed in the fireplace, and there was evidence on the table that staff was busy preparing the next meal, yet there was no one about.

"That's odd," she reflected as she took in the empty kitchen. "William, do you know where everyone is?"

"No, my lady, I do not."

She moved down the small hallway to peer out the two windows. Squinting through the murky glass, her eyes widened at the sight of a familiar green shawl.

"Jane," she whispered. Turning, she spied William watching her. He must have noted her odd behavior, because a frown marred his smooth face.

Calm down, Amelia! He'll never let you out that door if you keep acting like this.

In her best Lady Stanton voice, she looked down her nose at William (difficult to do when he towered over her) and said, "I'd like to go outside, William. See if Mrs. Dowling is about."

"My lady…" William began, "his lordship is waiting for you. I need to take you to him."

"No," Amelia insisted, resisting the urge to peer out the window again in hopes of spying Jane. "I need to find Mrs. Dowling." She only prayed Jane was still out there when she got out. *If I get out.*

"I should go with you, my lady." William shifted from foot to foot. "Or at least, tell me what you wish from Mrs. Dowling, and I will give her your message later."

She scurried to the main room of the kitchen and pulled out a stool, dragged it down the hall, and placed it by the door.

"Here." She pointed. "You sit on this stool with the door ajar, and I will go and find Mrs. Dowling and speak to her myself."

At William's continued doubtful expression, she crossed her arms and tapped her foot. "William Douglas, I didn't want to do this, but if you don't sit here and allow me to speak with Mrs. Dowling privately, I will tell his lordship what I saw you and Katy Ferguson doing the other day when she was supposed to be cleaning the downstairs and you were supposed to be watching the front door." Amelia glared at him, upset she had to use the one advantage she had over William to go out to the gardens, but it had to be done.

Poor William whitened to the color of new milk and gulped, his Adam's apple bobbing. "You saw that, my lady?"

"Yes, I did, and if you want to keep it secret, you'll let me leave right now." She pushed him onto the stool.

William sat and swallowed even harder. "He'll kill me, my lady, if something were to happen to you, and I weren't there to stop it."

She huffed out an impatient breath, afraid with every passing minute Jane would be gone by the time she convinced William to let her enter the garden unattended. "What could happen to me in the garden? It's walled, for goodness' sake, and you'll be watching from here and can rush to my aid if anything goes wrong."

"You promise you'll turn back if something isn't right?"

"Yes, yes. I promise. Now will you let me go?" The sound of her foot tapping on the hard stones of the floor echoed like thunder throughout the small hallway.

He nodded and opened the door. Amelia rushed out into the garden and glanced around for the sight of Jane's vivid green shawl. Rushing between the rows of newly planted seeds, she thought she spied who she was looking for toward the rear of the garden where several clinging ivies had started to climb up the walls.

"Jane!" she yelled as she raced toward the wall. "Wait!" But by the time she reached the wall, the only sight greeting her was the fluttering green of an old, ragged cloth someone had tied to a stake to ditract birds from destroying the garden. As Amelia looked up and down the garden, she noticed similar flutterings of differently colored cloths interspersed throughout the garden. Jane had never been here after all.

Heedless of the damage to her gown, she sank onto the ground next to the stake responsible for her hurried flight out into the garden in the first place. She knew she had seen a figure in the garden, not just the color of Jane's shawl. Hadn't she? Amelia rubbed her forehead and tried to think. Maybe Jane really was all in her imagination as Tavis had suggested. It felt so real. Jane was more than a figment of her imagination—wasn't she? She was so deep in concentration Mrs. Dowling approached unnoticed.

"My lady?" Concern was etched into the round features of her portly cook. "Young William said you wanted to speak with me?"

"I…I did. Yes, I do." Amelia glanced around in confusion and spied William disappearing behind the heavy wooden door.

"Let me help you up, my lady," the cook said as she offered her outstretched arm to Amelia. Grasping it, Amelia rose and looked around the garden. "I came to see you but couldn't find you, Mrs. Dowling."

"That's because I was working in a sheltered spot just over there," she explained, pointing to a location off in the distance. "I keep my herbs over there. Some of them need a bit more coddling than others, so they get a special spot near the kitchen where they can absorb some of the heat from the stones. William knew where to find me, though."

Amelia sent a silent thanks to the amorous William for his intervention. Had he not found Mrs. Dowling when he did, Amelia might still be sitting on the ground questioning her sanity. The cook's arrival brought a welcome reprieve from her distracted thoughts. "You know a lot about plants and herbs, Mrs. Dowling?"

"I should say so." Her stout chest puffed with pride. "The local healer uses many of my herbs for her remedies. Says as how I can grow the plants that will grow for no one else."

"Will you show me?" As mistress, she wanted to become more acquainted with the servants and their interests. Mrs. Dowling's interest happened to coincide with one of her own.

At the wall backing against the huge Ben Ballywith, Amelia examined the section Mrs. Dowling claimed to have been working behind. It extended straight out from the corner where the kitchen wall and the mountain met to a distance of some fifty feet beyond the kitchen. On closer inspection, Amelia saw a sort of double wall was formed, where a shorter wall protruded from the side of the kitchen and butted out in front of the longer expanse that wrapped around the entire back courtyard. The two walls blended perfectly with one another, making it nearly impossible to see the two distinct sections. It was behind this shorter one where Mrs. Dowling took Amelia.

"Here's where I keep my medicinal herbs. It's these who need the extra care throughout the year." She named several of the herbs she was planting, and Amelia recognized one or two.

"What's that one over there?" Amelia asked, pointing to a group of small plants closest to the kitchen walls.

"That is belladonna, sometimes called the Devil's Berries because if used incorrectly it can cause death." Mrs. Dowling bent down and started to pick up her gardening tools from where she'd left them lying about.

"How fascinating." Amelia looked at the innocuous little plant growing in the shelter of the garden. *What is my cook doing growing a poisonous plant amongst the other medicinal herbs?*

"One of nature's great deceivers, it is."

Amelia regarded the little cook at her curious choice of words. She didn't think she had ever heard a plant referred to as a deceiver. "What do you mean?"

"People are always taken in by beauty, never expecting it to be false, but more often than not it is, at least in nature. Like with the belladonna. Its beauty is part of what makes it so dangerous. Fragrant flowers and delicious black berries lure the unsuspecting to sample its delights. Too much, though, causes a painful death." Mrs. Dowling shrugged as if a horribly painful death from belladonna was inconsequential.

Amelia shivered. "Then why do you grow it?"

Mrs. Dowling finished storing her gardening implements and brushed off her apron. "Because even something as dangerous as belladonna has its uses, as long as you know how to control it, with only tiny amounts." She sprinkled a fresh covering of hay over the new plants for added warmth. "You can't blame the poor plant, either, as it's only natural it has some sort of protection, just like every other living thing does. It's no different than a rose's thorns or a skunk's odor, I imagine."

As Mrs. Dowling spoke about the belladonna, a seed of hope blossomed in Amelia's breast. Jane had said she needed to break the curse, but Amelia had learned after years of trying it was an impossible task. But what if she did as Mrs. Dowling suggested and learned to control her curse in small doses, like the belladonna? In a situation where she needed to protect herself or a loved one, could she restrain her curse enough to defend those she loved most? It was an exciting idea to contemplate.

Ridding her hands of the last of the hay, Mrs. Dowling asked Amelia, "Now, what can I do for you, my lady, since I imagine it wasn't to help me plant or to listen to me talk your ear off about my herbs?"

Tucking away the beginning of an idea, Amelia explained her needs. The two women walked back to the kitchen, and after some rapid preparations she and William were once again on their way to the stables.

Chapter 18

"What did you discover about the footprints we saw in the tree grove?" Tavis asked Wickes while he rubbed down Wickes's tired mount.

It had been almost a week since the incident in the garden with Jane, and upon learning of it, Wickes had grown agitated, muttering to himself about how the size and the shape of the footprints were a perfect match. When Tavis pressed his friend for more information, Wickes refused to talk. Instead he saddled up his horse and raced off to London, leaving Tavis to question who had been on his grounds and how Wickes knew them.

Because despite Amelia's assertions Jane was a spirit, both Tavis and Wickes believed Amelia's mysterious specter was flesh and blood rather than whatever ethereal mist formed the spirits of the dead. Tavis hoped his friend's trip to London had yielded some useful information about the two sets of footprints he'd found leading into and out of the tree grove. He was done waiting for answers, especially when his wife's safety was concerned.

"Not much," Wickes admitted, leaning against the stall door. "Before leaving for London, I stopped in the village and talked with some of the locals to see if any strangers had come around these parts asking questions about you or Lady Stanton."

"And?" Tavis slammed the stall door and grabbed

a pitchfork, with which he began forking up a pile of hay and throwing it into the horse's stall.

"And nothing. Whoever was in the tree grove made sure to keep out of town to avoid suspicion. We have no way of knowing who was actually there. Hell!" He snorted, throwing his hands in the air. "It could have been two villagers playing a prank on your wife."

"But the information was too specific, Tom. It has to be someone who knows Amelia and her curse, knows Amelia is here with me, and is familiar enough with the property to avoid detection while entering and leaving." He leveled a hard glare at Wickes. "You and I know there's only one person who fits that description."

"Tavis," Wickes warned. "We don't have enough proof."

"What further proof do you need?" Tavis shouted. "He lied to us about who he was and has been working with Westby all this time. And he nearly raped my wife. It has to be Meeks!"

Wickes looked ready to say something but held up his hands in defense. "Granted, Meeks seems like the obvious choice, but what would he gain by sending in an old woman to talk to your wife? From what your wife described, nothing untoward happened. If anything, this mysterious Jane person was trying to help Lady Stanton, not harm her, and if what you say is true about Meeks, then wouldn't he have harmed her, had he the chance?"

Tavis conceded Wickes was most likely right. There was no sign of foul play, and in spite of her initial scare, Amelia seemed unaffected. From what he knew of Meeks, the man wouldn't have stopped at scaring Amelia. No, he would have done whatever he could to finish what he started all those months ago.

"What of Harry the Horse?" Tavis insisted. "You thought you knew something of him."

"I did, and it turns out I was right when I told you Harry the Horse died several years ago in a shipping accident."

"Who was he, then?"

"He was a smuggler, one of the best I've ever seen. He started as a shipping merchant operating out of London. During the war, he became wealthy sending supplies and artillery to the British soldiers in France. For years, he was the foremost shipping merchant in all of London because he delivered his goods twice as fast as any other merchant, and at a quarter of the cost."

"I heard of him," Tavis added, thinking back to his years as a soldier. "He stamped his initials, HMH, on all the crates of supplies we received on the Continent. The soldiers, too, always eagerly waited for his ships to pull into port because they knew he would deliver their letters home faster than any other ship to England could do. We called him the Stallion of the Sea."

"His speed earned him his reputation, but it was his smuggling that earned him his notoriety. What most people did not know is he also had a secret operation on the western isles of Scotland that earned him the real money, allowing him to undercharge his legitimate customers in London. Using the extensive island system off the coast, he was able to hide his stash of goods in tiny coves and inlets up and down the western shore."

"How was he not apprehended? Someone must have seen what he was doing and grown suspicious about his activities."

"Who would tell? You know as well as I the

western coast of Scotland is populated by poor fishermen and crofters who are barely eking a living at the edge of the restless sea. They are one bad storm away from extinction." Wickes paused for a moment, and Tavis wondered what Wickes wasn't saying. Whatever it was passed, and he shrugged. "I don't blame them in the least. They had to do what was necessary."

"Aye, that's true," Tavis agreed, trying to imagine how hard a life that had to be. To what lengths would he go to protect what was his? Thinking of Amelia, he knew there was nothing he wouldn't do to keep her safe, healthy, and fed. Understanding dawned, and Tavis realized what Wickes was intimating about his countrymen. "They helped him, those fishermen on the coast. They helped him conceal the smuggling."

"We know he had a network of smugglers who moved his cargo before the royal navy could find it. He was always one step ahead of us because somehow, and we were never able to discover how, before he died, he received information whenever the royal navy was patrolling the coast."

"Thus allowing him sufficient time to contact his ring of smugglers who moved whatever Harry was smuggling before the navy arrived."

"Precisely." Wickes's mouth thinned, and Tavis imagined how his friend felt at being outsmarted by a patriot turned traitor. Wickes loved his country and was an honorable man who demanded no less from everyone else. Because of this strict code of honor, it had been difficult at times to follow his leadership during the war. As a young man, Tavis had wanted to drink and carouse with his fellow soldiers to forget about the horrors of war, but Wickes had discouraged that practice, saying sobriety and good judgment were essential to survival in a combat situation. Though he hadn't always agreed with Wickes, Tavis respected his commanding officer and listened to him in all matters.

As the war progressed and the first bloom of patriotism receded, Tavis saw the truth to Wickes's caution. Soldiers who lacked Wickes's discipline and ethics turned cruel and directionless. Normal acts of war transformed to barbarism as these men, burdened by terrific acts of violence, lost sight of who they were in the battle for supremacy.

Tavis owed everything to Thomas Wickes because it was his moral compass that provided order and meaning during those dark days of killing and disorder. Wickes reminded him—and all of them, in truth—what it was to be a man with dignity and honor. Because of Thomas Wickes, guilt did not consume Tavis and he was able to live with the acts he had committed during the war. Some of his compatriots, those who had not heeded the warnings, were not so lucky.

Wickes sighed and slumped against the wall, reminding Tavis his friend had ridden all night to arrive at Ballywith early this morning. He must be exhausted. "Why don't you head up to the house now, change and get something to eat?" Tavis suggested. "We can discuss more after you've had a chance to rest."

Yawning and nodding his head in agreement, Wickes slapped Tavis on the back and ambled toward the house through the gardens. Looking down the path from the stable to the main house, Tavis saw the petite figure and flaming hair of his wife, followed closely by the taller, broader frame of one of his footmen. He knew Amelia hated having an escort, but until this mess with her father was cleared up, he didn't want her going anywhere without him or a guard.

Despite her pique at this new arrangement, she had been nothing but good-natured and content this past week. So much so he wanted to surprise her with a ride in the country and a visit to the village of Stanton to do some shopping. He knew she had been restless, cooped up in the castle and always shadowed by a footman, so he thought a treat was in order.

"Was that Mr. Wickes I saw you talking to?" Amelia queried as she entered the stables. "I have yet to meet him, Tavis," she scolded. "He left so quickly last time that I didn't have a chance to, and on the way back to the house this time he took a different path so I didn't even get a good look at him." She set her basket on a small stool and teased, "If I didn't know better, I'd say he was avoiding me."

Bending over the basket, she rifled through the contents. "I thought you might be hungry after a busy morning working with the horses, so I brought us a picnic lunch." She held up a sturdy blanket in triumph. "Aha! I knew it was in there."

Before she could spread it out on the floor, Tavis grabbed her hand and leaned in for a swift kiss. "How about we take a ride instead?"

****

Tavis was a god among men. At least that's how he felt riding across his lands with his wife beside him. Amelia's simple pleasure as they rode for hours across rolling hills and through dappled meadows made his heart swell and put his mind at ease. She was such easy company and delighted in the unfettered freedom of a day outside the castle walls.

Now they were sitting by a small stream, the horses grazing nearby and the two of them sharing their cold picnic under a flowering apple tree. It had been a perfect day, in Tavis's mind, until she brought up traveling to London to see her parents.

"No, Amelia," he stated, shaking a chicken leg in her direction. "Absolutely not!" He threw the bone aside and wiped his hands on his lap. "It's too dangerous."

"But Tavis," she pleaded, "I need to see my parents and at least try to explain what happened." She scooted closer to him on the blanket. "Besides, once I'm there I can speak to Father about my dowry. Those funds will go a long way to helping rebuild Ballywith."

"I don't want you to worry about that, lass. Besides, I have a plan for rebuilding Ballywith. We nearly picnicked in it before I swept you away for our afternoon excursion."

Amelia scrunched her eyebrows in thought. "What? The stables?"

"One day Ballywith Stables will be synonymous with the finest horses in all of England and Scotland."

"You've been working so hard, Tavis, and I know you will succeed," she encouraged, "but I worry what will happen to Ballywith before the stables can start showing a profit."

He felt an unexpected surge of pride hearing her concerns for their estate. It told him, in spite of his recent doubts, Ballywith was her home and where she felt she belonged; otherwise she wouldn't care about keeping the estate afloat.

He leaned over and pressed a quick kiss to her

temple. "Like you said, lass, I will succeed. In fact, I've already sold the offspring of Majesty and Hyacinth. We just need to pray that new little miracle appears within the next eighteen months."

He didn't say it aloud, but he was a little anxious. Horse breeding was not an exact science. There was only so much he could do without actually assisting the horses in copulation. Thinking about the rich buyer who would undoubtedly take his business elsewhere if Hyacinth didn't breed, Tavis wondered if he needed to do just that.

"Weren't those two of the horses my father took from you?" Amelia asked with concern. He nodded, and she frowned. "My father's untimely prank involving them must have delayed your timeline and cost you valuable time and money."

He did not comment. The lie he'd told about those horses and that ridiculous wager returned to taste sour in his mouth. They were approaching dangerous territory, and he needed to proceed with caution. "Aye, a bit, but I don't want you to worry any. Hyacinth will be in foal before month's end. I have a feeling."

Amelia still appeared worried, but she did not press him further. "Will you breed Legacy's Daughter?"

"Your horse?" Tavis reached for some apple tarts and smeared them with honey. "I hadn't thought of it. You'll want to ride her, won't you? If she's breeding, you won't be able to ride her as much as you might like."

"Well, yes, but she has impeccable lineage." Amelia shrugged and poured herself a glass of wine. "If using her as a broodmare means the stables have a better chance at survival, then I would be willing."

"No. Legacy's Daughter is yours." He popped some apple tart into his mouth and said, "Your horse's dam, Legacy, was my horse when I was a boy."

"What?" Amelia stopped her wine glass midway to her mouth and stared at him. "How did my father end up with her foal?"

"From what I can figure, my father must have kept Legacy and her foal for years even though he had told me they were sold. He really did hate me. Anything I loved he took from me. My brother, my home with my aunt, my horse…"

He stopped, surprised by the lack of bitterness he felt discussing his old man's negligence and abuse. Usually he became so angry he had to hit something to lessen the sting of his father's betrayal, yet this time he felt only pity for the old bastard and the wretched, lonely life he had lived.

It's Amelia. She centers me and reminds me there are people who care even if my father didn't. His eyes burned and his throat constricted in such a manner he needed to swallow several times lest he embarrass himself by doing something as unmanly as crying. Throwing down his napkin to cover his discomposure, he reached for his wine glass and drained it in one swallow before adding, "Your father obviously picked up Legacy's Daughter when he took the other horses."

"Legacy's Daughter is really your horse, then," she said, worry marring her smooth brow.

"No, she's yours." She started to protest, but he cut her off by leaning over and kissing her parted lips. At one time, he might have wanted to have Legacy's Daughter for his own, but she was and always would be Amelia's horse. Since discovering the whereabouts of

Legacy, he had the fanciful idea his old horse knew he and Amelia were meant to be. Otherwise how else could he account for his horse's foal being given to the woman he married?

"I like to think Legacy knew we were fated to be together, so she sent her daughter to you until we were ready to meet." He shrugged self-consciously as he shredded a blade of grass he'd picked, embarrassed at having shared such a silly idea.

Amelia grabbed his hand and squeezed. "Thank you, Husband. She means even more to me now that I know where she came from."

Satisfied, Tavis leaned back on his arms, glad to have been able to share with his wife his plans for the estate. Discussing Legacy's Daughter with her was also a relief. He had never liked the horrible lie he'd told her about why he had stolen those horses. Even though she accepted it, he felt guilty about concealing things from her. At least this way he was able to share a part of himself without hiding everything.

Stretching his arms over his head, he debated against taking a quick nap before he began the pleasurable business of seducing his wife. He yawned as the combination of a full stomach and tiredness from a hard morning of working with the horses caught up to him, and he decided a nap wouldn't hurt. That way he'd be refreshed and ready to make love to his wife when the mood struck.

Meanwhile, Amelia hummed a song under her breath, its soft melody soothing him into a comfortable state of relaxation. He watched her graceful movements as she packed the remains of their meal into the basket. Moving to Tavis's side, she rested her head on his chest, and he felt her sigh.

"What is it, love?" he asked as he stroked her hair, a new favorite pastime of his.

"I'm just happy. I never dreamed I could be so content, but marriage to you has shown me how much I was missing before. I might have thought myself to be content without love, but I know I was lying to myself because this, what we have together, this is truly happiness." She nestled more closely to his side, wrapping her slender arms around his waist.

His hand stilled, and he propped himself up to better look at his wife. "What did you say?"

She smiled a secret, womanly smile as old as Eve. After a lengthy pause in which he felt as if Amelia were gauging his mood, she tilted her head to the side in a gentle benediction. "I think you're ready to hear it now."

"To hear what?"

"That I love you," she said, her expression open and sincere. "That I think I've waited for you my whole life, to love you, if that makes any sense."

Tavis was dumbfounded. Elated, to be sure, that she loved him in return, but dumbstruck. With no indication of his own feelings for her, she was brave enough to admit what she felt. What a precious gift she had given him. What an amazing woman he had found!

He must have looked terrified, or at the very least shocked, because she laughed and patted his arm. "It's okay, Tavis. You don't have to say it in return. I just wanted you to know how I feel. One day, I hope, you will feel the same about me."

Feel the same about her? he thought foggily with the part of his brain that had just been blown away by her declaration, while the remaining part of his mind, the part that still had some sense, screamed, *We do! We do love her! Tell her now!*

No matter how he tried, the words he longed to tell her did not come. Instead he crushed her to him, reveling in the familiar comfort of her embrace. "I need to love you, lass," he rasped, his deep brogue thickening as emotion overtook him. "I need to feel you around me."

He loved her in the waning afternoon sunlight as the apple blossoms danced and twirled overhead, weaving their perfumed fragrance around the two lovers. How long he loved her, he couldn't say. Time seemed to lose all meaning in the sheltering protection of Amelia's arms. He wanted to love her all night, to show his wife in actions what he felt in his heart. Yet when she trembled on the verge of release and her passion-filled voice cried out, "I love you!" Tavis let go, knowing that, after years of searching for his place in the world, he had finally come home.

Chapter 19

Tavis drummed his fingers on the side of his leg and snuck longing glances out the window, wishing he were anywhere but here.

Wickes is a lucky bastard.

If Tavis hadn't had plans, he could be with him right now, on his way to town, instead of in his sitting room with these two visitors who had unexpectedly arrived about an hour past.

But no. I had to stay home because I decided to tell Amelia today that I love her. Almost a week had passed since their magical picnic in the woods and Amelia's surprising profession of love. Since then, he had wrestled with his own feelings and how best to share them with his wife. He'd asked Wickes, who laughed and suggested Tavis tell her while they were making love. Tavis didn't think that was quite right, especially since Wickes was a confirmed bachelor and had never been in love. He wanted it to be special, something she would remember always, so he gathered his butler and his footmen and even the stable hands into the kitchen to ask them what to do. After some awkward foot shuffling and embarrassed throat clearing, young William spoke.

"I haven't had a special lass yet, my lord, but my ma always liked it when Da brought her flowers." William scratched his head and shrugged. "Pick a bouquet for her and tell her how you feel."

"No, that won't do," Luke, his upstairs footman, interjected. "You have to buy her something, my lord." Luke thought for a moment and then snapped his fingers. "Buy her a fancy bauble. Women love shiny things. It will make her feel pretty and loved, knowing you spent your hard-earned coin on her happiness."

"You boys know nothing," Gerard, the butler, said with asperity. "Women want to feel special. You must first feed her senses by creating an atmosphere of elegant simplicity. Arrange her favorite room with flowers from the garden. Light hundreds of candles to create a romantic atmosphere, and there should be gentle music playing. Perhaps a violin? Have Cook prepare her favorite dishes to tantalize her taste buds. When she is sated from food and wine, then you tell her."

"Ha!" Mrs. Dowling snorted from her place by the fire where she was peeling potatoes for the night's meal.

"Do you have something to say?" Gerard demanded. "What does a crabby old spinster possibly know about love?"

Mrs. Dowling wiped her hands on her apron and waddled over to the huddled group of men. With wooden spoon in hand, she tapped Gerard on his chest. "I know a sight more than an old decrepit fart like you."

While Gerard huffed and rubbed his chest, Mrs. Dowling turned to address Tavis. "You love her, my lord, and she loves you, aye?"

Tavis nodded warily, not liking how his cook was waving that spoon in front of his face.

"Then tell her. Everyone else knows how you feel

about her. It's about time she does too."

In the end, Tavis was so nervous he took all of their advice, spending the better part of a week arranging everything to be perfect for Amelia.

Of course now that he and everything else was ready, his wife was nowhere to be found, and he had visitors, visitors who would undoubtedly take offense if he were to whisk his wife away for a day of carnal pleasures.

Not to mention their presence is an unwelcome distraction from the more important task of locating Meeks.

Both Tavis and Wickes agreed that the sooner they found Meeks the better. Not only was he a traitor and a rapist, but they needed to question him about his activities with Lord Westby. Without him, they had no case against Westby, but if Meeks testified, they could use his statement to implicate and try Westby for treason. Of course that was assuming Meeks complied, which, given Meeks's loyalty to Westby, Tavis thought unlikely. It was a frustrating endeavor, to say the least, and one Tavis wanted to end.

He sighed, the large gust of air breaking the silence of the still room, and then smiled weakly when his guests narrowed their eyes at him in displeasure, an expression that hadn't altered much since their arrival. Not that he blamed them. What parents looked fondly on the man who stole their daughter from under their noses?

Lady Westby shifted again in her seat and sniffed, a noise he had not grown accustomed to despite the frequency of its occurrence since the good lady's arrival. Apparently nothing pleased Lady Westby, especially not him. With her pert nose raised in the air sniffing her disdain, she took great pleasure in telling Tavis how much she disliked him, his home, and his god-awful country. Contrarily, Lord Westby remained silent, only speaking once to grunt a greeting to Tavis when he welcomed them to Ballywith. Between the stony glares, the obnoxious sniffing from Lady Westby, and the mute hostility from Lord Westby, Tavis was ready to make his escape and damn the consequences.

The door swung open, and Tavis prayed it was his butler coming to summon him away on some urgent business, but it was Amelia. As happy as he was to see her, he was now well and truly stuck.

"Father! Mother!" Amelia said in stunned surprise. "What are you doing here?"

"Is that any way to greet your parents, Amelia?" sniffed her mother. "After we rushed from home and traveled for days, on insufferable roads, in a cramped carriage, only to arrive in Scotland, of all places." She paused to wrinkle her nose and sniff disapprovingly at Tavis. "And all you have to ask is what we are doing here?"

"Yes," Amelia replied as she sank into a vacant spot next to Tavis. "Only two days ago I sent you a letter with Mr. Coombes, my husband's solicitor, explaining everything, but it can't have reached London yet. How did you know where to find me?"

Noting her shaking hands and pale complexion, Tavis handed her a cup of tea, which she took with a grateful smile. Perversely, he felt better knowing she was as affected by her parents' unannounced visit as he was.

Lady Westby's teacup rattled in its saucer as it hit

the side table with more force than necessary, and she turned her flashing eyes to Amelia. "Your sister Beatrice told me, after I spent weeks worrying whether you were alive or dead. So, yes, we are here because I needed to see for myself you were safe."

Pointing an elegant finger at her daughter, she said, "You run away and elope, not even leaving us a note of your whereabouts, only for us to find out you've married and are living in Scotland!" Lady Westby's cheeks bloomed with the deep red of irritation as she turned the full force of her anger onto Tavis's wife.

"I'm sorry, Mother," Amelia stammered, having obviously taken note of her mother's heightened color and agitated state of mind. "Had I been thinking clearly, I should have left you a letter."

"Humph!" Lady Westby snorted, a pleasant change from her incessant sniffing, and crossed her arms over her chest. "It would have been nice to know if you were well or not, Amelia." Lady Westby speared Tavis with a hostile glare. "Now that I see who you were with, this lying Scotsman, I wonder at how safe you really have been all this time."

Tavis stiffened, not liking the implication he was not only a liar but incapable of protecting his wife. True, he hadn't told the entire truth when last he spoke with Lord and Lady Westby, but that didn't make him a liar. "I beg your pardon, madam—"

"Now, Anne," Lord Westby soothed, breaking his silence with the interruption. "You know this is the match we had hoped for between Amelia and Lord Stanton. Maybe it didn't happen in the manner in which we had envisioned; however, the outcome is the same. Be happy for them, my dear," he said. "It's obvious the two are deeply in love with each other and have found their own happiness together."

Lord Westby knew how to appease his wife, for Lady Westby softened at his words, finally lowering her crossed arms to her sides. "A girl shouldn't keep secrets from her mother, Howard. I should have known where she was and what she was doing." Her eyes sparkled with unshed tears. "I'm her mother."

"Don't take it too hard, Annie-girl. I imagine they were too overcome with love for each other to think much about anyone else." His expression when he looked over at them ordered the two to agree.

"Oh, yes, Mother," Amelia reassured. "Once I met Tavis, I could think of nothing else." She smiled dreamily at her husband who had taken her hand between his own to bestow a tender kiss upon her knuckles.

"I, too, was captivated from the moment I first met your daughter, Lady Westby. I thought of nothing else save her." Though he spoke to Lady Westby, his words were for Amelia alone.

"You were very naughty, though, Lord Stanton," Lady Westby said with a trace of her old, sly smile returning to her lovely face. "You never once let on that you had already met Amelia when we conversed in the ballroom."

Tavis flashed Lady Westby his most charming smile, the one Amelia told him made her weak in the knees. "I did not know who she was, Lady Westby. We met by chance out under the stars. At first I didn't even know if she was a real flesh-and-blood woman or an otherworldly goddess sent to tempt me with visions of a delightful dream I thought I could never have." He looked at Amelia with all the love he felt in his heart, too full of joy to contain his emotions any longer.

His eyes held Amelia's as he continued to weave his tale of accidental meeting to Lady Westby. "We shared an enchanted dance out under the stars, and like the mythical goddess I believed she was, she disappeared once our dance was over. As she left I called out desperately, 'Who are you, my lady? Please gift me with your name.' I needed to know what name I should whisper when I begged the gods to return one of their own to Earth for me."

Tavis turned and looked at Lady Westby, who was watching the two of them with starry eyes and clasped hands. "I thought she hadn't heard me, you see, for it was quiet so long after my cry into the darkness. Then I heard it. A faint sound carried on the wings of a warm breeze reached my ears and filled my heart with hope. 'Lady Amelia Westby,' it sighed. I tell you I hoped, Lady Westby, because I knew her then to be a woman of flesh and not the ethereal dream that would forever be out of reach."

"Why then did you say nothing when we met, Lord Stanton?" Lady Westby asked.

"Yes, do explain, Lord Stanton," Lord Westby asked, a hard, assessing glint in his eyes. "Why, upon realizing you had met our daughter, did you not inform us of this acquaintance?"

With a silent curse, Tavis returned Westby's hard look with a genial smile of his own. Westby knew Tavis was painting a pretty picture for his wife to lessen the hurt of Amelia's elopement. Instead of staying quiet and allowing his wife to believe what she would, he insisted on poking holes in his explanation, damn him.

Deciding his options were to either punch his new father-in-law across the jaw, an act sure to bring disapproval from his wife, or ignore the man, Tavis chose the latter (in spite of the former's definite appeal). Ignoring Lord Westby and his question, Tavis continued his story and addressed Lady Westby. "I was reeling from meeting your daughter, Lady Westby, too overcome with emotion to describe what had happened."

"Now really, Stanton," Lord Westby protested.

"Shh!" Lady Westby admonished her husband. "Let him finish." Turning back to sweetly smile at Tavis, she said, "Go on, Lord Stanton."

"After leaving the ballroom, I was understandably distraught at having missed our formal introduction, and so I prepared to depart. Imagine my surprise to find Amelia wandering outside looking for me. It was as if Cupid himself blessed our union. I stole her from you, I know, and for that I should apologize." He took a breath and squeezed Amelia's hand in his own. "But I can't because to do so would make it seem I regret my actions, and I don't."

Lady Westby drew in a sharp breath, and he could see her becoming angry again. Tavis hurried to conclude, lest she begin yelling or crying again.

"I don't regret taking her, Lady Westby, because running off with your daughter meant I got to know this incredible woman that much sooner. It meant I finally met the person who has become my partner and friend for life." He looked down at Amelia and smiled into his wife's shining eyes. "It meant I finally found the woman I love."

"You love me?" Amelia whispered, those brilliant

green eyes searching his own for proof he spoke the truth.

"Aye, lass," he said as he placed his forehead on her own. "I love you. I think I have been waiting for you to love my whole life." His words, almost the exact ones Amelia had used to describe her feelings for him, spread peace throughout his being. For a man who had always thought love was a weak, unnecessary emotion, he finally understood its power. It centered him and gave him strength; it filled the gaping hole of emptiness in him with all the goodness and light Amelia brought into his life.

"I love you too, Tavis," Amelia said. "More than I ever thought possible." He gathered her into his arms, loving the feel of her within his embrace. When they separated, he was surprised to find tears streaking down his face. She wiped them away with her fingers and gave a happy, watery laugh when he did the same to her.

Enfolding her into another embrace, he kissed her and once again addressed her parents. "So you see, my lady, I have no regrets, for how can I regret a decision which has brought me such happiness?"

Lord Westby, who had watched this display of affection between Amelia and Tavis without speaking, spoke. "You love her?"

Tavis was seized by the urgency of Westby's question and wondered at the lines of tension bracketing Westby's mouth and eyes. The man sat on the edge of the settee as if Tavis's answer were of the utmost importance. Tavis was under the impression Lord Westby was an indifferent parent, much like his own had been, but this intensity about him and his affections for Amelia told a different story. It showed him a father who had strong emotions for his child. Despite their past, Tavis had to respect the man's concern for his daughter's welfare.

"With my body and soul, I love her, my lord," Tavis responded.

Those tight lines of tension on his face eased, and Westby's body sagged. "Then I give you my blessing, Lord Stanton, and wish the two of you well."

Lady Westby's voice wobbled, "It's all well and good for you to give them your blessing, Howard, and for you to regret nothing, Lord Stanton, but I will always regret not being there for Amelia on her special day, even if it was an elopement."

"Oh, Mama," Amelia cried, rising from her seat to rush over to her mother's embrace. "I wish you could have been there, too." When they parted, tears streaked down both women's cheeks. Mother and daughter laughed and embraced again.

Westby rose, as did Tavis. The two stared at each other over the bent heads of their wives, and Tavis knew that in spite of Westby's blessing on their elopement his day of reckoning was soon at hand. He nodded his understanding and went to his wife. Putting his arm around her and his mother-in-law, he asked, "Perhaps when we are in Town in a month we could have a wedding celebration at your home? Maybe such an entertainment would put to rest some of the gossip surrounding our elopement."

"Can we, Tavis?" Amelia asked him with shining eyes full of excitement.

"What a grand idea!" Lady Westby squealed, clapping her hands.

Lord Westby joined the little circle and placed a hand on his wife's arm. "Why don't you and Amelia sit down and discuss the details." Lady Stanton nodded, and he leaned to press a quick kiss on the top of her head. "Tavis," he said, "I'm in need of something a little stronger than tea. What do you say, Stanton?"

"Of course, sir," he replied, clapping Westby on the back. "Let me show you what I have in my study." Opening the door for Westby, Tavis ushered him out and led him down the hallway to his private study. Westby entered and wandered around the room, looking at the furnishings and the paintings on the walls before settling in a comfortable chair near the fire.

Tavis poured each of them a glass of whisky and then sank warily into a chair opposite Westby, who raised his glass in salute. "To you and Amelia!" He tilted his glass and drained the contents in one swallow. Still Tavis waited, his glass untouched, for the moment when Westby flew at him in a rage.

Westby must have seen the look of apprehension on his face because he threw back his head and laughed. "I'm not going to kill you, Stanton, no matter if you did break our deal." He clunked his glass down on the table and leaned toward Tavis, waggling a finger in front of his face. "And you stole my horses, too."

"Those horses were mine, and you know it. Besides, I explained to you what happened, Westby, with me and Amelia."

"What a pretty story that was, too." Westby hooted. "A mythical goddess, my foot. What storytellers you Scots are!"

Tavis thought back to the night he and Amelia met and recalled his impressions upon seeing her. "It wasn't all a story. But I thought it would be easier for Lady Westby to accept if I painted a prettier picture than what actually happened."

Westby sobered. "For that, I thank you. You have no idea what it's been like at home since Amelia's disappearance." He grimaced. "Had you not professed your love for my daughter, I might have had to kill you solely for the pain you caused my wife," he said mildly. "She was distraught, you see." Westby grabbed the bottle Tavis had brought over and poured himself another glass.

"Westby, I never meant to break our deal. I wasn't lying when I said our elopement just happened."

"No, no," Westby interrupted. "Don't apologize. I wanted you to marry her, and you did. For that you have my undying gratitude. That you took her from the house sooner, so much the better."

"What do you mean?"

"She wasn't safe at home anymore," Westby said, staring at the swirling amber liquid of his half-empty glass. "I needed her to leave as soon as possible. That's why I used the papers against you." He shrugged but didn't apologize for the blackmail. "As you so eloquently said, I have no regrets. I would do it again if it meant protecting Amelia."

"Like you protected her when she was almost raped in her own home?" Tavis demanded. At Westby's surprised look, Tavis growled, "Aye, she told me about that. I have half a mind to beat you to death for failing in your duty as that woman's father." Westby whitened in the face of Tavis's red-hot rage. "You were supposed to protect her, not blame her for what happened!"

Westby straightened and leaned in closer to Tavis.

His eyes had taken on a wild look that made Tavis back away in nervousness. "But don't you see? That's why I found you."

"To what?" Tavis asked in confusion. "Protect her? Of course I will. With my life. But it doesn't explain why you didn't when she was under your care."

"I…I couldn't," Westby whispered. "My hands were tied."

"By whom? Who do you take your orders from, Westby?" Tavis demanded. When his father-in-law resisted still, anger coursed through Tavis's veins, and he lashed out violently, hoping his rage would spur Westby into confessing. "You will hang for treason, Westby!" he yelled. "Not even your title will save you from that fate."

Westby grimaced, and his lined face grew even paler. Tavis was betting on Westby's fear of hanging to outweigh his fear of whoever was leading their smuggling operation.

"What does it matter now if I tell you or not? I'm a dead man either way."

"Tell me now who is really in charge, and I'll see you are only exiled and not hung."

Westby flinched and looked around the room, even though it was only the two of them in the room. Shaking his head, he stammered, "No, no, I can't… They'll kill me!"

Tavis's control on his temper snapped, and he grabbed Westby's lapels to yank him up. Once they were eye to eye, Tavis said with deadly calm, "And I'll kill you if you don't, so tell me who he is!"

"It's—" But whatever Westby was about to say died on his lips as a shot ripped through the window by

223

the fireplace and struck Westby down, silencing him and his confession.

Chapter 20

A sharp crack disturbed the peacefulness of the sitting room where Amelia and her mother still sat talking. "What was that?" Amelia gasped, looking at her mother in surprise. "Did you hear that noise?"

Her mother shook her head. "It sounded like a gunshot, but it couldn't be, so close to the house. Besides, no one would be hunting at this time of year, would they?"

Amelia's face blanched. "Oh, no! Tavis!" Jumping up from the settee, she lifted her skirts and ran out of the room and down the hall to where Tavis and her father had retired half an hour previous. "Tavis!" she screamed down the hall. "Tavis!"

A door slammed, and Tavis rushed to meet Amelia and her mother, who had followed closely behind. "Amelia!" Tavis stopped her from going any farther down the hallway. "I need you to take your mother and go down to the kitchen."

"But Tavis, we heard a gunshot. What happened?"

"Your father's been shot," he whispered. "It came from outside the window. I don't know who or why, but he's been injured. Wickes is back from the village and is tending to him now."

"Howard?" Lady Westby whimpered. "Shot?" She wobbled and clutched at Amelia's arm for support. "I need to see him." Lady Westby tried to go farther down the hall, but Tavis stopped her with one strong arm.

"I need to know you are safe, Amelia. Please," he begged, "go to the kitchen, and as soon as I know anything, I will come and find you." Amelia started to protest, but Tavis stopped her with a hard kiss. "I can't do my job unless I know you and your mother are protected. Do you understand? I need you where nothing can happen to you."

Hearing the note of desperation in his voice, Amelia realized how afraid Tavis was. She nodded once and grabbed her mother.

Tavis motioned to two footmen entering the hall from belowstairs. "Take Lady Stanton and Lady Westby down below, to the kitchen," he ordered. Tavis strode over to a side doorway and returned moments later with two large rifles. Handing one to each of the footmen, he said, "Return to the kitchen and guard both of these women with your lives. If I find out you let something happen to either one of them because you let your guard down, I will kill you myself with my bare hands. Do I make myself clear?"

Though pale and trembling, both nodded and ushered Amelia and Lady Westby through the hallway and to the lower level.

"What's this?" bellowed an irritated Mrs. Dowling upon seeing Amelia and her mother enter the kitchen escorted by two armed guards. "I haven't time for any nonsense right now, what with unexpected guests and the evening meal ready to be cooked!" She shooed at the two footmen and planted her floured hands on her ample hips. "My lady, I can't have this much disruption in my kitchen. I did explain to you last time about announcing your visits, didn't I? I can't have you popping in whenever you want, no matter if you are the lady of this house."

Amelia led her mother to a small table in the back of the room. Seating Lady Anne, she took the shawl from around her shoulders to wrap around the shaking ones of her stunned mother before she returned to Mrs. Dowling, who stood tapping her foot.

"There's been an accident, and my father's been shot." Amelia recounted the events to her cook as best she knew them from what little Tavis had told her. "Which is why his lordship wishes us to remain below in the kitchens," Amelia concluded.

A grim-faced Mrs. Dowling harrumphed, muttered something like, "Such goings on," wiped her hands on her apron, and started barking commands to her gaping kitchen staff. Soon the room was again a flurry of activities with everyone working as ordered. Amelia watched through a bewildered fog as she sank next to her mother.

With dinner preparations delegated and underway, Mrs. Dowling waddled over to a shelf near the ladies and pulled down a small leather sack and a pair of pointed scissors. Amelia heard her cook muttering under her breath about her herbs. "Yarrow to stop the bleeding. Garlic, I think for infection. Not much remains…hmmm…maybe ginger?"

"Do you know of something to help my father?" Amelia asked.

The cook's face turned thoughtful. "I may have one or two herbs to help stop the bleeding and ease some of the pain he must be in—that's of course if the bullet didn't already do its job." She patted Amelia on the shoulder before taking her bag and her scissors down the hall to the garden.

"Wait!" Amelia called, jumping up to follow the retreating form of Mrs. Dowling. "Let me help you." Amelia ran down the small hallway after the cook. By the time she reached the door, Mrs. Dowling was already outside, and Amelia had her hand on the door ready to follow.

"My lady!" called William and the other footman, stopping her from her hasty exit. "His lordship was very clear you were to remain in the kitchen under our protection."

"William," she pleaded, looking at her protector. *No longer young.* It was funny how the moment Tavis had placed a gun in his hand, William's face matured, changing from the sunny, smiling countenance of a carefree young man to the harsher, more serious expression of this man before her. "If I stay in here, I'll go crazy with worry. Please," she asked, "allow me to do something useful instead of waiting and worrying."

It seemed like forever, waiting for William to contemplate her request, but in a moment he nodded his agreement. "Fine," he said, sighing. "But Luke and I go with you, my lady."

"Thank you."

William wasn't through giving his orders. "If something doesn't feel right to either me or Luke, you will go back inside with no questions asked."

"Yes, yes," Amelia said, eager to be doing something useful instead of this uncertain waiting.

William shook his head and pinned Amelia with a stern look. "No, my lady. This can't be like last time when I told you to stay close and you yes-yessed me. Remember that time? You slipped away, and I caught hell from his lordship for having lost you, pardon my language. I had to muck out the stables." He stared at Amelia until she flinched and looked away.

"I said I was sorry," she mumbled, remembering her guilt when she discovered how William had paid for her act of rebellion.

"I know you did," William replied, "but this is serious, and if something were to happen to you because you didn't listen, I can guarantee you his lordship will not accept my apology as nicely as I accepted yours."

Amelia knew William was right. This was serious. Her father had been shot in her own home, and even though Tavis hadn't told her what danger still existed, she knew it had something to do with her father. Amelia shivered and hoped William was just being overly cautious and no more danger lurked outside.

"Will you do as we say, my lady? Will you listen and go inside if there is any danger?"

"I promise, William, to do as you say."

"All right, then. Let's proceed."

Had it not been so serious a situation, it might have been comical the way the three of them walked out to the garden and around the side of the house. With William in the lead, Amelia behind his tall frame and almost nose to shoulder blades with his back and then Luke right behind her to protect her from the rear, the three were so close together their steps had to synchronize or they might have tripped and fallen.

When they rounded the corner to the sheltered garden where Mrs. Dowling kept her special plants, Amelia didn't see her cook. Peering out from behind William's back, she searched for Mrs. Dowling's robust figure amongst the darkening shadows. All she could see, though, was what looked like a large, misshapen sack lying on the ground. But when that sack moved, Amelia gasped and broke away from her escort to run to the heap.

"Mrs. Dowling!" Amelia yelled, shaking the seemingly lifeless form of her cook. "Can you hear me? Mrs. Dowling?" Amelia pressed her ear to the cook's chest and was reassured to hear the familiar thumping of a heartbeat. It was slow but regular, and Amelia took comfort Mrs. Dowling was alive.

"Amelia!" William shouted. "Get back to the house —now!"

Her head snapped up and looked to where William and Luke had been standing moments earlier. Instead of the two men she expected to see, she saw four, and it took her a moment to realize they were fighting a fierce battle. Though the footmen appeared to be outmatched, they were not giving up without a fight. Using their size and strength against the other much more skilled fighters, William and Luke were at least able to prevent the two men from reaching her.

Amelia's eyes widened in terror as one of the unknown men knocked Luke over the head with the butt of his own rifle. William braced up the injured Luke, caught Amelia's eyes amidst the chaos of the fight, and shouted, "Run!"

Giving one last look at the unconscious cook, Amelia hiked up her skirts and ran toward the small opening between the two walls. While the bulk of the fighting blocked the majority of the exit, Luke and William's positioning created a small opening behind them for her to slip through safely. Ducking her head, she sprinted through the opening and ran back to the house. She had just reached for the doorknob when rough fingers grabbed her from behind and her world went black.

****

Once assured of Amelia's safety in the kitchen, Tavis grabbed his rifle and ran out to check the perimeter of the house. Judging from the angle and height of the bullet entry, the shooter had been within several hundred yards of the house and somewhere up high. Tavis found the window the bullet had entered and jogged away from the house to a sparsely wooded area bordering the western edge of his property. He had to walk only fifteen feet or so before he found where the shooter had stood. It was a small hill with a flat top. At one end lay a large log someone had moved from elsewhere, as there were only small saplings surrounding the flat surface. The shooter, Tavis assumed, had moved it to steady the barrel of his rifle. On closer inspection, Tavis noted faint scorch marks on the top of the log, confirming his suspicions.

A close look at the earth on top of the hill revealed the light indentation of footprints, large but smaller than his own. Farther back on the hill was another set of footprints. The markings of these shoes were easy to see, as the indentation was heavily made into the soil.

Someone who weighed at least fifteen stone must have made those footprints, while the first set of footprints were made by a much leaner man. A marking toward the rear of the imprint caught Tavis's eye. It was a large X situated in the middle of the heel, a mark Tavis remembered well. It was the same mark he and Wickes had found in the footprints from the tree grove.

These men had been on his estate before, and Tavis had a good idea who they belonged to. Satisfied for the moment that there was nothing more to learn, he returned to the house to see if Westby still lived.

Mounting the stairs two at a time, Tavis found Wickes in a spare guest room at the top of the stairs, stitching up an unconscious Westby.

"Is he going to live?" Tavis asked.

Wickes grunted. "He's lucky. The bullet passed right through his shoulder. I was able to stanch the bleeding before stitching it up." He finished tying off the bandage and went to the wash basin, where he removed the blood from his hands. "Of course there is still a chance of infection," he said. "I'm reluctant to fetch a doctor until we know more about this situation, but if we don't, he could take a fever during the night. Either way, it's not an ideal situation."

"Amelia mentioned our cook is knowledgeable about herbs and such. Maybe she'll have something to ward off infection."

"It wouldn't hurt to ask," Wickes said. "But first, tell me what you found."

Tavis recounted his observations and told Wickes some of his suspicions regarding what he saw.

"Are you sure it was two people?"

"Quite sure. Not only were the prints of different sizes, there was the obvious weight difference. And they are the same footprints we saw earlier. I'm positive."

"How was Westby acting before he was shot?"

"Agitated. He was nervous and kept saying, 'They'll kill me.' "

"That accounts for the two sets of footprints,"

Wickes muttered, "but that doesn't explain who Meeks is working for."

"We've been working under the assumption Meeks was working for Westby. That can't be right, given what happened to Westby, along with what he was saying. The question now is who is Meeks working for if not Westby?"

"You definitely think Meeks is the shooter?" Wickes asked as he began to pace restlessly across the floor.

"I would say so. That would account for the lighter impressions I found on the ground."

"Meeks is a good shot, isn't he?"

"One of the best I've seen," Tavis replied without hesitation, having witnessed the man's skills with a gun on the Continent. "At least that tells us who shot at Westby, but it doesn't explain the other man or why they want to silence Westby in the first place."

"Amelia," came a hoarse whispered voice.

Both men whipped their heads around and looked at the bed where Westby lay. Going to his side, Tavis saw Westby had regained consciousness. Though his eyes were barely open, his breathing had changed and was more rapid and shallow, a sure sign he was awakening and in pain.

"What did you say?" demanded Tavis. "How does Amelia have anything to do with this?"

Westby was silent so long that Tavis thought perhaps he had passed into unconsciousness again. Finally, though it must have pained him to do so, Westby replied, "He...wants her. Broke our deal, though. No Amelia, no deal."

Wickes eyed Tavis before leaning over the

prostrate form of Westby and asked, "Who wants her? Meeks?"

Westby nodded. "Jeremy is…obsessed," Westby managed to get out between shallow gasps. "Couldn't give her to him…couldn't do that to…to my girl."

If what Westby was saying was true, then Jeremy had made a deal with Amelia's father involving Amelia marrying Meeks in exchange for…what? That remained unclear.

"What was the arrangement you made with him?" Tavis asked, disliking Westby all the more for using his daughter in his illegal activities. "What were you going to get for marrying Amelia off to him?"

"Their…silence," he wheezed. "And protection for my…my family."

Tavis's eyes narrowed at Westby's reference once again to there being more than one other person involved in this mess. "Who is Meeks working with?" he shouted. Noticing Westby's eyes had closed once more, Tavis leaned over and shook him on his uninjured shoulder, hoping to rouse him enough to get the answers he and Wickes needed. "Damn it, Westby! Who is the other man?"

Westby's head tossed on the pillow, yet Tavis did not relent. Grabbing the older man by the edges of his tattered and bloody shirt, Tavis yanked him up and shook. "Tell me who he is!"

"Tavis!" Wickes's sharp voice cracked through the still room as he placed his hands on Tavis's upper arm to prevent any further assaults on the injured man. "Enough! We'll never get anything from him if you kill him before he can talk."

Westby moaned, his head slumping forward onto

his chest. He began to mumble, "Hurry…hurry. Get the horse. The horse. Hurry."

"What are you saying?" Tavis commanded. "You're not making any sense!" Tavis shook the man again, but when he only repeated the same phrases, Tavis dropped him back on the bed in disgust. "We'll get nothing more from him now anyway."

Wickes gave Tavis a disapproving look and pushed past him to examine the older man, who lay pale and unconscious once more. Leaning over, he checked the older man's pulse and assessed the bandage for new blood. "Fortunately, he's still alive. You didn't reopen the wound despite how hard you tried." He straightened and walked to the door to motion in the maid who had been waiting outside. "But I think we had best seek out the cook, just in case."

"You're right. I'm sorry," Tavis apologized.

Catching sight of the maid, who had taken up her position by the side of Westby's bed, Tavis groaned as he recognized the she-devil Margaret. Realizing now more than ever he needed to be discreet, Tavis held his tongue, though there was plenty more he wanted to say about his father-in-law's cowardice and treachery. No one besides the two of them knew about Westby's illegal activities. Until they could find out who Meeks was working with, today's events needed to be seen as some sort of freak accident, which meant if he didn't want anything getting back to his wife via Margaret he needed to remain silent.

As Wickes finished giving instruction to the grim-faced Margaret, Tavis worked out a story to tell Amelia and her mother. He decided to tell Amelia it was a hunter who had come too close to the estate. As they left the room, the ever-disapproving Margaret said nothing to him, but the glare she shot him spoke more than words ever could. He nodded once in understanding of her silent warning, and the two men left the room to find the cook.

Eager to see Amelia and offer his comfort, Tavis wasted no time in descending the stairs to the kitchen. At first, he saw nothing. Thick smoke poured from the great fireplace and obscured his view. Waving his hands in front of him, he shouldered his way through the haze to the doorway in the back hall and flung it open. The smoke poured out, thinning as it dissipated, allowing Tavis to see what had previously been concealed.

Several maids rushed back and forth, carrying buckets of water to douse the flames at the fireplace. One maid carried clean cloths over to the battered and bruised figure of his cook, Mrs. Dowling, while another wrapped bandages around his injured cook's arms. In a growing panic, he searched for Amelia's familiar red head with the two footmen he had sent to protect her, but he saw only the bloody and beaten faces of William and Luke as they stood guard over his mother-in-law.

Lady Anne was pale. She held herself around the middle, clutching what looked to be Amelia's shawl around her as she rocked back and forth in her chair. He looked at his two footmen for some sort of explanation, but they turned their heads away, refusing to meet his eyes. An overpowering feeling of dread settled in the pit of his stomach as he regarded the hunched figure of Amelia's mother. Bending down, Tavis grabbed one of her hands and asked, "Amelia?"

"They've taken her," she replied in a low broken

voice. "Amelia is gone." She buried her face in her hands, and her body shook as the tears she had so bravely fought against burst through.

Chapter 21

"Tie her up," a gruff voice said. "Make sure it's tight, too. I don't want her escaping." Heavy footsteps retreated into the distance, and as Amelia regained full consciousness, she heard the far-off sound of a door opening and then closing. In spite of her groggy state, she felt the rough scrape of rope against the skin on her wrists. Someone with blunt fingers yanked her arms and tied them behind her back and then moved lower to bind her legs together at the ankles. She blinked to get a better look at her surroundings and experienced a moment of true alarm when all she saw was darkness. It wasn't until she felt a soft weight on her face that she realized a dark cloth covered it.

Where am I? And who took me? A rising feeling of panic threatened to engulf her, but she tamped it down. Becoming hysterical would solve nothing. She needed to be calm and rational if she wanted to survive.

Since sight eluded her, Amelia strained to catch any noise, no matter how faint. It took her several minutes of intense concentration, but she identified the muted footsteps of at least one other person besides the one who was tying her up. And what was that sound? Amelia listened more closely and heard a muffled roar breaking over and over again. Realizing she must be hearing the surf washing up on shore, Amelia deduced she was near the coast. Sniffing tentatively, her conclusion was confirmed by the briny smell of salt water on the air.

What did Tavis tell me? Amelia tried to focus and remember what Tavis had said about Ballywith's location in relation to the Atlantic Ocean. She thought he'd told her it was a half day's ride to the west, so assuming she'd only been unconscious for several hours and not days, that's where they must be.

Her captor having finished tying his final knot, he stood; she felt a large presence near her right shoulder. When he yanked off the covering from her face, she craned her neck to see behind her. Blinking to accustom her eyes to the sudden light that illuminated the small space, it took her a moment to recognize the familiar countenance of Jeremy Michelson.

"Jeremy!" she gasped. "It was you?"

"You didn't think I'd let that bastard Scot get away with taking what's mine, did you? After all, your father promised you to me."

Amelia struggled in vain against her bindings. "He did no such thing, Jeremy. Besides, I told you I would rather die than marry you."

Rough fingers grabbed her by the chin and forced her to look into cold, calculating eyes. "He did promise, Amelia, and I mean to make him keep his word."

She jerked to free her chin from his fingers, but Jeremy held tight, bruising the delicate flesh of her face. "You lie!" she spat. "What reason could he possibly have for such an agreement?"

Releasing her face, Jeremy placed his own fingers on his chin in pretended contemplation. "Hmmm, perhaps it's because your father is a traitor and has been selling Crown secrets to the French since the beginning of the war." He chuckled humorlessly at Amelia's outraged expression. "We promised to keep his secret as long as you were given to me." Placing one hand on the back of her chair, Jeremy leaned over until his face was mere inches from hers. "Didn't you ever wonder why I was invited to live at your home? Why your father didn't ask me to leave after our little misunderstanding?" he asked, referencing the time he'd almost raped her.

"That's not t-true," she stammered but with less conviction than before. "My father is a good man. He would never betray his country."

This time Jeremy laughed long and hard. "Oh, but he did, Amelia. Willingly and repeatedly. He had his chance to do the honorable thing years ago, but your father was too eager to reap the rewards of our…venture."

"You must have tricked him, then," she said, unable to reconcile the man who had raised her with this portrait Jeremy painted of a cold-hearted criminal.

"It's time to grow up," he said as he stalked over to a small window to Amelia's right. "Your father is nothing more than a common criminal who knew exactly what he was getting into when he signed up."

Tears welled in her eyes as she shook her head in disbelief. How had he lied to her family for all of these years? She closed her eyes and willed herself not to cry, refusing to give Jeremy the satisfaction of seeing how much his words hurt. Breathing in deeply, she counted her breaths to still her pounding heartbeat. For several moments, she remained silent as she cleared her cluttered mind. Then a whispered voice echoed in her mind, startling her out of her misery. *Then why did your father break his deal? Find out what happened, Amelia. Do not give up hope!*

"I don't understand," she murmured to herself. "If I was supposed to marry you, why did my father seek out someone else for me?"

His handsome face distorted into a disgusted sneer at Amelia's whispered question. "Because your father grew a conscience in his old age. Said he could no longer stomach getting rich off the blood of fallen English soldiers." Jeremy's sneer deepened. "We were willing to let him leave our organization so long as I became a part of his family. You, Amelia, were his collateral, his promise to us he would remain silent."

Returning to Amelia's side, Jeremy wrapped his fingers around her throat and applied gentle pressure. Amelia shuddered at the soulless look he gave her as he watched his own fingers where they lay on her pale skin. His voice was mild while he explained, "As long as he remained silent, you were safe. The minute he revealed our secret was the moment you died."

Amelia gasped and struggled for breath as the fingers encircling her throat squeezed harder. "But when he secured you the hand of that bastard Tavis McGuire, he sealed his own death."

"Jeremy," she gasped. "I…can't…breathe." An unholy light had entered his eyes, almost as if he enjoyed causing her physical pain. She thought for sure he would choke her to death. Her vision blackened at the edges, and just when she felt herself slipping into unconsciousness he abruptly let her go. Blessed air rushed back into her lungs, and she coughed and spluttered.

She pulled in deep breaths of air, her mind trying to

piece together what Jeremy had just revealed. If what he said was true, then her father had misgivings about his role as traitor. He also must have decided she was more important to him than saving his own skin, which is why he arranged an acquaintance between her and Tavis. That one selfless act instilled within her a small kernel of hope, a reason to continue fighting. But she needed to be calm, and she needed to stall until she thought of a way out of this mess.

"Unfortunately, because of your husband and the stalwart Mr. Wickes, I did not have a clean shot at your father and was not able to kill him." He sighed in regret. "Which means I will have to postpone killing you until after I am able to finish your father." Trailing one smooth finger down the side of Amelia's face, he said, "Or I could make him watch as I kill you and then end his life. That has a ring of justice about it." Taking her bottom lip between his thumb and forefinger, he pulled hard; Amelia winced. "Then your husband can watch, too, as I take your life before his eyes."

Oh, God, no! Amelia couldn't allow Jeremy to go back to Ballywith. Not when her mother and her husband were still there, and her father, even though he might be a lying traitor. Jeremy was just crazy enough to kill them all. She had to protect them, but how? *Lie*, came that same whispered voice. *Tell him a lie.*

Lie? Amelia thought. She had not had the chance to practice lying since her discussion with Mrs. Dowling that day in the garden. What had Mrs. Dowling said about belladonna? Every plant and animal has a way to protect itself. Why not her? Couldn't she tell a lie to protect those she loved?

Wetting her lips, Amelia croaked out past the pain

and swelling in her throat, "He's dead."

"What's that?" Jeremy asked from where he stood again by the window.

Not feeling the dizziness or pain in her stomach which usually accompanied a lie, she swallowed and tried again, louder this time. "I said he's dead. You killed him."

Striding toward her, he boxed her in with his arms. "That's impossible," he said, his nostrils flaring with each agitated breath he took. "I am an excellent marksman, and I know when I've made a kill shot. That was not one."

Firming her jaw, she flashed her eyes at him in anger. "Believe me when I say you killed him." She swallowed again, pushing past the rising bile from her churning stomach. "I saw the blood pour out of him and heard his last shuddering breath. He's dead." Biting her lip, she breathed in to relax her clenching stomach. Soon the beads of perspiration on her forehead disappeared, and Amelia held Jeremy's stare without flinching.

He is waiting to see if I'll become ill from a lie.

"You know I cannot tell a lie, Jeremy," she said refusing to back down.

Jeremy believed her, for he backed away and allowed Amelia to take in a deep, steadying breath.

"Well," Jeremy said, "that saves me the trip back to Stanton to finish him off, and it allows us more time to wed before we depart for France."

"Wed? I am a married woman, Jeremy, or have you forgotten?"

"So little you know, Amelia. You may be legally wed here in Scotland"—he practically spat out the word

'Scotland'—"but in England you are not. We will marry by a special license and then sail for France, where I will bed you first and then kill you."

The sound of the door opening signaled the return of the unknown man who had ordered her to be restrained. Once again, his heavy gait pounded on the wooden slats of the floor as he came ever nearer to where she sat trembling in fear. At least with Jeremy she knew where she stood—he would keep her alive long enough to marry her and rape her. Though frightening, it allowed her enough time to figure out how to escape. This stranger with the heavy steps and the raspy voice, he was unknown, and it was that element which scared Amelia most. For how could she protect herself against what she did not know?

"Change of plans. I found a priest who'll do the service here at dawn," he said, his rough voice coming from behind Amelia and sending prickles of dread along her skin.

"Will it be legal?" Jeremy questioned. "I want her to be mine when she dies, so McGuire knows it was I who took away what he loves the most."

"It'll be legal. I found someone to forge a special license for me."

"In this backwater?"

"Any job can be done for a price, Son. All you have to do is ask."

Son? A dreadful suspicion started to form in her mind. Loud footsteps approached, and Amelia swung her head to see who the other man was.

"Time to cover her, Jeremy," he ordered. Amelia was able to make out his profile from the corner of her eye. He was a large, beefy man with a bald head and a bulbous nose, yet she still could not make out the entirety of his features or recognize him from what little she saw. "I want her silent until dawn." The man moved in front of Amelia with a black sack in his hands, and Amelia got her first good look at him, from the top of his shiny head to the familiar red, puckered scar running the length of his right cheek.

"You!" she gasped as the man covered her face with the funny-smelling bag that made her so tired, plunging her once again into darkness. She felt the cords tighten around her neck, sealing in the dizzying fumes of the bag. A moment before she blacked out she wondered what Jeremy's father was doing alive and in Scotland when he was supposed to be dead at the bottom of the sea...

Chapter 22

"Wait!" a feeble voice cried from the top of the stairs.

Tavis turned and spied the ashen, strained face of Lord Westby. Margaret had her plump arms around the man's waist to support him should he topple and fall. "I'm coming with you."

"The hell you are!" Tavis swore. "You're no good to me like this. I'll make better time on my own."

Westby made his way down the stairs, each step an obvious effort. His wife, Lady Anne, sped to his side, wrapping one of her own arms about his waist. "You don't know where to look for her or even who has her."

Grabbing his pack bag and slinging it over his shoulder, Tavis glared at Westby. "I know they headed west. I'm going to ride that way until I find them, and when I do"—his eyes narrowed to small, furious slits— "I'll cut their throats open and watch them die." Turning on a heel, he headed for the door with Wickes close behind him.

"I know who has her and where they took her!" Westby's desperate voice penetrated the thick fog of anger that had engulfed Tavis the moment he realized his wife was gone. Striding back to Westby, who now clutched the railing at the bottom of the steps, he demanded, "Where is my wife, Westby, and who took her?"

"You already know Jeremy Michelson, better known to you as Jeremiah Meeks, was one of the men. The other"—Westby gulped, and his already ashen face went even grayer—"is his father, Henry Michelson, or Harry the Horse, as he is sometimes called."

Tavis stepped back from Westby and looked at Wickes in confusion. "That's impossible. He was drowned at sea."

Wickes stared at Westby with a speculative gleam in his hawk eyes.

Tavis asked, "Tom, you're not surprised by this? You knew?"

Without taking his eyes from the pasty, sallow face of Westby, Wickes replied, "With his lucrative shipping firm and his contacts across Europe, we have long suspected Henry Michelson of selling Crown secrets. When news came of his unfortunate death at sea, there were many who believed he had faked his own death, to let the suspicions die with him, but we never had any proof." Wickes crossed his arms across his chest and ordered, "What do you know? Tell me everything."

"No," Tavis cut into Wickes's interrogation. "You can question him later. Right now, I need to find Amelia. Where did they take her? What are their plans for her?"

"There is a village by the name of Oban on the bay of the Atlantic several hours west of here. It used to be nothing more than a few rundown cottages with poor fisherman living hand to mouth doing their best to survive. About twenty years back, all of that changed when an anonymous investor opened a distillery. Henry, ever the opportunist, started running ships out of the bay, carrying loads of whisky to England and beyond. At the time, he bought one of the cottages right on the bay, to better watch his investments. That's where he'll have taken her before he sets sail again for France."

"To what purpose?" Tavis asked, though he feared he already knew the answer.

"As I said, Jeremy is obsessed with having Amelia, and he was furious she ran off with you. He will want to wed her. Then he...he'll rape her." Westby gulped and Lady Anne gasped, shaking her head as tears filled her eyes. "And then," Westby continued, his voice no more than a harsh whisper, "he'll kill her."

Tavis closed his eyes on a silent prayer for his beloved wife, and without a word more to anyone he turned and walked out the door.

****

It took several hours of hard riding, but Tavis and Wickes arrived in Oban as faint streaks of pale blue colored the sky behind them, signaling the dawn of a new day. Finding Henry's cottage was easy, as the town was still so small that not many cottages dotted the shoreline. They tied their horses to some trees fifty yards or so from the cottage and snuck up to the western side of the building nearest the water.

There was a feeble light coming through one of the windows, and Tavis poked his head up to look through it. What he saw instantly relieved him, for tied to a chair in the middle of the room was Amelia. Although a black cloth covered her head, which caused him to fear they had arrived too late, he saw the slight rise and fall of her chest indicating she still lived.

Beckoning to Wickes, he managed to tell him through hand motions Amelia was within and alive.

While he hadn't seen anyone in the room with Amelia, he didn't want to risk endangering her further by attempting to rescue her now, in case there was someone inside he didn't see. The two men worked out a plan, and Wickes crept off to take his position on higher ground. Tavis was preparing to move away from the window also when he heard movement from inside the cottage.

"It's time to wake up, my beloved," Jeremy's unmistakable voice came through the open window to Tavis, who still lurked below.

"Wha—? Whaz goin' on?" Amelia asked foggily.

Had she been drugged?

"Dawn is upon us, and soon we shall be wed."

"I don't wanna marry you. Jus' kill me now."

"Now, now, my dear," Jeremy soothed, "is that any way to talk to your bridegroom?"

"Get your hands off me, Jeremy!" Amelia yelled, her voice loud and clear as the fog of whatever drug affected her wore off. Tavis tensed, his hand poised over his gun, ready to fire if need be.

"Just a little preview of our wedding night, Amelia." Jeremy laughed.

"I'd rather die!"

"Oh, you will."

"Now?" she pleaded.

"And ruin my fun? I'll kill you, my dear, but only when your husband has arrived. I want him to watch me do it." A dark tone crept into Jeremy's voice. "Might even make him watch as I spread your legs apart and plunge my cock inside of you. Now, won't that be fun, hmmm?"

Tavis ground his teeth together in absolute fury,

but as long as Jeremy was in there with Amelia, he needed to stick to the plan.

"He won't come."

"Of course he'll come," Jeremy replied. "I know him. He loves you, so he'll have to come to save you."

"He doesn't love me."

Tavis's jaw dropped at Amelia's blatant lie. She knew he loved her. It was only yesterday he'd told her so in front of her parents. Why did she say something so untrue? Did she honestly believe it?

"What do you mean?" Jeremy asked. "I thought the reason you ran off with him in the first place was because it was love at first sight."

Amelia snorted. "He may have told me that, but really he wanted his horses, the ones my father had taken from him. I just happened to come along and spoil his plans."

What is going on?

She was still conscious, so she wasn't lying; otherwise she would have fainted. Had she somehow found out what he had really been doing at the ball when they first met?

"So if you are planning to take revenge against my husband by killing me, Jeremy, you are wasting your time. I tell you, he will not come. Even if he did, he doesn't care."

There were several long minutes of silence in which Tavis heard rapid pacing across the floorboards. "Regardless," Jeremy said, "with or without McGuire present, we will proceed as planned." He heard Jeremy's footsteps fade, and then a door slammed, leaving the room once again silent.

"Tavis…" Amelia's whispered voice came to him

through the window. "Please hurry and find me."

Tavis didn't know what to think. First she said he didn't love her and wouldn't come for her, and now she was wishing he would. Had she been lying before? But if so, why wasn't she ill?

After peering through the window once more, Tavis hoisted himself over the ledge and into the room. Stepping quietly over to his wife, he placed his hand over her mouth and, in a low voice, cautioned her to be silent. "Shh, Wife. It's me."

She struggled against her bonds and twisted her head to stare up at him in burning hope. He released the bonds about her wrists and at her legs. When she was free, she launched herself into his arms. "Oh, Tavis!" she sobbed into his chest. "I knew you'd find me! I knew it!"

He held her to him and breathed deeply of her familiar scent, taking comfort in her words and in the feel of her body warm and alive in his arms. "Then why did you say otherwise? Why did you lie?"

Amelia sniffled and wiped at her eyes. "I knew Jeremy was obsessed with taking his revenge in front of you, and I thought to buy myself some time if I said you didn't care about me. I thought maybe if he believed you weren't coming he'd keep me alive for a little bit longer, at least until you found me."

"You lied?" Tavis asked. "How is that possible?"

"I broke my curse, Tavis. On my own." she whispered, her face beaming at her accomplishment. "I discovered if I have to I can lie to protect myself or those that I love."

"You broke your curse?" Tavis leaned in to kiss his wife on the lips. "You're amazing! I love you so much,

Amelia."

"I love you, too, Tavis."

"We need to get out of here," he said, changing the subject. "Is there another way out besides that door?" he asked scanning the room for another exit.

"Why can't we leave through the window you came in through?"

"I barely made it through myself." He tapped her nose with his finger and shook his head in dismissal. "No, we can't go out that way."

"What about…" But her words died in her throat at the sound of approaching footsteps.

****

"Quick! Hide, Tavis! He can't find you here!"

"Sit in the chair and pretend to still be tied. I'll take care of the rest." Tavis hid behind a tall bureau in the corner of the room, the shadows helping to conceal him. Amelia did as she was told and resumed her position in the chair with her arms behind her back and her ankles crossed. Lowering her head so Jeremy didn't see the excited fervor in her eyes, she waited.

"The priest has been delayed. Father has gone to look for him," Jeremy announced, "so I decided why wait until after we're married to get on with it?"

Amelia watched with mounting horror as Jeremy started to unbutton the flap of his breeches. "I want to enjoy you more than once before I have to kill you, after all." He reached into his breeches and then stopped, laughing with good humor. "How foolish of me. You're still tied. Can't spread those plump thighs if you're strapped to the chair." As he bent over to release her ankles, Amelia acted. Raising her leg in a sharp upward motion, she slammed her knee into Jeremy's nose. A satisfying crunch echoed throughout the room.

"You bitch!" he screamed, holding onto his nose, blood streaming down his face. "You broke my nose!"

Amelia stood and walked up to Jeremy, who continued to writhe and moan in pain. She grasped his shoulders and thrust her knee into his groin. He screamed and fell to the floor doubled over in pain. "That's for trying to rape me, you bastard!" She had reared her leg back to kick him in the stomach when strong arms encircled her waist, pulling her trembling frame back into the solid strength of her husband. Turning her easily, Tavis cradled her head on his chest.

"That's enough, lass," Tavis's whispered voice said in her ear. "You defended yourself well, but that's enough. It's not in you to be violent, love. He's not worth it, Amelia. Let go of your anger." He continued whispering soothing words into her ear while stroking her back in long sweeping motions. Amelia sobbed, her body shaking from the shock of the last several hours. Under Tavis's tender ministrations, her tears soon stopped, though her eyes still glistened with moisture when she lifted her head from her husband's chest. "I want to go home, Tavis."

"As soon as I've taken care of him, we can go home. I promise."

She closed her eyes to block out the sight of Jeremy's beaten body so she could regain control of her nerves. All too soon, though, the image of his cold, sneering face as it had loomed above her floated into her mind's eye, and she feared these events were not going to be easily erased from her memory.

A loud commotion at the door startled her and had her husband spinning her behind his back. As she buried her face in his back, she felt his arm tense, heard the cock of the pistol, and…

"Jesus, Tavis! It's me!" Wickes yelled. "Put the damn pistol down!"

Lowering his arm, Tavis inquired, "What took you so long?"

"Had I known you were going to storm the cottage, I would have been here sooner," he said. "As it was, I simply sat and watched while Michelson Senior left the house, my pistol cocked and ready. I wanted to fire, but I didn't know what was happening here, and I didn't want to force his hand." Wickes gestured to Meeks, who lay barely conscious on the ground. "I came rushing in when I heard a woman scream. I thought Amelia was in trouble."

"That was Meeks you heard. Amelia incapacitated him when he tried to rape her yet again," Tavis said.

Wickes whistled in appreciation. "You are quite a woman, Lady Stanton."

She smiled in reply and studied Tavis's elusive friend for the first time. Tall and broad-shouldered like her husband, he also had blue eyes, but where Tavis was dark, Mr. Wickes had light blond hair more like that of her sisters. Though she couldn't put her finger on it, she felt as if she had met Mr. Wickes before. It was something about his eyes. She had a fanciful idea that if he were angry, those eyes could turn a man to stone… Gently shaking her head, she nodded toward Mr. Wickes and acknowledged his words. "Thank you, Mr. Wickes. It's nice to finally meet you."

He bowed and smiled. "It's my pleasure." Amelia wasn't sure, but he almost seemed relieved at her words. Surely not. She was just overly tired and reading into Mr. Wickes's actions when really there was no reason to do so. After all, he was her husband's friend and had ridden all night to rescue her. It was just her overactive imagination playing tricks on her. And if a nagging doubt persisted, she was too overwrought to pay much attention to it right now.

"I imagine you want to take your wife back home," Mr. Wickes said, addressing Tavis and rousing Amelia out of her musings. "I'll deal with Meeks here, while you tend to your wife."

"Are you sure, Tom? Michelson is still out there. I don't want to leave you outnumbered."

"He'll be no problem," was the reply, accompanied by a sneer at Jeremy. "I'll tie and gag him and then sit and wait for 'father dear' to come home," Wickes said with a wicked grin on his rugged face. "We'll have a nice, long chat, he and I."

Amelia knew Tavis wanted to argue further, but Mr. Wickes waved them off. "Go! Take care of your wife. I'll see you in a week or so, after this is all straightened out."

Needing no further encouragement, Tavis wrapped his arm about Amelia's waist to escort her out the door. Amelia was going home.

Chapter 23

"You've been avoiding me, Daughter," Lord Westby said, startling Amelia out of her reverie.

In the fortnight since her abduction, Amelia had indeed avoided being in the same room with her father. At first, she was too tired and shocked from her ordeal to worry much about what she'd learned of her father's activities. She spent several days healing, both physically and emotionally, in her chambers under the watchful care of her husband. After that, she reasoned her father was recovering himself, often sleeping most of the day away from heavy doses of laudanum for the pain in his shoulder. He had been insensible and unable to talk to her, or so she told herself. However, several days had passed since the doctor declared him well enough to leave his room and be in company.

During those times when he had enough strength to venture out into the house, Amelia was simply elsewhere. Sometimes she went into the garden or the kitchen, much to the annoyance of Mrs. Dowling who, having fully recovered from her own ordeal, was as commanding as ever. Amelia realized the futility of hiding from her father forever, but she had hoped to avoid this confrontation for a while longer, perhaps even until after he left her house.

Amelia turned and gave her father a chilly stare before glancing at the book she had been reading. It appeared her time was up; however, that didn't mean she needed to make it easy on him. He had much to account for, after all.

Lord Westby sighed and pulled up a chair next to Amelia, who sat pretending to read yet, although now she was too agitated and the words swam around on the page. "Your husband tells me you broke your curse. I'm proud of you."

She fumed at his praise and flipped another page. Amelia didn't want him to be proud of her. In fact, she didn't want anything more from him ever again. "Yes, it seems all those London doctors you dragged me to were wrong. The curse was breakable. I just needed sufficient motivation to do so."

"May I ask what finally motivated you enough to overcome it?"

"I lied to protect my loved ones—Tavis, Mother, and even you." Amelia laughed bitterly. "How lucky for you that I did not know of your duplicity before I was abducted. Otherwise I never would have been able to lie so convincingly to Jeremy, and you would most likely be dead. He was coming back to kill you, you know."

She closed her mouth with a snap to contain the boiling rage threatening to burst free. There was more she wanted to say, but she didn't know how to say it without screaming, something she had never done to her father. These foreign emotions overwhelmed her normally calm and ordered existence, and Amelia disliked the lack of control they brought. For her own peace of mind, she had to maintain her composure, so she remained silent, ignored her father, and resumed turning the pages of her book.

Sara Ackerman

A heavy silence followed her last statement before her father spoke again. "You were always one to pick up a book when you had a lot on your mind. Your mother and your sisters tend to become a bit hysterical when something bad happens, but not you. You take a book to a quiet spot and read until your mind can work through whatever is bothering it. I've always admired that about you, Amelia."

With a crooked finger, Amelia continued turning the pages, trying not to listen to the soothing timbre of her father's voice, a sound as familiar to her as her own heartbeat. How many times had they sat like this, Amelia curled up with a book and her father nearby talking calmly to her? He always did know how to untangle the jumble of emotions she felt, the gentle cadence of his speech smoothing the frayed edges of disappointment and pain until once more she was in control of herself. He was her hero, and she adored him.

All that had changed the moment Jeremy told her that her father, the man she respected and admired, was actually a traitor and a liar. Nothing he said to her now changed that fact, yet still she listened.

"I did that, too, when I was a boy. Took a book to read and think. I needed to immerse myself in someone else's words until the ideas in my own head started to make sense. You first did that after you were cursed. I don't recall the exact details now, but you told the truth to your mother about something, and it upset her. She cried and called you the Devil's own for having such a wicked tongue. While I comforted your mother, you ran from the room and went to the library. I found you hours later, curled up on the window seat much like you are now. I remember watching you read, your tiny head

258

bent over the pages of the book, a line of concentration furrowing your brows, and thinking to myself how much you were like me."

Slamming her book closed, Amelia jumped up and glared at her father. "I am nothing like you!" she hissed. "Nothing! I would never sacrifice my home and country for money, so do not think to compare my actions to yours ever again!" She stalked off and stood in front of a large, side window, leaning her head against the cool pane of glass.

"Amelia," her father began, rising to follow her, "please, let me explain."

"Explain what, Father?" Amelia whipped her head around and pinned her father with her hot, accusing stare. "What possible reason can you give to explain your actions?"

"I was young, Amelia, taken in by my older, more dynamic friend. I was a quiet boy, and my only real friends were found in the pages of a book. Henry's family worked for mine, so he was often about. I used to envy how commanding he was, how all the other boys in the village looked up to him. When he took an interest in me, I was flattered. I would have done almost anything he asked of me."

"Bollocks!" Amelia shouted, her tight rein on her temper snapping. "Don't stand there and lie to me, Father! That story might have worked with Mother, but credit me with having enough sense to recognize when someone is lying to me!"

Lord Westby's eyes flashed with the same fire as Amelia's. He firmed his mouth and nodded. "Fine. You want the truth? The truth is, Amelia," he said, advancing toward her until his face loomed over hers,

"I was greedy and I was a coward. I knew exactly what I was doing, who I would be hurting, and I did it anyway. Is that what you wanted to hear?"

"At least it's the truth! You owe me that much!" she yelled into his face, her hands balled into trembling fists at her side. The urge to strike her father, to make him feel a small fraction of the pain she felt, was overpowering, so Amelia backed away from him, moving to the opposite side of the room. Clutching at the back of a chair for support, she asked the question that had been eating at her since her abduction. "So tell me, Father, now we're being honest with each other, did you really intend for me to marry Jeremy?"

His gaze slid away from hers, and he hesitated for a moment, but he nodded.

"Why?" she cried, unable to credit that her father had forged an alliance between that unholy monster and her. "You knew how he treated me, knew what would have happened to me if we married. How could you agree to such a match?"

"I had no choice, Amelia! To keep us alive one of you had to marry him. It was supposed to be Beatrice, but when she refused and ran off with Lord Easton instead, I had no other option. Evie was still in the schoolroom. Should I have condemned a child to such a fate? Did I choose wrong?"

In spite of her anger she realized the truth of his statement. Thinking of Evie, her bright, vivacious sister, in the hands of such a man as Jeremy Michelson made her ill to her stomach. He would have crushed her spirit within a fortnight, eventually killing the brilliant spark that made Evie so unique. Her father was right. It had to be her.

"Is that why you…you blamed me when he tried to…to rape me?"

Tears streaked down his face, and he whispered, "I am so sorry, Amelia. I didn't protect you from him. I have never been more ashamed than when I saw what he did to you. I was doing my best to keep you all safe, and had I said anything…" Her father's voice trailed off, and he shuddered, a look of terror distorting his features. "It would have been much worse."

A hysterical laugh bubbled forth, and she pressed her hands over her mouth to suppress the sound. "I see," she said. "To keep us safe you aligned yourself with traitors and thieves. You allowed a maniac to live with us and control your home and family. And finally, you sold your daughter to a madman to protect us from a situation of your own making." Amelia pretended to ponder this information, tapping her chin in thought. "Yes, it makes perfect sense, Father. How silly of me not to see it."

She looked at him then, not as the man she had set upon a pedestal when she had been a young girl, but as a man who was fallible and made horrible mistakes to protect those he loved. Though she knew he loved her, Amelia was unable to reconcile his actions with his profession of love for her and her sisters.

As she contemplated his beloved face, now suddenly lined and old with age and grief, she mourned the loss of the man she called father. "You are not the man I thought you were, Father," Amelia quavered. "I..I don't know if I ever knew who you really were, but I don't like this man, whoever you are." She turned away from him and walked to the door, ready to be done with this conversation and its painful revelations.

Before her hand had reached the knob, he called out to her. "I knew it, Amelia, and was ashamed of who I was. That's why I found Tavis for you. I knew he could protect you when I couldn't. Tavis is the type of man you deserve—strong, honest, brave. He is the kind of man I wanted to be for you."

Amelia turned her head away from the door to look at her father. "But you were, Papa," she whispered, all her suffering and heartbreak evident in those few words. "You were that kind of man to me, and whether you had ten pounds to your name or ten thousand, I still would have loved you." She opened the door and stepped through.

"And now?" came her father's anguished question, stopping her in her tracks.

Amelia paused and thought. She thought about the deceitful life he had built for his family, of all the pain he had caused and of the lives he had ruined. Then she knew what to tell him, the perfect revenge for her father, the liar. "Of course I love you, Father," she replied, regarding him through tear-filled eyes. "I will always love you."

"Is that the truth, Amelia, or…are you lying?" he asked, the weight of broken dreams and fractured hopes etched into every line of his face.

Closing her own stinging eyes to block the sight of her father, stooped and broken with age and despair, Amelia pushed back the bile that rose up so familiarly in her throat and said, "You'll never know, now, will you?"

With a soft click, Amelia closed the door and fled down the hallway, heartbroken and alone.

Chapter 24

"Come in!" Tavis commanded from behind his desk. He had several weeks' worth of paperwork to catch up on after the whole incident of Amelia's abduction. Several days beyond that he'd spent helping her to recover. Now he finally had some time to do much-needed paperwork. Whatever the interruption, he hoped it could wait.

"Tavis," his father-in-law said as he opened the door to his study. "I was hoping to have a word with you before I leave tomorrow."

"Of course, Westby. Take a seat." Tavis gestured to an empty seat across from him. Since Westby seemed disinclined to talk immediately, Tavis took the opportunity to continue adding sums in his ledger book. He had finished adding one column when Westby finally broke his silence.

"I've talked to Amelia."

Tavis became worried. He knew Westby had wanted to talk with Amelia alone, but Amelia had proved elusive. He also knew what Westby had to say would be devastating to his wife, so his anxiety for her welfare was more than justified. "Oh? How did she take it?"

"Badly," Westby declared. "I told her the truth, which is all I can give her now. I hope one day she will forgive me."

Tavis remained silent. He had his own opinion about Westby, though no matter how he felt, he knew Amelia must be feeling so much worse. Changing the subject, Tavis presented Westby with a formal document. "Here is your written confession. All you need to do is sign and you will be a free man."

Part of what angered Tavis so much about Westby was the deal he'd made with Wickes. In exchange for his full confession and testimony about Henry Michelson and his smuggling ring, Westby, who was dead according to Michelson and the rest of the world, would remain deceased and exiled forever to the Americas. Tavis disagreed with that decision, preferring to let the courts mete out justice accordingly, but Wickes overruled all of his objections, saying there was a better chance of catching Michelson if Westby lived, arguing that even in America Westby could still provide useful information.

Taking the plume from Tavis, Westby signed his confession, which Tavis retrieved and tucked away in a desk drawer. Pulling out some other papers, he said, "Here are the documents you will need to board the ship to America, including your new identity and several hundred pounds. That should see you through until you can establish yourself as a man of business there."

Westby took the documents and put them into the pocket of his coat.

"Will Lady Anne be joining you?" Tavis inquired. Before telling Amelia, Westby had been required to account to his wife for all the danger he had let loose on Amelia. Needless to say, she did not take his confession well.

"I don't know. She still hasn't spoken to me since we talked two days ago. I told her I depart tomorrow and asked her to join me." He shrugged. "I imagine I'll be sailing alone." Westby sank into his chair.

Tavis waited.

"There's the matter of Amelia's dowry still to discuss, and—oh!" Westby patted his jacket pocket. "And the papers I had on your father." Pulling out a large envelope, he laid it on Tavis's desk. "That's everything I had."

Tavis grabbed the packet and stepped to the fire, into which he immediately threw the envelope Westby had given him. Breathing deeply, Tavis watched in relief as the flames licked away the last remnants of his father's stupidity.

"Before we left London, I had my solicitor draw up some papers detailing Amelia's settlement." Westby pulled out another envelope, which Tavis opened. "All of that is Amelia's."

Face set in a grim line, Tavis pushed the papers back to Westby in distaste. "If it's all the same to you, I'd rather not take blood money."

"It's not. My wife had a large settlement, and early in our marriage we agreed to set aside those funds to dower whatever children we had. You have my word this money is not tainted." Westby pushed the papers back toward Tavis. "Please," he begged, "allow me to give this to my daughter."

In spite of his reluctance, Tavis retrieved the papers and folded them into his drawer. "Now if you'll excuse me, Lord Westby," Tavis said, "there is much yet for me to do."

Westby remained seated, though, in spite of

Tavis's blatant request for the man to leave. "There is one other thing, Stanton," Westby hedged, "that I would tell you before I leave. It's about the curse."

****

Tavis didn't know what to think about the news Westby gave him. He had disliked the man before he knew this, but now he loathed the man. For a father to do that to his own children was unconscionable. Then the man had the nerve to swear him to secrecy.

"What good will it do for them to know this now?" Westby argued. "It will only hurt them more, and they have already been hurt enough by me."

Westby broke down at that point and started to cry, prompting Tavis to agree, if only to see the man quit his study and leave him in peace.

He sat thinking for a good half an hour after Westby left, deciding whether to share what he'd learned with his wife. After his last and final mission for the War Office, he never wanted to keep a secret from her again. It was too difficult, yet he agreed with Westby's logic. Telling Amelia would pain her, and she had been through enough. He didn't want to see her hurt any further.

Finally rising from his desk, he left to seek out Amelia. It didn't take him long to find her, the garden behind the kitchen having become her favorite place to sit and think. There she sat on a small wooden bench, knees drawn up to her chest and red curls flying about her head in the breeze.

He approached her with caution and called her name lest she startle. Turning her head, she smiled, a sad lonely smile, and opened her arms to him. Tavis needed no further invitation as he hurried over and scooped her up, settling her onto his lap as he sat. She nestled her head on his shoulder and wrapped her arms about his neck. There they sat for several minutes, both content to be with one another after the scare of thinking they would never see each other ever again.

"I had news from Wickes," he said.

"What did he say?"

"Jeremy is dead, killed by his own father, and in the confusion of the fight, Wickes was injured, too."

"Will he recover?"

"I should think so, but he's angry at himself for letting Michelson get away. Apparently when Wickes went down, Michelson swam out to a ship and left the harbor."

What he didn't tell Amelia was that there was another person in the harbor that night, a small woman with striking blonde hair and cool, blue eyes, who fought like a soldier. She followed Michelson and was presumably on the ship with him. Tavis had an idea of who the mystery woman was, but he remained quiet, not wishing to further upset Amelia with his suspicions; however, if he was correct, that would explain how Amelia's sister claimed to know so much about him even though they had only met once.

"Father spoke to me," Amelia said. Tavis nodded and waited for her to continue. "I think he wanted my forgiveness, Tavis, but I just couldn't give it."

"You know I've always hated my father, Amelia." He rested his chin on the top of her silky curls. "I hated him for years for abandoning me when I was a babe. But that hate didn't change anything. It didn't make my father a different person or a better man. It didn't give me the childhood I longed for. All it did was make me lonely, bitter, and closed off to love. The moment I forgave my father was the moment I realized how much I loved you. Until I let go of my anger and resentment, I wasn't free to love you as you deserved."

"You think I should forgive him?" she asked in surprise. "You think I should forget about all the horrible things he did?"

"No, love," he said. "It's up to you to decide whether you forgive him or not. I only wish to remind you that forgiving your father…well, that's not for him."

She raised her head off his chest and studied him with confusion swimming in her green eyes. "I don't understand."

"Forgiveness is for you, not the other person. It's when you finally let go of all the hurt and anger that has burned within you, and you allow yourself to feel love. As long as you feel resentment toward your father, it owns you, body and soul. It's a terrible curse to bear, and one you will never be free of as long as you hold on to negativity and hate."

Cupping his cheek with her hand, she searched his face for the truth of what he said. "How did you become so wise?" she asked.

"You taught me, my love. Everything of importance I know is because of you."

Reaching up behind his neck, she pulled his lips down to hers in a tender kiss of love and renewal. "I love you so, Tavis," Amelia breathed, wrapping her arms about him. "Don't ever let me go."

He hugged her closer to his chest and pressed a swift kiss to her cheek. "Never, Amelia," he promised fiercely. "I will never let you go."

Chapter 25

"Wait!" Amelia shouted. "Father, wait!" Tavis and Westby turned to watch in astonishment as she hurried across the hallway and down the stairs to the waiting coach.

"Amelia?" Westby asked in amazement. Stepping down from the coach, he looked at his daughter through misty eyes full of disbelief. "What are you doing here?"

Amelia grabbed Tavis's hands and lifted her chin. "I've come to say goodbye and to say you may write to me once you've reached America. I...I can't promise I will ever write back, but you may write to me."

Westby lowered his head. "Thank you, Daughter. I will write to you every day. You may depend on it." Bowing to Amelia and Tavis, Westby once again prepared to board the coach.

Impulsively Amelia leaned forward and caught her father by the hand and squeezed it. "I wish you a safe journey, Father." Her eyes sparkled with unshed tears, but she smiled, a small tentative smile, at her stunned father.

Westby smiled in return and nodded his head, tears already gathering in his eyes. Squeezing back, he whispered, "I wish you a good life, Amelia. Full of happiness and joy." Then, turning away, he boarded the coach and with a tap to the driver was gone. Amelia stayed in the drive and watched until the coach disappeared from sight.

"That was a good thing you did, Amelia," Tavis said, coming up from behind to wrap his arm solidly about Amelia's waist. "I know how hard it was for you to forgive him."

As if they were of one mind, the two turned and wandered down the path to the stables. "In spite of what he did, he is still my father, and I…I won't ever see him again." She shrugged and wiped at her eyes. "I couldn't let him go without saying goodbye."

"And your mother?" Tavis asked. "I noticed she did not accompany your father to America."

"Someday maybe she'll forgive him, but not now. She's too angry at all the lies he told her over the years and at what nearly happened to me. Mother will return to London a widow and try to put the pieces of her life back together again. It's what we will all have to do."

Amelia was saddened at the price of her father's actions. Forbidden to return to England, he was dead to all of their acquaintances. Her mother was alone for the first time in over twenty years, starting a life for herself as a widow, taking sympathies from friends and family when in reality her husband was alive and living in exile in America. What a horrible mess he'd made, and all because he lied. To his family, to society, but worst of all to himself.

She grabbed Tavis's hand and held on, allowing his strength to bolster her own flagging spirits. He squeezed back and said, "There's something I need to tell you, something I have been keeping from you."

He looked suddenly nervous, and Amelia realized she didn't even care anymore what his big secret was. She had figured out most of it during her abduction, but if Tavis needed to tell her, she was happy to listen.

Clearing his throat, he told Amelia all of his secrets, secrets he'd been keeping since they met. Through it all, she listened without speaking, and when he was done, she spun to face him. Grabbing his arms, she demanded, "Promise me that, no matter what, there will always be honesty between us."

"Sometimes that is just not possible, Amelia," Tavis hedged. "If your father had told your mother what he was involved in, do you honestly think her knowing would have changed anything?"

She thought about that for a moment and realized he was right. Had her father told her mother anything about his illegal activities, he would have put his wife in danger. Amelia would not have met Tavis. She would most likely be married to Jeremy, abused or possibly dead.

"It wouldn't have been better," she admitted stopping outside the stable doors, "yet I fail to see how telling a lie is better than answering honestly. I thought you valued my honesty."

"I do Amelia, more than anything." He led her inside and down to Magnus's stall. She rubbed his velvety black nose, and he bobbed his head, nickering his appreciation.

"However," he grunted, cinching Magnus's saddle under the great beast's belly, "there's a difference between outright deceit and a little white lie to protect the ones we love."

"When would lying be necessary?"

"What if you don a new frock and ask me whether it unfavorably accentuates certain features of your body?" He leered and grabbed her buttocks, leaving no doubt in her mind as to what he referred. "You honestly want me to answer yes?" His eyes sparkled in delighted mirth, and she swatted him on the arm.

"I have superior taste, my lord, and would perish before purchasing an unflattering gown." She wiggled out of his embrace. "And I have never asked you that, either!" She pinched him for good measure.

He laughed and finished bridling Magnus. "But of course, my dear. How foolish of me to suggest it."

Amelia narrowed her eyes at his playful goading and plotted a tease of her own, one that was sure to prick his manly ego.

She followed him into the next stall, where he was gathering her horse's tack, and leaned against the wall, her arms crossed over her chest. "Then when you run to me in a panic because you have found some gray streaking your temples, you want me to say it's merely a trick of the light?"

"I don't have gray hair yet." He dropped the saddle onto her horse's back before bending over to peer at his reflection in the silver stirrups, running his fingers through the thick dark hair at his temples.

"Of course not, dear," she said, giggling. "What was I thinking?" As his indignant expression turned to mock outrage, she backed away, lifting her skirts and fleeing the stall for the relative safety of the former one and the solid protection of Magnus's furry body.

Tavis followed her in hot pursuit and soon had her cornered. He gathered her into his arms and growled, pretending to bite the sensitive skin of her neck and shoulders while his nimble fingers launched a frontal attack to the tender flesh of her ribs. Helpless against his ticklish assault, she squealed and struggled to get away, bumping into Magnus in the process. The horse huffed and stomped his hooves, irritated by the commotion in the stall. Tavis, taking pity on the poor beast, grabbed his reins and led him out of the stables.

Once both horses were outside, Tavis made some adjustments to their stirrups and turned to her. "You see what I mean? Too much honesty can lead to as many hurt feelings as not enough."

"You wish for us to lie to each other?" she asked, still puzzled by his plea for dishonesty.

"Nay, Amelia," he smiled, lifting her onto her saddle. "Not lie to each other. Just recognize when a little lie is more appropriate than a harsh truth." With an ease born of practice, he mounted and spurred his horse into motion. She flicked the reins, and Legacy's Daughter walked also, following the comfortable, easy pace Tavis set.

"I will always want to protect you, Amelia," he said, reaching over to grab one of her hands, "and if I know I can prevent causing you pain, I will do whatever it takes to see you safe and happy."

"I think I understand what you mean," she said at last. "When Jeremy threatened to kill you, I would have said or done anything to keep you from harm. I lied because I loved you."

Still, worry gnawed at her, and questions tumbled inside her head. She had lived too long with the burden of honesty and didn't know how to proceed without its familiar constraints. What if she couldn't change? How would their marriage survive without absolute honesty? Her brow furrowed, and she blurted, "But what if—"

He squeezed her hand, silencing her concerns with a swift kiss. "What if I said you were my heart and soul and I will love you forever?" he asked, his sapphire eyes brimming with fathomless devotion. "Would you believe me?"

"Yes," she said, her anxiety melting with that one declaration. "With all my heart."

"If you can believe that, Amelia, that's the only truth we need. The rest will come."

Then, spurring his horse to a gallop, he raced ahead, and Amelia, not wanting to be left behind, flew after him, her copper curls streaming in ribbons of liquid gold behind her.

Epilogue

Six weeks later

"What are you reading?"

Amelia started at the unexpected sound of her husband's voice and turned to find him standing just over her shoulder.

"A letter from Mother. She writes to say she arrived safely in London and has decided to move in with her widowed sister." Amelia's brows furrowed, and she worried her lower lip with her teeth as she reread the last lines of the letter.

Tavis joined her at her perch in the window seat of the library. "That's good news, so why do you look so worried?"

She waved her hands in front of her to dismiss his concern. "It's nothing." She smiled while tucking the paper into the folds of her skirt.

"Your curse may be broken, my heart, but you will never make a good liar." He reached for her hand and placed a soft kiss on it, lessening the sting of his words.

Amelia grimaced and then sighed. "Mother writes that Evie has gone to visit our uncle in Surrey."

"That's certainly nothing to worry about."

"Except Evie hates our uncle in Surrey." She blew out a frustrated breath. "Plus she hates Surrey even more than she does our uncle."

"Is your mother concerned?"

"No, but she was upset that Evie didn't even inform her betrothed before leaving Town." Nibbling on her thumb, Amelia wondered why Evie had decided to leave home.

"I'm sure there is a perfectly good explanation for her sudden absence, Amelia, and it's nothing to concern yourself about." He removed her hand from her mouth and tucked it into his own.

She smiled brightly and said, "You're right, Tavis. I'm just being silly." But her smile must not have reached all the way to her eyes, for he asked, "Was there more?"

"Only that Beatrice has left Town and no one knows quite where she went. Do you think something might have happened to her?"

"Wherever Beatrice is, I am sure she is capable of taking care of herself," Tavis comforted. "Besides, wasn't she the one who taught you how to defend yourself?" She nodded. "Bea will be fine. Stop worrying so much, my heart." Taking the letter from her lap, he set it aside and looked curiously at a small, wrapped parcel lying beside her on the window seat.

"Did she send you a package, as well?" Tavis questioned as he took the package in hand.

In her haste to read news from home, she had forgotten all about the present accompanying her mother's letter. "Yes, she mentioned it in her letter. I just haven't opened it yet."

Untying the string, she peeled back the wrapping to reveal a beautifully woven shawl. Her heart pounded, and she felt the blood rush from her face, leaving her lightheaded and suddenly ill. With trembling hands, she reached out to touch the fabric, only to pull her hand back sharply in fear. Because despite her mother's letter saying she'd recently purchased it for her, Amelia had seen this shawl before.

"How pretty," Tavis said as he grabbed a corner of the cloth and held it up to the side of her face. "Look. It's the same color of green as your eyes. I have never seen anything like it before."

Still, Amelia remained motionless, eyeing the shawl with equal parts awe and fear. "I have," she whispered, thinking of her meeting with Jane all those weeks ago. She hadn't seen her since and had eventually convinced herself Jane was a figment of her overworked imagination. But this, this was proof of her existence because somehow—and she didn't know how—her mother had purchased Jane's shawl for her.

Jane...Why didn't I see the connection before? Amelia Jane.

Was it possible? Was Jane Amelia's future? She touched the smooth edge of the wrapper and felt a spark tingle up and down her arm. She snatched her fingers away.

That certainly explains Jane's uncanny knowledge of me and my husband. What it all meant she did not know nor, she was surprised to discover, did she care. Unlike her curse, which she had spent years trying to decipher, maybe this was one mystery best left unsolved.

Gathering the shawl in his hands, Tavis rose. "Here, I'll put it on you." As he unfolded the layers of fabric, a small note floated to the ground. He bent to pick it up and read, "It will only work once. Use it wisely."

"That's odd," he said with a frown. "Whatever does it mean?"

Amelia laughed and knew then her suspicions were correct. "Oh, nothing, I imagine. Someone's idea of a joke, perhaps." Taking the shawl and the note from his hand, she tossed them aside. "Besides, it's much too warm today to wear a shawl."

Later, after she'd had the time to look at everything and examine what it all meant, she would find a special place to store the shawl so it would be ready in case her suspicions were correct. But not now. Now she needed to be here with her husband, not worrying about her sisters and not thinking about a distant future and a magical shawl.

Wrapping her arms about Tavis's neck, she asked, "Tell me, Husband, what brings you out of the stables on such a fine day as this?"

His lingering confusion and worry about the mysterious note fled at her question, and he smiled, his eyes sparkling with excitement.

"Hyacinth is breeding!"

"Oh, Tavis!" she squealed, throwing her arms around his neck. "How wonderful!"

He had worked hard this last month and a half to prepare Ballywith Stables to be a national name amongst horse enthusiasts and racers. He had spent hours writing letters to contacts he held throughout England and Scotland, informing them of his venture. Within weeks, three interested parties had arrived at Ballywith, and he had secured much-needed funding from these backers. Now that their first horse was breeding, it would be only a matter of time before requests for Ballywith horses came pouring in from all over England and Scotland.

Catching his lips with her own, Amelia kissed Tavis fiercely. "I'm so proud of you," she said when she pulled back. "When will she foal, do you think? In nine months like me?"

"By the beginning of next July." He rubbed his hands together, missing the important news she shared. "Why do you ask? Do you want to help with the foaling?"

She took his hand and pressed it to her stomach. "I ask because I was hoping to be the first female since your mother to have a baby at Ballywith, and it looks like I will be."

His eyes grew wide as comprehension dawned, and his mouth opened and closed, though no sound emerged. Eventually, he spluttered, "You mean… you're going to…we're going to…?"

With tears of happiness filling her eyes, she nodded. "He or she should arrive early spring of next year." Tavis slid from his seat and knelt before Amelia. Hugging her waist, he placed his head in her lap and held her. Then he leaned over and pressed a soft kiss to her barely rounded abdomen. When he looked up, his own eyes were wet and full of emotion.

"I'm going to be a father!" he whispered. Jumping up, he pulled her into his arms and swung her around. "I'm going to be a father!" he shouted. Pressing a tender kiss to her forehead, he cradled her to him. "Thank you, Amelia. You have given me more than I ever dreamed possible. Every day I thank my lucky stars you agreed to run away with me even though you knew next to nothing about me, not even my real name."

"I should be the one thanking you," she replied. "Before we met I was miserable, and it took a chance meeting with a stranger to show me the truth of what I had become. It was your words and actions that awakened within me a fierce desire to live my life on my terms and not at the mercy of my curse. That's why I ran away with you, Tavis, and I have not once regretted my decision."

When he looked like he wanted to protest, Amelia placed her forefinger over his mouth to quiet his protestations. "I know it still bothers you that we started our relationship with a lie, Husband, but know it was that lie which showed me the truth. It was that lie which gave me wings to fly."

Twining her hands around his neck, she kissed her husband, sharing all the joy she had found since meeting him, knowing in her heart he was the only truth she ever needed.

A word about the author...

Sara Ackerman is an ESL teacher in Wisconsin. *Little White Lies* is her debut novel.
Visit Sara at:
http://seackerman.com

www.ingramcontent.com/pod-product-compliance
Lightning Source LLC
Chambersburg PA
CBHW070837280626
47161CB00015B/721